"Perhaps I could take over the front desk?"

"That's a generous offer, but I think it best if I handle this," Seth said.

Abigail stiffened. "Are you saying you don't think I can handle the job?"

"It's not so much you personally as that I really don't think this is an appropriate job for any young lady."

"Why ever not? I've studied the work Mr. Crandall does, and even relieved him a time or two when he had to tend to his sister. So I actually have some experience."

She called that experience? "It was inappropriate for Mr. Crandall to leave you in charge."

"You obviously want me to prove myself, Mr. Reynolds. But in return, will you give me your word that this is just a first step? And you will train me on the responsibilities of a hotel manager?"

"Agreed," he said without hesitation. If she could handle the desk job, then he'd humor her with the additional training.

But at the end of the day, someone else would be hired as hotel manager. Someone who was not Abigail. That was how it had to be.

Winnie Griggs is the multipublished, award-winning author of historical (and occasionally contemporary) romances that focus on small towns, big hearts and amazing grace. She is also a list maker and a lover of dragonflies, and holds an advanced degree in the art of procrastination. Winnie loves to hear from readers—you can connect with her on Facebook at Facebook.com/winniegriggs.author or email her at winnie@winniegriggs.com.

Books by Winnie Griggs

Love Inspired Historical

Texas Grooms

Handpicked Husband
The Bride Next Door
A Family for Christmas
Lone Star Heiress
Her Holiday Family
Second Chance Hero
The Holiday Courtship
Texas Cinderella
A Tailor-Made Husband
Once Upon a Texas Christmas

Visit the Author Profile page at Harlequin.com for more titles.

WINNIE GRIGGS

Once Upon a Texas Christmas

HARLEQUIN® LOVE INSPIRED® HISTORICAL

Recycling programs for this product may not exist in your area.

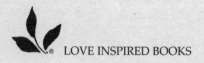 LOVE INSPIRED BOOKS

ISBN-13: 978-0-373-42551-8

Once Upon a Texas Christmas

Copyright © 2017 by Winnie Griggs

www.Harlequin.com

Printed in U.S.A.

Do not bear a grudge against others, but settle your differences with them, so that you will not commit a sin because of them. Do not take revenge on others or continue to hate them, but love your neighbors as you love yourself.
—*Leviticus* 19:17–18

Dedicated to my fabulous agent,
Michelle Grajkowski, who is not only a
great advocate for my work but also a great friend.
And also to my wonderful husband,
who is not only incredibly supportive but has
never once complained about the amount of time
I dedicate to my writing career.

Chapter One

Philadelphia
October 1899

"Check and mate." Seth Reynolds leaned back in his seat, a satisfied grin on his face. It wasn't often he could defeat his employer and friend.

Judge Arthur Madison raised a brow. "So it is. I must say, after I captured your queen I thought I had you."

Seth began setting the pieces back on the board. "That was the plan. I'm prepared to sacrifice anything, even my queen, if it ensures a win."

As the older gentleman helped reset the board, Seth surreptitiously massaged the damaged muscle in his left thigh, a constant reminder of all he lacked in the eyes of the world.

"Speaking of winning," the judge said without looking up, "how's the Michelson deal coming along?"

Seth knew the prying question was well-meant, so he didn't get his back up. "I've received an extension on the balance owed until year's end."

The judge looked up. "I'd be glad to loan you the money."

If anyone else had offered, Seth would have rebuffed him soundly. But Arthur Madison wasn't just anyone else. "I appreciate that, sir, but this is something I must do myself." Achieving the goal he'd been working toward for over a decade wouldn't mean anything if he didn't do it on his own.

The judge's expression shifted. "You're only in this bind because you took in your nephew last year. That proves all anyone needs to know about your measure as a man."

Seth brushed aside the words. Taking Jamie in after the death of his sister was simply something family did. No matter how estranged he and his sister were. Besides, his being a man of honor wasn't what he needed to prove. "Don't worry, I have the matter well in hand."

The judge raised a brow but otherwise didn't pry.

Which was why Seth felt obliged to expand. "This hotel job in Turnabout, Texas, is what will help me finalize the deal. I just need to wrap things up by the end of the year. My bonus, along with hiring the right person to serve as hotel manager, will seal the deal."

And he *would* get both done before year's end.

No matter what it took.

An hour later, Arthur Madison stood at the window, watching Seth walk away. It was satisfying to see how far the young man had come in the eleven years he'd known him. From a determined but untrained scrapper to a competent man of business. To see him on the road to becoming a business owner in his own right was quite gratifying.

But even though he had the utmost respect for Seth, he also worried about him. He'd long suspected the most crippling scars Seth bore were not the physical ones responsible for his limp. He only knew bits and pieces of Seth's history, but he'd never doubted what an inherently good person the young man was. Then again, his opinion was colored by the fact that he'd first met Seth when the then eighteen-year-old had saved his life, at considerable risk to his own.

Now it was his turn to save Seth.

Seth's entire focus was aimed at showing the world he was as good as any man who could walk unhindered. He was driven to the point that he didn't seem to know how to enjoy what he already had. Someone had to give him a nudge in the right direction before it was too late.

And if he could help a certain young lady in the process, so much the better.

Arthur glanced again at the letter on the corner of his desk. Abigail was the opposite of Seth in many ways—sweet, optimistic and a bit naive—but she was also intelligent, spirited and had a mind of her own. Like Seth, she also needed a bit of a push to set her feet on the right path.

The plan forming in his mind could be described by some as meddlesome. But he'd employed a similar tactic with his granddaughter six years ago. That had worked out even better than he could have hoped. Could success repeat itself? After all, just as with Reggie and Adam, he would merely set the stage. The rest was up to them.

Speaking of setting the stage… He sat, then reached for a pen and paper.

My dear Abigail…

"How is the hunt for a job going?"

Abigail Fulton grimaced as she set her letters and parcel on the pharmacy counter. "I've checked with nearly every business here in Turnabout and no one is hiring."

Constance Harper, her best friend, gave her a look that seemed equal parts sympathy and amusement. "Surely you're exaggerating. I can't believe you checked with *every* business in town. For instance, you never checked with me."

Just this week, Constance's long-held dream had come true when Mr. Flaherty had retired and turned over the keys of the apothecary shop to her.

Abigail patted her friend's hand. "Don't even think about offering me a job. You can't afford to hire me, not for a wage that would allow me to move into the boardinghouse."

Constance gave a reluctant nod then smiled. "Give it time, something will come up."

"That's just it—I'm running out of time. I absolutely *have* to move out of Everett and Daisy's home by the end of the year."

Constance's expression turned skeptical. "Has Everett or Daisy said anything to make you feel unwelcome?"

"No, not at all." Not yet anyway.

Living with her older brother had been fine when Abigail was fifteen and Everett was single. But she was twenty now and Everett had a wife and two children. Lately, she'd begun to feel she was taking up much-needed room. Better to work this out herself than to wait for them to bring it up themselves.

"Daisy and Everett are expecting another child."

"Oh, that's wonderful." Constance's smile faded. "Aren't you happy?"

"Of course. They're wonderful parents and have enough love to encompass a houseful of children." Abigail sighed and leaned her elbows on the counter. "But I can't justify taking up a room in their home any longer."

Constance frowned thoughtfully. "Actually, I'd think

having you around to help would be more important than ever now."

Daisy ran the local restaurant and Everett produced the town's newspaper. Abigail helped out where she could, which was her way of repaying their kindness to her.

"I'll still help when I'm needed, of course. But it's past time I get out on my own and gave them the space they need. I just need to prove to someone that I'd make a good employee."

"Of course you would." Constance sounded almost indignant.

It was easy for her friend to feel that way—she had an important job and was a respected businesswoman.

"After all," Constance added, "You've been running the town's only library since you were fifteen years old."

Abigail waved a hand dismissively. "It barely makes pin money, certainly not enough to allow me to support myself." Then she fingered her collar. "Actually, there is a job coming available that would meet my needs."

Constance eyed her suspiciously. "You don't sound happy about it, whatever it is."

"I ran into Hilda Burns earlier. Seems she and Joseph Melton are engaged. *And* they're planning a Christmas Eve wedding. Which means, come mid-December, Mrs. Ortolon will be looking to hire someone new."

Hilda's job consisted mainly of cleaning and cooking at the boardinghouse and using her "free time" to run errands for Mrs. Ortolon. Not only was the work near-drudgery, but it was common knowledge what a hard-to-please employer Mrs. Ortolon could be.

Constance apparently sensed something of her feelings because she touched her arm sympathetically. "You don't have to decide immediately. You have two and a half months to find something else. Think of it as a last resort." She paused a moment. "When is the baby due?"

"February." Abigail lifted her chin. "All right, I either find something else, or the boardinghouse job it is." She firmly believed there was always a way if one looked hard enough. She need only convince one local businessman she could bring something to his business he hadn't realized he needed. It would take a bit of imagination, but she was convinced she could find her niche if she just looked hard enough.

Time to change the subject. She touched the parcel she'd set on the counter. "I have something here from Judge Madison."

Constance shook her head. "It's beyond me what you two can have to say to each other. I can't think of a thing you have in common."

Abigail grinned. "I'll have you know we enjoy a very lively correspondence on a wide variety of subjects."

She'd first written to Judge Madison when she learned how he'd given her brother his second chance, a chance that brought him to Turnabout. She'd wanted to thank him, tell him how well it had turned out, and let him know it had given her a fresh start as well.

To her surprise, he'd written back and they'd enjoyed a regular correspondence ever since. She found him charming, intelligent and quite intriguing. Even though they'd never met face-to-face, he'd become like the grandfather she'd never had. And her letters to him had become almost like entries in a diary, sharing hopes and dreams she didn't tell anyone else.

"It looks like it contains a book of some sort," Constance observed.

Abigail frowned. It wasn't unusual for Judge Madison to send her books. In fact, ever since he'd learned about her subscription library he'd periodically sent books from his personal collection. But in her last letter she'd asked him not to send her any more—she simply didn't have room for them. Had he forgotten? Or simply not believed her?

"Let's see." She opened the parcel and her breath caught. It was a copy of *Birds of America* by John James Audubon. "Oh, Constance, look." She stroked the cover, anticipating the beauty of the images inside. Perhaps she could find room for one more book...

It took her a moment to notice there were also two letters in the parcel. The first had her name on it, the second had the name Seth.

"Who's Seth?" Constance asked.

"I have no idea." Curious, she set aside the book and second envelope, then quickly unfolded the one with her name.

My Dear Abigail,

I will dispense with the normal pleasantries because I have a business proposition for you and I want to get right to it. As you know, I invest in properties from time to time. I recently became aware that the Rose Palace Hotel was on the market. So yes, I have bought the place.

She looked up at her friend. "He's bought the Rose Palace from Mr. Crandall."

"I didn't even know it was for sale. Mr. Crandall must be planning to accompany his sister to Chicago when she goes to the hospital there."

Abigail nodded and turned back to the letter.

The current owner is already in the midst of enlarging the facility, which suits my needs. I have

noted the growth Turnabout has undergone in re-
cent years and I believe this will be a good invest-
ment. I am sending Seth Reynolds, an acquaintance
of mine, to oversee the remainder of the work.

Abigail glanced at the second envelope. That must be
who this was for. But why send it to her?

Here is where my offer comes in. I want to hire
you to take charge of the decor, matters such as
paint colors, wallpaper, curtains and the like. I
would also like you to assist in the interviewing
and hiring of new staff. I'm sure your familiar-
ity with the local citizenry will prove invaluable.
In return, I am willing to provide you with something that will solve a problem you are facing. You
mentioned that your library had outgrown its space
in your sister-in-law's restaurant. So, as payment
for your assistance, I will allocate a room on the
hotel's ground floor to permanently house your library, free of charge.
I have not yet mentioned your involvement to
Mr. Reynolds since I was unsure of your response.
If you agree, please give him the enclosed note
when he arrives as it will explain matters to him. If
you decide to decline, simply send me a wire saying so and there will be no hard feelings.
I don't know the exact date of Mr. Reynolds's
arrival, but it should be within a few days of your
receipt of this letter. He has one small task to complete for me and then will head your way.
On a side note, I have decided to spend Christmas in Turnabout with my granddaughter and

great-grandchildren. I look forward to finally meeting you in person.

So much good news, it was hard to take it all in.

She would have willingly helped the judge for free. But to have a new place to house her library was exciting!

And she was finally going to be able to be of service to the man who had done so much for her family.

And she'd also have the opportunity to meet him in person when he came for Christmas.

To know that he trusted her to handle the furnishings and decor of his hotel was gratifying. It was a big responsibility but she was absolutely determined to do him proud. Besides, it would be fun. She was already thinking of possibilities.

And then there was Mr. Reynolds. If he was anything like the judge himself, it would be a privilege to work with him.

Since Mr. Reynolds's arrival date was uncertain, she'd make sure to meet every train coming from that direction until he arrived—the man deserved to be greeted properly.

In the meantime, she'd learn what she could about the hotel—perhaps she'd write a piece for the *Gazette* about the history of the establishment and the renovations taking place.

And the judge's letter had given her an idea for how she just might solve *all* her problems.

"Well?"

Abigail glanced up at Constance, who was not so patiently waiting for an explanation.

A big grin slowly spread across her face. "I think I may have just found the answer I've been looking for."

* * *

Seth shifted, leaning a shoulder against the train window, trying to get more comfortable. The conductor had assured him the stop for Turnabout wasn't much farther, thank goodness. He was eager to get started on this new job—the sooner he completed it, the sooner he could finalize the deal on the Michelson property and get on with the rest of his life.

He stretched out his left leg as much as the space allowed. Sitting for such a long time tended to tighten up the muscles around his old injury.

He glanced across the aisle and noticed the boy perched there appeared fascinated by his cane. The lad reminded him of Jamie, at least in appearance—the same dark hair, brown eyes and sturdy build. But that's where the similarities ended. This boy had that fearless air about him, that buoyant spirit reserved for the very young or very innocent. It was something Jamie no longer seemed to possess.

Losing your parents at such an early age did that to a child. As Seth knew only too well.

The shrill train whistle sounded. Finally!

Seth straightened in his seat as he waited for the train to pull to a stop. Then he grasped his cane, using it to lever himself upright. As expected, he found himself leaning on the silver-topped device more than he liked. Experience told him it would be hours before his cramped muscles eased. But he was used to such inconvenience and wouldn't let it slow him down.

Grabbing his valise with his free hand, he headed for the exit. As he carefully stepped onto the platform, Seth assessed his surroundings. The depot was a mid-sized painted structure fronted by a wooden platform with three benches lined against the building. A freight wagon waited at the end of the platform, no doubt ready to take on cargo from the train.

There were people on the platform but it wasn't crowded—nothing like the bustling throngs he'd waded through when he departed the Philadelphia station.

One person in particular drew a closer look—a young lady in a bright blue dress whose hair was an interesting shade of red. But that wasn't what had snagged his attention—it was the bright, hopeful look she wore, her air of pent-up excitement, as if she was meeting someone she couldn't wait to see. A family member? Or a sweetheart?

What would it be like to have someone waiting for *him* with such happy anticipation?

He impatiently shrugged off that fanciful thought and moved toward the depot. The first order of business was to acquire directions to the hotel. He'd just step inside and ask—

"Excuse me, sir, are you by chance Mr. Seth Reynolds?"

Startled, Seth turned to see the young redheaded woman focusing on a balding gentleman who'd just stepped off the train.

The man she'd addressed gruffly dismissed her. "Sorry, young lady, but you're mistaken." With a tip of his hat, he walked away.

The woman sighed and turned back to the train.

Why was she looking for him? She appeared too young to be Judge Madison's granddaughter. But he must have arranged to have someone meet him. It was both unexpected and unnecessary. But he couldn't just leave her standing there.

Seth steeled himself to ignore the pain in his leg and took a firm step in her direction. "Excuse me."

She turned and met his gaze. The impact of her bright

blue eyes startled him. A stray curl had escaped the confines of her pins and fallen over her forehead. For just a moment he had the absurd desire to tuck it back in for her.

"Yes?"

Her question brought him back to himself. Taken aback by the undisciplined direction his thoughts had taken yet again, he tugged sharply at one of his cuffs. "I couldn't help but overhear you just now. I'm Seth Reynolds."

"Oh." For a moment, all she did was stare.

Which gave him time to study her. Hair the color of mahogany and blue eyes that held a touch of green. Her clothes were well made but not the height of fashion. She wasn't a beauty in the traditional sense—her mouth was a little too large, her forehead a bit too broad. But there was something about her...

When the silence drew out, he gave a sardonic smile. "I take it I'm not what you expected." Was it the cane that had tied her tongue? Had the judge not explained?

His words brought a touch of color to her cheeks. "My apologies. It's just, Judge Madison said you were a friend of his, so I assumed you'd be nearer his age. But that was silly of me. I'm sure he has friends of all ages. Just look at me."

Definitely not the man's granddaughter then. "So, you're a friend of Judge Madison's? Did he send you to meet me?"

She waved a hand, smiling as if he'd said something amusing. "Not exactly. But I couldn't let a friend of the judge's show up with no one to welcome him. So I've been meeting trains ever since I got his letter."

Was the woman always this chatty?

Then she gave him another friendly smile. "Actually, he's hired me to help with the renovations at the Rose

Palace. You and I will be working together—isn't that wonderful?"

She delivered that bit of information as if she thought it would make him happy.

It didn't.

Chapter Two

Seth tried to make sense of her words. Did the judge think he couldn't handle this job alone?

The redhead's smile faltered slightly—his lack of enthusiasm must have shown on his face.

Before he could say anything, however, she pulled an envelope from her skirt pocket and held it out to him.

"My apologies for springing this on you—Everett says my mouth sometimes gets ahead of my thoughts. Perhaps you should read this letter from Judge Madison before we go any further. I think it will explain matters."

He accepted the proffered letter, his mind trying to make sense of her convoluted story. Who was Everett and why did he have any relevance to this? "Thank you, Miss…"

"Oh, I'm so sorry, where are my manners? I'm Abigail Fulton."

"Well, Miss Fulton, if you will excuse me?" He executed a short bow and managed to make it to a nearby bench without leaning on his cane too heavily.

So, Judge Madison had arranged for him to have an assistant. Having someone to help with matters concerning the locals would no doubt be useful. But Seth had always selected his own assistants if he felt he needed one. And this young lady would definitely not have been his choice. She looked like she would be more at home in a Sunday school class than a business office.

Besides, her presence could prove to be a distraction. He glanced her way again. Already she was claiming more of his attention than he usually gave strangers.

Because she was such a chatterbox, of course.

More troubling was the fact that Judge Madison hadn't mentioned this to him personally. Had he thought Seth lacking in some way? Or did he have some other reason?

Perhaps she was a friend of his granddaughter's, someone he was attempting to help in some way. He supposed that was the man's right.

Whatever the reason, Seth decided he could be gracious about it. Judge Madison had always been good to him, had been willing to take a chance on him when no one else would. He could extend the same courtesy to this young lady.

So long as she did her job adequately.

He unfolded the letter and scanned the opening. Then he halted and started over, carefully taking in each word.

I trust you made the trip to Turnabout in good form. As you have no doubt gathered, there are a few matters I failed to clarify before you left. This was partly because they were not yet definite, and partly because I thought it best you not form any preconceived notions before meeting Miss Fulton.

That being said, I have asked Miss Fulton to handle the decor aspects of the renovation and to partner with you on staffing decisions.

His jaw tightened. That could throw a hitch in his plans. Just how involved would she want to be in the staffing process?

It is my hope that this will be a mutually beneficial arrangement for you both. It will relieve you of the burden of making design decisions, allowing you to focus on overseeing the construction. And the combination of her knowledge of the local townsfolk and your understanding of the skills required should make for a highly effective partnership as you two work on the staffing.

You will receive your usual bonus at the project's completion and Miss Fulton will earn the means to achieve one of her own dreams.

Seth frowned. What did that mean?

Working with Miss Fulton should not prove an onerous task. Despite her youth, I have found Abigail to be an imaginative, witty and charmingly spirited young lady. I believe she will be a fast learner and an able partner.

I look forward to seeing the results of your collaboration when I journey to Turnabout in December. If you should have any questions or concerns, you know how to reach me.
Sincerely,
Arthur Madison

As Seth read, he grew more and more incredulous. The judge wanted Miss Fulton to handle the decorating? He'd thought his employer wanted to give the hotel an air of sophistication and elegance. What did this provincial miss know about hotel decor? She'd probably never stayed in a truly elegant hotel in her life. If he had to keep a close eye on her choices it could actually lead to more work for him rather than less.

He realized he'd stiffened, so he deliberately relaxed. If this was what Judge Madison wanted, he'd just have to make the best of it.

She'd just better not get in the way of his plans.

Abigail watched Mr. Reynolds as he read the letter. He was certainly a different sort of man than what she'd expected. For one thing, he was younger than she'd imagined—he looked to be roughly thirty. And unlike the judge, who was so warm and forthcoming in his letters, this man seemed aloof and guarded.

To be fair, though, that might be due to travel weariness. And her announcement *had* seemed to catch him unawares.

His silver-handled walking stick had at first seemed an affectation. But then she'd noticed the slight stiffness of his gait as he moved to the bench and she'd realized the cane was more than a mere accessory.

Though his expression remained closed as he read the letter, she sensed he was displeased with the news. What was he unhappy about—sharing responsibility for the work, sharing it with a woman, or something else?

When he finally lowered the letter, he seemed lost in thought.

Abigail cleared her throat. "Is there a problem?"

Mr. Reynolds glanced up as if he'd forgotten she was there. "Not at all." He folded the letter and slid it inside his jacket as he leveraged himself off the bench with his cane. "My apologies. I suppose I'm tired from my travels."

His expression gave away nothing of his thoughts. Then he met her gaze. "May I ask how you came to know Judge Madison?"

She'd prefer to discuss their assignment, but she supposed it was a logical question. "Of course. We've corresponded regularly for going on five years now."

He raised a brow at that. "Corresponded? So, you've never actually met."

His tone remained neutral but something about his demeanor made her feel defensive. "Not in person, no. I'm looking forward to having that pleasure when he visits in December. But I believe we've gotten to know each other quite well in all the ways that matter."

"I see." He tugged on the cuff of his jacket. "With your indulgence, we can discuss how best to proceed with this…partnership after I've had a chance to freshen up a bit."

"Yes, of course."

"I'd appreciate it if you could direct me to the hotel."

He seemed eager to be rid of her. But she had other ideas. "I'll do better than that. After you make arrangements to have your baggage delivered, I'll walk you there—it's on my way."

"On your way?"

"To the town's restaurant. My sister-in-law owns and operates it and I promised to help her today."

A few minutes later, as they walked down the sidewalk, Abigail pointed out the various businesses they passed. The man said very little in response so she did her best to keep the conversation going on her own. She noticed, however, that his gaze seemed to take in everything, so his silence apparently wasn't due to disinterest.

Perhaps he just wasn't the talkative type.

Finally, as they approached the hotel, she pointed

straight ahead. "The Rose Palace is that red brick building up there."

She could hear the sounds of construction above the
other town noise, but since the work was taking place on
the far side it wasn't visible from their vantage.

She cut him a sideways glance, trying to discern his
thoughts as he studied the building, but as before, his
expression gave very little away.

When they reached the entrance, he gallantly opened
the door and let her precede him. At least there was nothing wrong with his manners.

The curtains were open so the lobby had a cheery,
sunshine-filled warmth to it. Abigail smiled—it was as if
the place was putting its best face forward for his benefit.

"Can I help you folks?"

The question came from Mr. Crandall, standing at his
usual post behind the guest book on the front counter.

Abigail led her companion forward. "Good day, Mr.
Crandall. Allow me to introduce Mr. Seth Reynolds, the
gentleman Judge Madison sent to oversee the renovations."

She turned to him. "Mr. Reynolds, this is Edgar Crandall, the former owner of the Rose Palace."

Mr. Crandall held out his hand. "Welcome to Turnabout and to the Rose Palace. We have a room all ready
for you."

Abigail took that as her cue. "I'm sure you'd like to get
settled in, and I need to head to the restaurant. Perhaps we
could continue our conversation over a late lunch." She
smiled. "In fact, you could meet me there. It has some
of the best food you'll find in these parts and it's a short
walk from here. Mr. Crandall can direct you."

He leaned casually against the counter. "Actually, I'd

prefer to eat here. I want to get a feel for the quality of the hotel's current menu offerings."

Even leaning against the counter, he managed to maintain his all-business air.

"Of course. Shall I return in, say, two hours?"

He nodded. "I look forward to resuming our conversation."

Now why didn't she believe that?

Abigail made her exit, trying not to lose heart.

Mr. Reynolds wasn't the friendly, open person she'd been hoping for. Perhaps after he'd had time to rest from his trip he'd thaw a bit. Otherwise it might be difficult working with him for the next few months.

For all his standoffishness, however, there was something about him she found intriguing. And it wasn't just that he was handsome, which he was, in a brooding sort of way. There was something she'd seen in those cinnamon-brown eyes of his, something that tugged at her, that spoke of a buried vulnerability behind his guarded attitude. There was his limp, of course, but it went deeper.

One thing was certain, he hadn't been pleased to learn she'd be working with him. How would he react when she told him she wanted the job of hotel manager?

She'd given it a lot of prayer and thought. In fact, she had thought of little else since she'd received the judge's letter. She'd even discussed it with Constance, testing the idea with her levelheaded friend.

The thought of managing a hotel on her own was daunting but exciting at the same time. If she could convince Mr. Reynolds and Judge Madison to give her the chance, however, she was absolutely convinced she could do it. After all, Constance had responsibility for the pharmacy and she was the same age.

True, Constance had gone to school back east to train

for her position. But it wasn't as if Abigail hadn't prepared in her own way. She'd spent every minute she could with Mr. Crandall, getting his insights into what the job entailed and what he saw as the main challenges. And Constance had agreed that she had a way with people that would serve her well in a job like this.

It was just a matter of convincing Mr. Reynolds of her suitability. And surely, if he was anything like Judge Madison, he would keep an open mind on the matter.

Seth ignored the urge to watch his would-be work associate leave. There was something about her that got under his skin. But he didn't have time for such distractions—he had to focus on his almost-within-reach goal.

He turned back to the former owner. "Mr. Crandall, let me say on behalf of Judge Madison that he appreciates your willingness to remain until we can transition to a new manager."

Edgar Crandall nodded. "It was the least I could do. It's good that you showed up today, though. I'm not sure how much longer I could have stuck around."

Seth frowned. "What do you mean?"

"Didn't Judge Madison tell you? The whole reason I sold this place was because my sister needs special medical care. I'm taking her to a doctor in Chicago as soon as possible. I told the judge I'd stay until his representative arrived, but I was beginning to think I'd have to renege and leave before that happened."

It seemed Judge Madison had neglected to impart yet another piece of crucial information. He knew his employer well enough to believe it wasn't an oversight. Which meant there was more to this than appeared on the surface. What was he up to?

For now, though, that question would have to wait.

He hadn't counted on having to hire new staff so soon. Maybe he could find someone to man the desk temporarily. "When are you planning to leave?"

"Norma and I will board the morning train tomorrow. We're already packed and ready."

"Do you have any recommendations for who can step in until we hire a permanent replacement?"

The man turned to retrieve a room key. "Abigail's been hanging around here the past few days, studying the place and trying to learn what she can about the different jobs."

He supposed that would make her insight into the staffing process more useful. "That was enterprising of her."

Crandall smiled. "You'll find Abigail is a fast learner."

Seth decided to change the subject. "How many guests do you have currently?"

"We're limiting our bookings to three guest rooms, the ones farthest from the construction. The noise level is a problem for the other rooms." The man handed him the key. "You'll be the exception. I have you in room six—top of the stairs and second room on the right." He cast a furtive glance at Seth's cane. "My sister and I occupy the first-floor suite. It'll be vacant starting tomorrow if you prefer to have that space."

Seth's jaw tightened at this reminder of his perceived infirmity. But he merely nodded and turned toward the stairs. Though he'd long ago accepted that this was how he would be viewed, he still felt the sting each time it happened.

As he climbed the stairs he stepped deliberately, regardless of the pain. It helped him to concentrate on the job ahead. He would take a look at the state of the construction as soon as he freshened up from his trip.

All in all, from his initial look, the atmosphere here

was overblown and cozy rather than elegant, rustic rather than refined. Nothing here spoke of sophistication and luxury.

Could he really count on Miss Fulton to handle the decor so that it was brought up to the judge's normal standards? And to get it all done in time to wrap up by the end of the year?

Why couldn't the judge have partnered him with someone who had more experience than the chatty young redhead?

How had his employer described her in his letter—witty, imaginative and charmingly spirited, a fast learner and an able partner? High praise from a man he'd always thought of as keenly perceptive.

But then again, the judge only knew her via correspondence. He'd never actually met Miss Fulton in person.

So, no offense to his employer, but he would form his own opinions about just how capable the woman actually was.

And so far, he was not impressed.

Chapter Three

"Did you have a chance to look around yet?" Abigail had just taken a seat across the table from Mr. Reynolds in the hotel dining room.

He inclined his head. "I did."

The man didn't seem to be any more forthcoming now than he'd been earlier. "And what are your thoughts?" she prodded.

"In my opinion, having everything completed by Christmas is an ambitious goal, but it is definitely achievable."

"Oh." Was this something he and the judge had discussed? "I know Judge Madison is planning to visit over the holidays, but I wasn't aware that that was our deadline."

He gave her an infuriatingly superior look. "It's always good to have an end date in mind when starting any project. And Christmas seems an appropriate one in this case, especially since Judge Madison will be in town."

Choosing to ignore his tone, she smiled. "I shall defer to you on that since I understand you have experience overseeing this sort of work."

"I have experience in many different areas."

Goodness, did the man have to be so stiff and solemn all the time?

Della Long, who had taken over the kitchen when Norma Crandall became too ill, arrived to take their orders. Abigail performed the introductions, then they made their selections from the very limited menu.

Once they were alone again, Mr. Reynolds picked up the conversational reins. "Mr. Crandall introduced me to Walter Hendricks, the man handling the construction."

Abigail nodded. "Mr. Hendricks and his two sons are good men and they do good work. You can see examples all over town, including the schoolhouse and the town hall."

"So you know them personally?"

"Of course. It's a small town. Most everyone here knows everyone else." His lack of conversation was making it difficult for her to discern how he felt about things. "Did you have the opportunity to inspect their work?"

"Briefly. I plan to inspect it in more detail over the next few days."

"Well, I'm certain you'll be pleased with what you see."

He merely nodded noncommittally.

Deciding things might go better if she learned something about him personally, she changed the subject. "I actually have a favor to ask."

He raised a brow. "And that is?"

Abigail smiled at the touch of wariness in his tone. "It's nothing onerous, I assure you." She retrieved a small notebook and pencil from her pocket. "My brother, Everett, owns the local newspaper and I help occasionally. I'd like to interview you for the next issue."

Mr. Reynolds frowned. "I can't imagine anything about me would be noteworthy."

Was he just being modest or did he really think so little of himself? "Everyone has a story of some sort to tell. Besides, folks are always interested to learn more when someone new moves to town. And the hotel renovation itself is big news around here." She opened the pad. "You don't mind, do you?"

His expression didn't change but she sensed his hesitation. Or was it annoyance?

He finally waved a hand, as if in surrender. "Very well, but let's keep it short. There's not much to tell anyway."

Careful to keep the note of victory from her expression, she smiled. "Thank you. Let's start with you telling me something about yourself—where you're from, your family, what exactly it is you do, that sort of thing."

"I'm from Philadelphia and my job is that of property manager for Judge Madison."

"And what does a property manager do?"

"Judge Madison doesn't care much for travel. Whenever something needs close supervision on any of his out-of-town properties, I act as his on-site representative and handle whatever needs attention."

"That sounds like a lot of responsibility. Judge Madison must have a great deal of faith in you."

He shrugged.

Definitely a man of few words. Moving on... "And your family? Are you married?"

"No."

Ignoring the little spurt of pleasure that gave her, she pressed on. "Parents? Siblings?"

"Deceased." His response was chopped and his tone warned against further probing.

"Oh, I'm so sorry." Was that why he seemed so closed off? She couldn't imagine being entirely on her own.

Even when she'd spent those long, lonely years in boarding school, she'd known Everett was out there and would come running should she need him. And she'd had holidays to look forward to, when the two of them could spend precious time together.

How long had he been on his own? "That must—"

But he cut her off, brushing aside her sympathy. "I lost them a long time ago. I'm used to being on my own."

As if that would make it any easier to bear. But she took the hint. "Well then, can you tell me how long you've worked for Judge Madison?"

"Going on eleven years now."

"And do you have any hobbies?" she asked, desperate to get *some* kind of personal insight. "Something you enjoy doing when you're not working?"

He made an impatient gesture. "I don't have time for hobbies. The judge keeps me busy. And that's how I like it."

The man was impossible! How could she get him to open up and give her more than these terse, uninformative answers?

Before she could ask anything else, Della returned with their food. Abigail set aside her pencil and notebook while the meal was placed before them. She wasn't getting much to work with anyway. This was going to be a very dry article unless she injected more life into it herself with personal observations.

Of course, he had to actually do something for her to observe before even that much was possible.

Seth had never liked talking about himself, so as soon as the waitress departed, he took the offensive. "I believe it's my turn to ask you a few questions."

His words brought a pleased light to her eyes. Apparently, unlike him, she *did* like talking about herself.

"Of course," she said, lifting her fork. "My parents are no longer around, but I have an older brother who's married with two children." She smiled. "I've already mentioned that Daisy, my sister-in-law, runs a restaurant." She touched the pencil on the table. "And Everett owns and operates the town newspaper. I work with both of them from time to time."

Interesting, but not the information he'd been after. "You said you and Judge Madison have been corresponding for a number of years. What initiated the correspondence?"

"That's a fun story. He did an amazing kindness for my brother several years ago and I wrote to thank him. It continued from there. We discovered that we had similar tastes in literature and in food. He introduced me to Cervantes, and I introduced him to the joys of apple-pecan pie."

Interesting. What *amazing kindness* had Judge Madison done for her brother? But she didn't elaborate further so he moved to something else. "Do you have any experience doing the sort of work the judge is asking of you?"

"Not actual hands-on experience." She said that lightly, as if it was inconsequential. "But I've studied as much as I could find and it sounds like fun. I don't imagine it will be terribly difficult."

He found her offhand manner irritating. Then he remembered the judge's cryptic mention of allowing her to "earn the means to achieve one of her dreams." "What will you gain from doing this?"

She frowned—was it at his question or his tone? Had she picked up on his irritation? She might be more perceptive than he'd given her credit for.

"You mean, besides repaying a friend?" Her tone said that should be enough.

Then she smiled, her mood seeming to change with dizzying speed. "I run a small subscription library that's currently housed in Daisy's restaurant. Judge Madison offered me a ground-floor room here in the hotel to house it."

Yet another thing his employer had failed to mention to him. "So we'll need to account for that when we address the ground floor."

She nodded. "I've already looked around and found the perfect place."

Of course she had, but he wouldn't be ready to discuss that until he had a chance to evaluate things himself. "We'll certainly look at all the options when the time is right. We want to make certain the location benefits *all* parties."

She studied him thoughtfully, then nodded. "Of course."

They both focused on their meals after that, eating in silence for several minutes. At first he found the respite from her chatter soothing, but after a while the silence began to feel oddly oppressive.

Finally, he spoke up. "Tell me about this library of yours."

Her face lit up again. "It's a subscription library that I started about five years ago with just the books my brother and I owned.

"Over the years I've taken the money I earned through the subscriptions and purchased new titles to add to it," she continued. "And from time to time Judge Madison sends me some of his books as well."

She gave a sharing-an-insight smile. "He always says

he's just getting rid of some of his older books to make room for new ones, but I suspect he's just being generous."

Seth suspected she was right. The judge obviously had a soft spot for Miss Fulton. But he'd noticed the man often enjoyed championing lost causes.

She waved her fork, obviously unable to keep her hands still while she talked. "Anyway, it's not as large as the libraries you'd find in big cities, but now I'll have the space to expand it the way I want to."

What did she know of big-city libraries? "A worthy goal. And I suppose having the library here in the hotel could be viewed as a bonus for our guests."

She beamed at him. "Oh, I hadn't thought of that. What a wonderful idea. I could even waive my subscription fee for guests, at least for their first book."

Being the focus of that wide-eyed, admiring smile took him aback. He wasn't used to such attention. Scrambling to get his thoughts back under control, Seth brought the discussion back around to the job ahead of them. "The food here seems passable, but not memorable."

Miss Fulton grimaced agreement. "It was better when Norma ran the kitchen. But Della is trying. With some direction, and help with menu planning, she could be an excellent cook."

"You said you've worked in your sister-in-law's restaurant. Do you feel qualified to help in that arena?" Having the chatty Miss Fulton in charge of the kitchen might keep her busy enough to stay out of his way.

"Of course." She pointed her fork at him. "In fact, I've already been thinking about this." She leaned forward, her expression warming with enthusiasm. "Since we have so few guests while we're under construction, it makes sense to get their food orders the day before and then we can plan all meals first thing in the morning. It will make the best use of Della's time and our money."

That was a surprisingly good plan. "Doesn't the hotel dining room get outside customers?"

"Occasionally. I thought of that, too. One of our offerings could be a soup or stew, which can be easily stretched to serve additional people."

The woman continued to surprise him. Perhaps there was more to her than he'd first thought.

She lowered her fork. "But we have a more pressing staffing issue. Did Mr. Crandall tell you he's leaving tomorrow?"

So she knew about that. "Yes. And that's a key position that needs to be filled immediately, at least on a temporary basis." He would let his future hotel manager take care of hiring key positions like the permanent desk clerk.

"But don't worry," he assured her, "I can handle the job for a day or two. That should give me time to interview candidates and make certain I get the right person for the job." Though it would delay his efforts to inspect the property in the detail he needed to.

"We."

Her tone and expression were equally determined.

"I beg your pardon."

She met his gaze without flinching. "*We* will interview candidates. Judge Madison asked us to handle the staffing together, remember?"

What did this barely-out-of-the-schoolroom miss know about interviewing job candidates? "Of course. I'm sure your insights will be most helpful." But he planned to establish from the outset that the final decisions would be his. His whole future rested on him ultimately hiring Bartholomew Michelson as the hotel manager.

Miss Fulton's face took on a suspiciously casual expression. "You know, you're going to be quite busy familiarizing yourself with the hotel and town for the next few days. Rather than you also assuming the manager duties, perhaps I could handle that piece for now."

He sensed there was more going on here than her being helpful. "You misunderstand. The position we'll be hiring for is desk clerk. I'll assume the role of hotel manager myself while the construction is ongoing, and fill it permanently once we're closer to the completion date."

"I see." She frowned, then seemed to rally. "Then, since we are sharing the responsibilities for the renovation, I think we should also share the responsibilities of the hotel-manager position."

Why ever would she want such a responsibility? Did she think it would give her some sort of prestige? "That's a generous offer but I think I should take care of this myself."

She stiffened. "Are you saying you don't think I can handle the job?"

"Do you have any experience in doing so?"

"I studied the work Mr. Crandall did, and even relieved him on occasion at the front desk when he had to tend to Norma."

"It was inappropriate for Mr. Crandall to leave you in charge when you're not employed here."

"But I *am* employed here. Did you forget already?"

He resisted the urge to roll his eyes. "That's for an altogether different function. I'm sure Judge Madison intended to have you work in a more behind-the-scenes capacity—certainly not to do actual hotel work."

Her eyes narrowed and her chin came up. "Judge Madison didn't tell you any such thing. And this partnership between us will only work if we respect each other."

He tried a different approach. "To be blunt, you admit

to having very little experience. And being hotel manager involves much more than working the front desk. In fact, in many larger establishments, the manager never works the front desk. And if I have to train you on those finer points, I might as well do the job myself."

"But this is the perfect time for me to learn. There are only three rooms occupied and the staff has been reduced to one maid, one cook and the night clerk. So supervision won't be as demanding."

"Which shows how inexperienced you are. With such a small staff, the hotel manager will not only need to help work the desk, but also see that all the smaller tasks get done, like tending to guest luggage, providing concierge duties and handling complaints."

Her gaze didn't falter. "All of which I'll absolutely be able to manage."

Stubborn woman. She obviously had a very high estimation of her abilities. "Do you honestly see yourself carting luggage and trunks up and down the stairs as required?" His conscience twinged as he admitted to himself that he would have trouble managing that himself with his injured leg. Too bad this place didn't have elevators.

Her expression tightened. "I'd find a way to manage."

He could see he'd need to act quickly in hiring a new desk clerk. "Perhaps a compromise is in order. We can divide up the front desk work between us—you take a portion of the hours and I take a portion." He could make certain she was on duty during the less busy time, and he could keep an eye on her as well.

She studied him, and for a moment he thought she'd dig in her heels. Then her expression shifted.

"Very well. You obviously want me to prove myself and I can understand that. But in return, will you give me your word that this is just a first step. When a suitable time has elapsed, and I've proven myself capable, you will train me on the responsibilities of a hotel manager."

"Agreed," he said without hesitation. If she could handle the desk job—and he wasn't convinced she could—then he'd humor her with the additional training.

And if she could eventually take care of some tasks, like managing small grievances that might pop up with the staff, it would free him to focus on the bigger picture.

After all, at the end of the day, Bartholomew Michelson *would* be hired as hotel manager when the time came to fill the position permanently. That was how it had to be.

Time to change the subject. "Do you have any thoughts on the decor?"

He wasn't surprised when she nodded.

"I've actually been thinking about that quite a lot since I received Judge Madison's letter. I want to draw on the word *rose* in the hotel's name for inspiration."

Seth winced as he had a sudden vision of pink splashes everywhere and overblown cabbage roses adorning every drape, carpet and bed covering in the place. "Before you go too far down that path, I should tell you I believe the place needs a new name."

"What's wrong with the current name? I've always thought Rose Palace has an elegant feel to it."

"On the contrary, Rose Palace conjures up a gaudy, old-fashioned image. Something more understated and sophisticated would better fit the image of an establishment owned by Judge Arthur Madison."

"Well, I think the name is charming, especially when you know the story behind it."

What was with her and stories? Was it because her brother was a reporter? "And that story is?"

"From what I've heard, the man who built this place had a daughter named Rose who spent her life confined to a wheelchair. That man not only named this place for her, but also designed the entire first floor for her benefit."

She waved a hand. "If you'll notice, many of the decorative carvings and embellishments are at chair-rail height. There are no raised thresholds, and the owner's suite is on the first floor."

"Quite sentimental. But I doubt any future guests will know that story." He ignored her outraged look. "We need a name that carries meaning today."

She leaned back, her expression issuing a challenge. "I suppose you have something more appropriate in mind?"

"Simple is better. Naming it the Madison or the Madison House after its new owner strikes me as an appropriate choice."

She wrinkled her nose, obviously unimpressed. "Is that really what Judge Madison wants?"

"He didn't say one way or the other, but I can't imagine he'd object. He usually goes with my recommendations on such matters."

Her face suddenly lit up. "I know. Why don't we call it the Madison Rose Hotel?"

It was his turn to be unimpressed. Why did she have to challenge him on every front? "The Madison Rose? That doesn't make sense."

"Actually, I think it has a nice ring to it. It embraces the hotel's history while acknowledging the new ownership." She stabbed a carrot with enthusiasm, obviously convinced she'd settled the matter.

He rubbed his jaw, deciding he should pick his battles. "As a compromise, I suppose it's not a bad choice."

She nodded as if his agreement had been a foregone

conclusion, then glanced around the room. "I still think we can use the rose as a theme for our decor."

That again. "If you're thinking of using shades of red or pink throughout—"

She waved a hand dismissively. "Not to excess. Just touches here and there. And I plan to interlace it with spring green. Trust me, it will be tasteful."

Seth withheld comment. Whether they were in accord on their definitions of tasteful remained to be seen.

While the conversation so far hadn't gone as she'd hoped, Abigail decided there was reason to be optimistic. Mr. Reynolds seemed willing to keep an open mind. And since he wasn't planning to hire someone to fill the hotel-manager position until the renovation neared completion, she had time to prove herself capable. If he himself trained her, how could he refuse to hire her when the time came?

The rest of the meal passed pleasantly enough. Once they'd finished, her companion pulled out his pocket watch and flicked it open.

"Do you have another appointment?" Abigail had hoped they'd have more time to discuss their working arrangement.

He put his watch away. "I've asked Mr. Crandall to have everyone gather in the kitchen at two o'clock for a short meeting."

He stood, placing his napkin on the table. "If you'll excuse me, it's almost that time."

She quickly stood as well. "I'll join you."

He raised a brow. "I assumed you already knew everyone."

"I do. But I think we should introduce ourselves from

the outset as partners. We can also let them know what to expect both during construction and after."

He didn't seem pleased with the idea, but he waved a hand toward the kitchen, indicating she should precede him.

Flashing her brightest smile, Abigail moved past him toward the kitchen. At least now he knew she intended to be a full partner in this undertaking.

People tended to treat her like a naive little girl to be patted on the head and humored. Hopefully, Mr. Reynolds would now take note that she was more than that.

If not, she'd just have to keep giving him reasons to take note.

Chapter Four

Abigail stepped into the kitchen to find all the staff assembled, looking as if they were about to meet their executioner.

She supposed it was natural for them to be concerned since they were exchanging one boss for another. Hopefully she and Mr. Reynolds would be able to set their minds at ease.

Since the construction began and the number of guests they were accommodating had been cut back, the hotel staff had also been reduced from six to three. In addition to Della Long, there was Ruby Mills, the maid, and Larry Scruggs, the night clerk.

Mr. Crandall stepped forward as soon as she and Mr. Reynolds entered the kitchen. "Folks, this is Mr. Seth Reynolds, who's come here as the new owner's representative to oversee all the construction work being done. And you all know Abigail Fulton. She's going to be working with Mr. Reynolds while he's here."

The man then turned to the three staff members standing behind him and introduced each in turn. When he'd finished, Mr. Reynolds took control of the conversation.

"I want to assure you that even though Mr. Crandall

is leaving tomorrow, everything will remain as it is for the time being."

Abigail noticed that the three employees were each reacting to Mr. Reynolds in their own way. All had obviously taken note of his cane. Larry couldn't seem to meet the man's gaze, Ruby appeared unable to tear her gaze away from the cane and Della appeared merely curious.

Mr. Reynolds continued speaking in the same businesslike manner, seeming not to notice anything amiss. "Over the course of the coming weeks, as we expand and redesign the interior of this hotel, we'll also be looking into menu and service changes that will add to the overall atmosphere we wish to provide to our guests."

Abigail almost rolled her eyes. Was he trying to reassure the staff or make them more anxious? "Not that there's anything wrong with the meals and service you've been providing," she said as he paused. "We merely want to try a different approach, something to go with the new look the hotel will have when the renovation is complete."

He shot her an irritated look, then continued as if she hadn't spoken. "I'll be talking individually with each of you over the coming days to discuss these changes and how they will affect your responsibilities. I'll also answer any questions you have and work up a timetable."

"In the meantime," Abigail added, "we know you'll continue to offer your usual high quality of service." She turned to the former owner. "We also want to let you know that we wish you and your sister the medical cure you're seeking in Chicago and that our prayers will be with you both."

The rest of the staff nodded and offered their well wishes. Even Mr. Reynolds had the grace to do the same.

After that the meeting broke up. As they moved back

to the lobby, Mr. Reynolds cut her a sideways glance. "I take it you don't approve of the way I handled the staff."

"Perhaps a bit more empathy in the way you deliver your information wouldn't go amiss."

"Mollycoddling employees rarely provides the desired results. They are Judge Madison's employees, not our friends."

"They can be both. And being kind isn't the same as mollycoddling. Employees who feel valued are employees who will go the extra mile for you."

"And just how many employees have you dealt with thus far?"

Her cheeks warmed. "None, of course. But that doesn't mean I don't know how to deal with people."

"*People* are not the same as employees."

Before she could respond, he changed the subject. "Would you be so good as to give me directions to the judge's granddaughter's home. I'd like to stop by sometime to pay my respects."

"Actually, I can do better than that," she said impulsively. "There's a group of four families here in Turnabout who have connections to Judge Madison. Reggie Barr, the judge's granddaughter, is naturally a part of that group. Tomorrow is Sunday and we all get together for lunch after the church service. Why don't you come as my guest?"

He seemed slightly taken aback at her invitation. Surely he wasn't so staid as to consider that too forward of her?

"I don't know—"

She quickly interrupted his protest. "I assure you, you'd be most welcome. And in addition to the Barrs, you'd be meeting a number of well-respected citizens of Turnabout in a relaxed, informal setting. And that includes the rest of my family."

And just maybe, once he got to know folks better, he'd drop some of his standoffish demeanor enough for them to become friends.

Seth didn't consider intruding on an established social gathering with a room full of strangers, no matter how congenial, to be a relaxing pastime. But she was correct, this was a way to get himself into the social mix of the town in an expedient manner. "Very well, if you're certain I wouldn't be intruding, then I accept."

"Wonderful. And I'll be happy to accompany you to the service tomorrow as well. I'm in the choir, but you can sit with my brother and his family during the service."

"Of course. Thank you." Seth had had an uneasy relationship with God for quite a while and didn't make attending Sunday service a priority. But he knew it would be expected of him.

Then he remembered something she'd said earlier. "I'm curious—how did there come to be four families here with connections to Judge Madison? I understand the Barrs—their connection is familial. And you mentioned he once did your brother a kindness. But that still leaves two others."

She nodded. "Actually, all four men, including Mr. Barr, are originally from the Philadelphia area, which, come to think of it, should give you some common ground with them."

"Four different men moved here from Philadelphia?" Something suddenly clicked. That's why the name Everett Fulton had sounded familiar. "Your brother, Everett, you said he runs the newspaper here—he was a reporter for a newspaper in Philadelphia six or so years back, wasn't he?"

She looked pleased. "He was. Do you know him then?"

"Only by reputation." There'd been a scandal attached to the man's name, something about an inaccurate article that led to a public figure's downfall. No wonder he'd moved so far away. But why had Judge Madison gotten involved? And did Miss Fulton know about the scandal?

"Everett had a rough time of it for a while." Miss Fulton said. "I'm not sure of the details—he doesn't like to talk about it so I don't pry. But things have really turned around for him since he moved here. Especially since he met and married Daisy. I've never seen him happier."

So she *didn't* know about the scandal. Perhaps that was for the best. Such knowledge would definitely dull the sparkle of her rose-colored outlook.

"As for the connection between the four families and Judge Madison," she continued, "he's the one who arranged for all four men—my brother, Adam Barr, Mitch Parker and Chance Dawson—to travel here together. His reasons for doing so are between him and the men." She grinned. "I've always thought it added an air of romance and mystery to the group and I used to spend hours making up stories about it in my head."

He certainly believed that—she seemed the type to romanticize even the most mundane of happenings. But it was interesting that all four men had traveled here together.

She brushed at her skirt. "I know you're probably still tired from your trip. Would you like me to come by here in the morning before the service or would you rather meet us in front of the newspaper office?"

"I'll come to you."

She gave him directions and then made her exit.

As Seth climbed the stairs he tried to get his thoughts in order. This job was turning out to be something quite different than what he'd anticipated, but not because of the work itself. Having to keep up with the unorthodox Miss Fulton was going to require a whole extra layer of his attention.

But he was confident he could handle it. Strange, though, that he was feeling more intrigued than irritated by the prospect. When had his attitude shifted?

He shook his head. All he needed was a good night's rest and he would be up to facing any silly scheme she tried to throw at him.

In fact, he was rather looking forward to it.

Abigail took her accustomed place with the rest of the choir at the front of the church the next morning. Her gaze turned Mr. Reynolds's way more often than was entirely proper, but she couldn't seem to help herself.

He'd met her, as planned, in front of the newspaper office. Punctual, of course. She'd introduced him to Everett and Daisy and had been a little surprised at his demeanor. While he'd been polite, he hadn't exactly been warm or neighborly. Of course, he'd been standoffish with her at first, too. But there was something different about this interaction that troubled her, something she couldn't quite put her finger on.

Perhaps it was just her imagination. Because Seth sat in the pew next to Everett and she didn't sense anything amiss now.

Reverend Harper moved to the pulpit and Abigail turned her gaze in his direction, determined to pay attention to the sermon.

Later, when the service had ended, Abigail was pleased to find Mr. Reynolds had waited for her rather than making his exit with her family. She linked her elbow to Constance's and pulled her from the choir. "Come on, I want to introduce you to Mr. Reynolds."

A moment later, they were face-to-face. "Mr. Reynolds, this is Constance Harper, who is also the reverend's daughter, the town's pharmacist and my best friend."

She turned to her friend. "Constance, this is Mr. Seth Reynolds, the gentleman who's come to oversee the renovations to the hotel."

Mr. Reynolds executed a short bow. "It's a pleasure to meet a lady who holds so many auspicious titles."

Abigail was delighted to hear Mr. Reynolds attempt to be charming, especially when it was aimed at her best friend.

Constance smiled. "Thank you. And welcome to Turnabout. I hope you'll enjoy your stay here."

"I'm sure I will."

They headed toward the front doors.

"Abigail has been talking of nothing else but the hotel since she received Judge Madison's letter," Constance said. "It sounds as if it will be quite grand when the work is complete."

"That's our plan."

So, he was back to short answers.

They had reached the door by this time, so Abigail introduced him to Reverend Harper and then they were out in the sunshine. Constance moved off to join her mother, leaving Abigail alone with Mr. Reynolds.

"Everett and Daisy have already headed to the restaurant. Shall we head that way or is there anyone here you'd like me to introduce you to?"

He swept a hand outward. "I'm at your disposal. Please, proceed as you normally would."

Since he didn't seem particularly eager to tarry, she

nodded and moved toward the sidewalk. "Then we'll head on over to the restaurant so I can help Daisy get things ready."

He fell into step beside her, and other than pausing for the occasional introduction or to exchange pleasantries, they didn't speak until they were out of the churchyard.

"Are these Sunday luncheons always held at your sister-in-law's restaurant?"

Surprised by his apparent interest, Abigail nodded. "We used to rotate the hosting duties among the families, but the group has grown so large that Daisy's restaurant is about the only indoor space large enough to hold everyone."

"How many people are in this group?"

Did she detect a note of wariness? "Not counting you, there are eleven adults and eight children."

"That's quite a crowd."

"Which is part of what makes it such fun." She gave him a reassuring smile. "Don't worry, before long you'll feel right at home."

She still detected a hint of tension in him, so she decided to change the subject. "Did the Crandalls get off okay?"

He gave a short nod. "They were headed for the train station as I left to join you for church service."

"I pray the doctors in Chicago can help Norma. And not just for her sake. She and Edgar are so close. They're twins, you know, which makes them doubly close."

Something flickered in his expression, something involuntary, there and gone before she could identify it.

They'd arrived at the restaurant, however, so she didn't have time to dwell on it.

Abigail made a few introductions, then left him in her brother's company while she headed to the kitchen.

She knew it was foolish to worry about how he'd fit in. Traveling as he did, Mr. Reynolds must be accustomed to finding himself in unfamiliar places with strangers for company.

Still, she felt responsible for him while he was here.

Seth watched Abigail head to the kitchen and for just a moment felt as if he'd been set adrift. Strange how he'd become accustomed to her presence after such a short acquaintance.

Which was absurd. He was used to being among strangers—in fact he normally preferred it. Strangers had little power to distract or disappoint you.

"What do you think of Turnabout?"

He turned to see it was Everett Fulton who'd addressed him. "From what I've seen so far, the place carries a certain small-town charm."

Everett smiled. "Quite different from Philadelphia, isn't it? But it definitely has its fine points."

"Your sister indicated all four families here have ties to Judge Madison."

"We do. About five or so years ago, Judge Madison was instrumental in convincing the men in this group to move here from Philadelphia."

Which was information Miss Fulton had already provided. He'd hoped for a little more, so he tried a little prodding. "I suppose he was working to improve his granddaughter's hometown even then."

Everett looked amused. "You could say that." The door opened and Everett waved a hand. "Speaking of the judge's granddaughter, she just walked in with her family. Come on, I'll introduce you."

Regina Barr turned out to be a confident, interesting

woman, with eyes that seemed to see more than the physical aspect of the person she was speaking to.

"It's a pleasure to meet you," she said as she shook his hand. "My grandfather has told me so much about you."

She released his hand and continued. "I'm sorry I didn't greet you properly yesterday, but I'm glad you could join us today. I trust my grandfather was well the last time you saw him."

"Yes, ma'am. And he sends his best to you."

"In his letters to me, he speaks very highly of you, and my grandfather isn't one to praise lightly."

Seth gave short bow. "You flatter me, ma'am. I have the utmost respect for your grandfather. He tells me you're a talented photographer."

She nodded, acknowledging his compliment. "It's something I enjoy." Then she handed the child she'd been carrying to her husband and accepted the hamper he'd been carrying in return. "If you gentlemen will excuse me, I'm going to see if they need my help in the kitchen."

After that, the other members of the group arrived in rapid succession and Seth was introduced to each in turn.

With practiced ease, the men rearranged the tables to form one long dining surface. After a moment's hesitation, Seth set aside his cane and pitched in. He was always self-conscious about his ungainly gait when he walked unaided, but that was no excuse for not helping.

The conversation among the men was convivial and while they made an effort to include him, much of it contained references to people and events Seth was completely unfamiliar with. But he listened and absorbed what he could. He'd learned long ago that it was always helpful to learn as much as possible about the people around you.

Seth was pleased no one tried to give him special treatment due to his limp. His assistance was accepted as a matter of course, a consideration he didn't always receive.

Once the tables were properly arranged, cloths were brought out, followed by the meal itself. Everyone pitched in, even the older children—obviously no one here considered setting up the meal to be women's work.

Once everything was set out, he went to retrieve his cane and found one of the children, a little girl who looked to be four or five, eyeing it curiously.

"I like your stick," she said when he approached.

"Thank you." He took it and leaned into it, relieving some of the weight from his aching leg. "I like it, too."

"Do you use it because you walk funny?"

Seth stilled, unused to being questioned so directly. But there was no judgment in this little girl, only curiosity. So he managed to smile and give her a simple answer. "Yes. It helps me to walk when my leg hurts."

She nodded, then skipped away to rejoin some of the other children.

Seth turned and stilled as he found Miss Fulton watching him. The idea that she might have overheard his exchange with the child left him feeling uncomfortably exposed.

"I see you've made the acquaintance of the judge's great-granddaughter, Patience."

He still couldn't tell if she'd overheard anything. "She seems a bright child," he said cautiously.

Miss Fulton nodded and then changed the subject with a wave toward the other end of the room. "I thought I'd give you a look at my library."

"Of course." He followed her across the room, deciding that she probably hadn't heard anything after all.

The three bookshelves that held her collection were crammed full, with many of the shelves weighted down with books stacked two deep. And the range of titles included was impressive.

"What do you think?" She studied him earnestly, as if his answer really mattered to her.

He wasn't used to such regard. He cleared his throat. "You have an impressively eclectic selection. There seems to be a little something for every taste and age level."

She smiled as if that had been a huge compliment. "Thank you. I try to have something for everyone, but as you probably noticed I've run out of room to add anything new. In fact, the last batch Judge Madison sent is stacked on a chair in my bedroom. I've had to ask him to stop sending books until I figure out a way to accommodate them."

Which must be when Judge Madison decided she needed a new space for her books. "Does your library get much use?"

Miss Fulton nodded as she fussily straightened a few volumes. "Absolutely. Several patrons have read every book I own, some more than once. And many have asked to be notified as soon as I acquire new titles."

The small desk in front of the bookshelves held an open ledger and he idly studied it, curious as to her record-keeping skills.

The page contained row upon row of neatly penned entries containing book title, checkout date, return date and the borrowing patron's name. The woman was surprisingly well organized for someone who seemed so flighty.

Perhaps there was more to Miss Fulton than he'd initially credited.

Then again, managing a small subscription library and managing the creation of a cohesive design for a major business were two entirely different undertakings on two entirely different scales.

A moment later everyone began taking their seats. It appeared all of them, including the children, sat together along the long row of joined tables, and Seth found himself seated between Miss Fulton and Chance Dawson, the youngest of the four men who'd journeyed here together.

Mitch Parker, who Seth had learned was one of the town's schoolteachers, stood and gave the blessing over the meal.

When the amens were said, conversation picked up again as the food was passed around the table. Apparently this group believed in keeping things informal.

As he passed the bowl of peas to Miss Fulton, he resumed their conversation about the library. "I see now why you're anxious to find a new place for your library. We'll have to decide on a space soon."

"I'm so glad you agree. Perhaps we can discuss it tomorrow."

"Of course."

The judge's granddaughter said something to her from across the table and their conversation ended. Seth took the opportunity to look around.

The group nearly filled up the restaurant. In addition to the four couples and Miss Fulton, an elderly couple, the Peavys, were there. They were apparently the housekeeper and handyman that lived with the Barrs. And there seemed to be kids everywhere, from infants to adolescents. In addition to Miss Fulton's sister-in-law, Mrs. Parker, the schoolteacher's wife, was apparently expecting as well. Seth hadn't been part of a family or even a community gathering of this sort in a very long time.

How would Jamie feel about being a part of a gathering like this? Of course, the boy no doubt took part in large gatherings for the students at his boarding school.

But did they have the same kind of family feel as this?

Throughout the meal, everyone did their best to make him feel comfortable, going out of their way to include him in conversations, explaining some of the references that were foreign to him, asking him questions that showed interest without being too personal.

But he knew himself to be an outsider here. Except when he looked at Miss Fulton. Strange how just glancing her way seemed to anchor him. Perhaps it was because it was she who had met him when he arrived.

When the meal ended, he helped put the restaurant back to rights, then turned to Abigail. "I should get back to the hotel so I can relieve Miss Mills."

The staff took turns watching the front desk on Sunday mornings so no one person had to miss services *every* Sunday. Today it had been the maid's turn.

"And when would you like me to come by and relieve you?"

Miss Fulton apparently took her role as his partner seriously. "This being Sunday, I can cover things until Mr. Scruggs comes by for the night shift. Why don't you plan to come by tomorrow morning?"

She nodded. "Perhaps we can also discuss what sort of budget I have for the furnishings and fabrics I'll need to purchase."

Her question caught him by surprise, though he thought he did a good job of covering it. He was uncomfortable with the idea of giving her a budget to manage on her own. But now was not the time to mention that. He'd begun to feel the effects of a headache.

"Of course. I can work out some preliminary figures based on what Judge Madison and I discussed for the overall project budget. We can discuss how to work things out in that area when I see you tomorrow."

A few minutes later he stepped outside and headed toward the hotel. The fresh air helped his headache some but he couldn't shake it completely. Perhaps he should have taken Miss Fulton up on her offer to help this afternoon.

Then he rolled his eyes. He'd never been one to let something as minor as a headache stop him before. Surely he wasn't letting the intriguing Miss Fulton get to him?

He had too much on the line to let himself be distracted by a sunny smile and spirited personality.

Chapter Five

Abigail always enjoyed helping with the cleanup after the Sunday lunches. Being together in the kitchen with the other women, listening to their stories and laughter, had always given her an all-is-right-with-the-world feeling.

If ever a girl needed role models for marital bliss she couldn't ask for finer examples. She hoped to one day join their ranks. Of course, she first had to find a man to love and be loved by in return.

Would that ever happen for her?

Once the kitchen was set back to rights and the other families made their exits, Daisy gave a tired sigh. She looked at her son and daughter playing with wooden spoons nearby. "I think these two are ready for a nap." She smiled Abigail's way as she rubbed her stomach. "And I may just join them."

"You need help getting them upstairs?" Abigail asked as she untied her apron.

Everett bent over to lift Danielle. "That's my job." He tickled the little girl, causing her to erupt in giggles.

Daisy took Wyatt's hand and Everett slid his arm around her, giving her an affectionate peck on the cheek.

A lump rose in Abigail's throat as she stared at the blissful family picture they made. Her brother had found his forever love and she'd never seen him so happy and content. Would she ever have that for herself?

Throwing off the poignant mood, she hung up the apron. "It's a beautiful day and I'm not interested in napping. I think I'll take a nice long walk."

With goodbyes quickly said, she headed out, turning toward the Harper home almost without conscious thought. A nice chat with her best friend was just what she needed to clear her mind.

Mr. Reynolds was a puzzle to her. The man could be so formal one moment, then relaxed the next. His interactions with the hotel staff were no-nonsense. Yet today he'd handled Patience's innocently indelicate question with surprising sensitivity. She'd also sensed being caught performing that kindness had embarrassed him.

Yes, the man was definitely a puzzle.

When she knocked on the Harpers' door, it was Reverend Harper who answered. "Hello, Abigail." He pushed open the screen door. "Come on in. Constance is in the parlor."

"Not anymore." Constance appeared behind her father's shoulder.

Abigail smiled a greeting. "I thought I'd enjoy some of this fall sunshine. Care to join me?"

Constance nodded. "Let me fetch my bonnet."

Ten minutes later they were strolling along the country lane that meandered behind the church. Abigail finally broke the silence. "What did you think of Mr. Reynolds?"

Constance gave her a wry smile. "Based on the five-minute conversation I had with him, he seems a nice enough gent. A little stiff perhaps, but that's understandable since he's new here."

She cut Abigail a sideways look. "The real question is, what do *you* think of him?"

Abigail gave the question careful consideration. "He's very business-minded in his approach, but earnest and willing to listen. As far as I can tell, he's also very good at his job." Then she waved a hand. "Which isn't surprising since the judge hired him."

"But do you like him?"

"I don't *dis*like him."

"That's not exactly an answer."

"I'm still trying to figure out how I feel. I got the impression he wasn't happy to learn I'd be working with him, but that could just be because he was caught by surprise. And his all-business demeanor can be a bit off-putting. But there's also something about him that's seems so honorable." She wanted to call it vulnerability, but that was ridiculous.

He was also handsome in a severe sort of way, but that wasn't something she needed to comment on, even to her best friend.

Thankfully, Constance decided to take the conversation on a tangent. "Have you told him yet about you wanting the hotel-manager job?"

"I hinted at it but didn't come right out and ask. However, I did ask him to teach me the job, and he's agreed."

"Well, that's promising."

"It is. But I can tell he's going to need a lot of convincing."

"You're smart and a quick study. I'm sure, once he's worked with you a while, he'll see how good a job you'd do."

"I sincerely hope so." She gave her friend's arm a squeeze. "Oh, Constance, I think this is something I'd really like to do. Working with the hotel staff, and the guests and everything else that goes with the job."

"Then I'm certain it'll all work out. I've never known you to fail at anything you've set your mind to."

Abigail sincerely hoped her friend was right. Then she gave Constance's arm a squeeze. "But enough about me. Tell me, has Calvin asked you to step out with him yet?"

She grinned as Constance began to protest, perhaps a bit *too* strongly, that there was absolutely nothing between her and Calvin Hendricks. And the rest of their walk was filled with inconsequential conversation.

When Abigail arrived at the hotel early the next morning, she found the night clerk still there.

"Good morning, Larry. Is Mr. Reynolds about?"

"I ain't seen hide nor hair of him this morning." Larry sounded put out, but that wasn't unusual for the curmudgeonly night clerk. "He told me I was to stay on duty until he relieved me, but I've got to get on home now."

Pleased that she'd made it here ahead of Mr. Reynolds, Abigail gave Larry a bright smile. "You can go on. I'm scheduled to work the desk this morning."

Larry didn't wait to be told twice. Almost before she'd finished speaking, he was around the counter and waving goodbye.

Abigail took his place and waited to see what kind of reception she'd get from Mr. Reynolds when he finally made his appearance.

Twenty minutes later he still hadn't shown up and she was getting worried. Where was the man? Maybe he'd slipped out of his room without Larry noticing. Had he gone over to inspect the progress of the construction work?

Mr. Reynolds struck her as a scrupulously punctual

person and she definitely didn't think he was one to over-
sleep.

Ruby came down the stairs and Abigail immediately
called her over. "Have you seen Mr. Reynolds this morning?"

"No, but I've been upstairs getting room three ready
for a new guest."

"Would you please keep an eye on the desk while I
check on something?"

Abigail headed for the kitchen, where she found Della
peeling potatoes. "Good morning. Have you seen Mr.
Reynolds today by any chance?"

Della shook her head as she set down her knife and
wiped her hands on her apron. "No, I haven't. He's not
come down for breakfast yet. He didn't eat much supper last night, either—sent his tray back with hardly a
thing touched."

Next Abigail followed the sound of the hammering
and spoke to Mr. Hendricks, who also gave her a negative response. Beginning to really worry, Abigail decided
it was time to take more drastic measures.

Abigail learned from Ruby that he'd moved into the
first-floor rooms the Crandalls had vacated. She quickly
headed for the suite and knocked. She waited several
seconds, then knocked again, this time more forcefully.

When she still didn't get a response, Abigail hesitated, chewing on her lower lip. Had he gone out to run
an errand? She could be worried over nothing. But what
if he hadn't?

Then she heard a sound that raised the hairs on the
back of her neck.

Chapter Six

Abigail heard the sound again, a low moan, and knocked harder this time. "Mr. Reynolds, it's Abigail. Are you all right?"

When she still received no response, she raced back to the front desk to fetch the master key. Propriety be hanged, she was going to find out what was wrong.

Clutching the key, she asked Ruby to join her, then hurried back to his door without waiting to see if she would comply. Abigail shoved the key in the lock, took a deep breath and threw open the door.

It took her a moment to orient herself. The owner's suite consisted of a sitting room with doors on either side—undoubtedly leading to bedrooms. She stared at the two closed doors for a moment, then heard a sound from the one on her left. Running over, she knocked, then waited a long anxious moment, but the only sound was that of Ruby coming up behind her. Finally, Abigail turned the knob and shoved the door open.

A small cry escaped her lips at the sight that greeted her. Mr. Reynolds lay sprawled on the floor next to the bed.

His complexion had a sickly pallor and his hair was plastered to his scalp by sweat.

"Oh my goodness." Ruby's voice held a touch of panic and she backed up a step. "You reckon he caught the same ailment as Miss Norma has?"

"No, of course not. What Norma has isn't contagious."

Abigail kneeled beside him. She pulled down his nightshirt to preserve his dignity, but not before she saw the awful scars on his leg. Her stomach lurched at the thought of what pain that must have caused him, but she immediately tamped that down. There were more urgent problems to focus on.

She felt his forehead and as she suspected he was burning up. "Listen carefully," she told Ruby. "I want you to get Calvin Hendricks so he can help get Mr. Reynolds back in bed. Then run to fetch Dr. Pratt. Ask him to please hurry."

With a nod, Ruby scurried off as if she couldn't get away fast enough.

While Abigail waited, she retrieved the washrag and basin from his bedside, then gently applied the damp cloth to his forehead. But her mind couldn't rid itself of the scars she had seen. No wonder he limped. It was a miracle the man could walk at all.

As she wiped his brow, she noticed a large knot on his forehead. He must have hit his head when he fell.

A moment later Calvin Hendricks came rushing up. "Ruby told me you needed—" He stopped at the threshold and she realized they must make a rather strange tableau. A heartbeat later, though, he came rushing the rest of the way in. "What happened?"

"Mr. Reynolds apparently took a fall. I need help getting him back in bed."

"Of course."

Calvin, who was both nimble and strong, managed to get Mr. Reynolds upright with only minimal assistance from her. Once they'd got him back on the bed, Abigail pulled up the sheet to cover him and turned to offer her thanks to Calvin.

"You want me to wait with you until Doc Pratt gets here?"

"No, thank you. Dr. Pratt should be here soon."

Calvin rubbed the back of his neck. "Leaving you here with him by yourself don't seem quite right. If you don't mind, I think I'll stay anyway."

Calvin Hendricks was one of the first people her own age she'd met when she'd arrived in Turnabout, and they'd been friends ever since. At one time she'd had a crush on him, but that had passed quickly.

She took Mr. Reynolds's hand, not sure if she was trying to reassure him or herself. "I think it's a waste of your time, but I have no objections."

A moment later the point became moot when Dr. Pratt bustled in.

She turned but maintained her hold on Mr. Reynolds's hand. "Thank you for coming," she said softly. "I wasn't sure what to do." From the corner of her eye she noticed Calvin slipping out of the room.

"I see you've been doing the right things. Do you know how long he's been like this?"

She shook her head. "Della says he didn't eat much for supper last night, but no one saw him after that until I found him on the floor this morning."

"On the floor, you say."

"Yes, sir. I think he tried to get out of bed, but lost his balance and fell. He has a bump where he must have hit his head when he fell."

"Hmm, yes. Why don't you step out while I examine him? And try not to worry, it may be nothing at all."

Abigail gently released Mr. Reynolds's hand then hesitated when he groaned. But Dr. Pratt waved her off with a reassuring "we'll be fine," and she reluctantly made her exit.

Trying to keep busy, she took the opportunity to check in with Ruby.

"How's Mr. Reynolds doing?" she asked.

"Dr. Pratt is with him now. We won't know anything until his examination is complete. In the meantime, I need you to watch the front desk."

Then she went to the kitchen, where she again had to answer questions on how Mr. Reynolds was doing. Once that was out of the way she got down to her reason for being there. "I know you already have today's menu planned out, but could you please work in a chicken-and-vegetable broth? It's what Daisy cooks when someone in the household gets ill so I figure it couldn't hurt to do the same for Mr. Reynolds."

"Don't you worry. I'll start on it right away. My ma always served it when we were feeling poorly, too."

"Thank you, Della. I know Mr. Reynolds will appreciate it."

By the time Abigail returned to Mr. Reynolds's suite, Dr. Pratt had finished his examination.

She didn't waste time on small talk. "What's wrong with him?"

"His fever is caused by an infection he didn't have treated properly. And added to that, he likely sustained a concussion when he fell."

She clasped her hands together in front of her, trying not to let her anxiety show. "Is it serious?"

"It can be. I've treated the infection and given him a powder to help make him comfortable, but I'm afraid there's not much else that can be done until the fever runs its course."

"What can I do?"

"Someone needs to keep an eye on him for the next day or so. Concussions can be a tricky business."

"I can do that."

He gave her a stern look. "Not by yourself. You won't do anyone any good if you make yourself ill as well. Besides, there may be some, shall we say, delicate ministrations he will require." He rubbed his chin. "Normally my wife would be available to help you, but she burned her hand on the stove this morning and needs to take care of herself. But Mrs. Peavy has helped from time to time with folks who need looking after. If you like, I can see if she's available to lend a hand."

Abigail's first instinct was to decline—she was certain she could handle the job herself. But she realized Dr. Pratt—not to mention her brother—would not allow it. So she gave in gracefully. "That would be most helpful. Thank you."

"In the meantime, try to get him to take in some thin broth and other liquids if you can."

"Della is already preparing a broth. Is there anything else I can do?"

"Pray, of course." He gave Abigail's hand a grandfatherly pat. "I'll check back in with you this afternoon to see how he's doing. In the meantime, if you think things are getting worse, send for me."

Once Dr. Pratt was gone, Abigail asked Ruby to bring her a pencil and some paper. First she wrote a note to Everett explaining what had happened and that she would be staying at the hotel until Mr. Reynolds was improved. She also asked him to find someone who could help out here at the hotel for a day or two.

Then she had Ruby help her move one of the comfortable upholstered chairs from the sitting room to Mr.

Reynolds's bedside. Sending the girl back to the front desk, she prepared to keep vigil.

She'd barely settled in when the patient stirred. Abigail immediately popped up from the chair and stood at the bedside.

He blinked up at her, squinting his bleary eyes, as if he had trouble focusing. "What are you doing here?"

She smiled down at him, once more gently brushing the damp hair from his brow. "Hush now. You've taken ill and have had a fall as well. I'm here to take care of you."

"Nonsense." He struggled to sit up. "I never get sick and I don't need a nursemaid."

She placed a hand on his shoulder, alarmed at the heat radiating through his nightshirt. "Well, it appears that has changed. Settle back down. Dr. Pratt has already had a look at you and recommends you not get up from here until you're a good sight better."

He tried to brush her hand away but the attempt was feeble. A moment later he finally quit struggling and settled back into an uneasy sleep.

Abigail watched him, wanting to help but feeling powerless to do so. She couldn't resist tracing the curve of his face with a finger. His chin was rough with stubble but it wasn't an unpleasant feeling. In fact, she rather liked it.

Suddenly he grabbed her hand. "Don't leave! Please don't leave me."

Startled, her gaze flew to meet his, but all she saw was a feverish, glazed look. She took his hand with one of her own and patted his face with the other. "Hush now, I'm not going anywhere."

Her touch seemed to calm him some but there was still signs of agitation. Finally, she resorted to something she'd seen Daisy do when one of her children was restless or ill—she began to sing softly. She selected the first song that came to mind—"Amazing Grace."

That seemed to do the trick. As she sang, she continued to hold his hand and watch his face. How vulnerable he looked.

He'd already endured so much pain in his life if those scars were any indication. If he'd come back from that, then he could come back from this.

That plea he'd made—*please don't leave me*—had sounded so desperate, so lost. She sensed that he hadn't been talking to her, that it had been dredged from someplace deep inside him, and her heart ached for his loss.

Someone left him before, someone he cared deeply for.

A family member? A sweetheart?

He finally quieted, and none too soon. Her voice ached with the singing she'd done and she'd drunk every drop from the pitcher. How soon before she could get more?

Less than an hour after she'd sent her note to Everett, Daisy showed up, carpetbag in hand. Abigail immediately moved to the door so they could talk without disturbing the patient.

"How is he?" Daisy asked in a low voice.

Abigail pitched her voice in the same hushed sickroom voice. "Still restless, though the fever doesn't seem as high as it was."

"That's a good sign, at least." Daisy raised the bag in her hands. "I brought a few things you might need if you're going to stay here tonight."

"Bless you!" Abigail gave her sister-in-law a quick hug, then stepped back. "Everett was okay with this?"

Daisy shrugged. "You know your brother. His first instinct was to march over here and inform you that you were not to spend the night here, no matter what the situation."

Abigail winced.

But Daisy patted her arm. "Don't worry. I reminded him that you were a grown woman and that you had very likely thought this through and were going to take precautions to protect your reputation." Then she raised a brow. "You have, haven't you?"

Abigail nodded. "You can tell Everett that Mrs. Peavy will be spending the night here as well."

That brought a relieved smile to Daisy's face. "I knew it. Won't Everett feel foolish when I tell him." Then she touched Abigail's arm. "By the way, Everett contacted Darby Kline and asked him to check in with you."

Abigail nodded. "Darby showed up about fifteen minutes ago and he's already been a big help. He was the perfect choice."

"I want you to take a break—freshen up, get yourself a bite to eat, maybe get a little fresh air. You have a long vigil ahead of you and you need to make certain you don't wear yourself out." She held up a hand before Abigail could protest. "I'll sit with him for a while."

Abigail reluctantly decided to do as Daisy instructed. After all, she also had a responsibility to check on the hotel operations.

But she planned to make it a very short break indeed.

Chapter Seven

Abigail stayed away only long enough to check on Della and Ruby. Della insisted she eat something, so she took a few bites of whatever dish the cook set in front of her—later she couldn't remember what it was.

She returned immediately to Mr. Reynolds's room, where she found Daisy right where she'd left her.

"How is he doing?" she asked anxiously.

"The same." Daisy gave her a severe look. "You were barely gone fifteen minutes. I told you to take a little time to rest."

Abigail shook her head impatiently. "I'm fine." Why were folks treating her as if she was the patient? "You've got a restaurant to run and this is my responsibility. So get along with you now."

Daisy gave her an assessing look. "Sometimes I forget you're a grown woman now." She straightened and gave Abigail a quick hug. "You be sure to send for me if you need help with anything."

Abigail had barely settled into the chair beside the bed when Constance arrived.

"Dr. Pratt asked me to bring this to you. It's a powder

to help ease his fever. Mix a teaspoon in some water and try to get him to drink it."

Abigail stood and gave her friend a hug, leading her away from the bedside. "Thank you. But who's minding the pharmacy?"

Constance waved a hand. "The world won't end if I close the doors for a short while." Then she turned to study Mr. Reynolds. "How is he?"

"A little better, I think." Or was that just wishful thinking?

Constance met her gaze and there was worry in her expression. "Is there anything I can do?"

"Pray."

"Of course. Would you like me to sit with him a little while so you can have a moment to rest? It's likely to be a long vigil."

"Daisy was here earlier and spelled me for a bit, but thank you for offering."

They both silently watched the patient a moment, then Abigail straightened and cut a sly gaze her friend's way. "Calvin was a big help this morning."

"Oh?" Constance's voice was just a little too casual.

"Mr. Reynolds had fallen to the floor and was unconscious when I found him. Calvin helped me get him back in bed. I never realized how strong young Mr. Hendricks is." She nudged her friend. "How about you? Have you ever noticed how strong he is?"

There was a telltale shadow of pink climbing up Constance's neck and into her cheeks. "Why should I have?"

A restless groan from Mr. Reynolds cut off Abigail's attempt at levity. She moved forward and gently brushed the hair off his forehead. His skin was still so warm. "I just feel so helpless to do anything," she whispered.

Constance gave her shoulder a one-armed hug. "You're doing plenty."

Since there was no acceptable response she could give to that, Abigail said nothing.

After another moment, Constance removed her arm. "Well, if you're sure there's nothing else I can do, I guess I'll go back to the pharmacy. But promise you'll send someone to fetch me if you need anything at all."

"I promise." Then Abigail had another thought. "Actually, there *is* something you can do."

"Name it."

"I usually bring the workmen a light snack about this time every day. If you wouldn't mind taking care of that, I would appreciate it. And I'm certain they would, too— one of them in particular."

She grinned as the color rose again in her friend's face. Constance and Calvin Hendricks had been eyeing each other for some time.

Constance tilted up her chin. "I'm certain I have no idea what puts these silly notions in your head."

Abigail bumped her friend with her hip. "No point denying it, I've seen the way you and Calvin look at each other when you think no one's watching." She made a shooing motion with her hands. "Just go to the kitchen and tell Della I asked you to take care of the refreshments for Mr. Hendricks and his sons. She'll know what to give you."

Constance rolled her eyes but nodded and bustled off.

The rest of Abigail's day passed with agonizing slowness. At one point Della brought a tray of food that Abigail ate. And Everett came by to check on her and offer some big brotherly advice.

But mostly it was long periods of sitting by Mr. Reynolds's bedside, singing or talking or reading to him. And often praying aloud.

When Mrs. Peavy arrived about six thirty, Abigail set aside the Jules Verne novel she'd been reading aloud. Seeing the way the woman glanced at the book, Abigail gave her a smile. "I don't think he understands what I'm reading but it seems to calm him."

Mrs. Peavy nodded. "I'll keep that in mind."

Abigail again took a little time to freshen up and eat something, but then she returned to Mr. Reynolds's suite. When Mrs. Peavy assured her she had things well in hand, Abigail retreated only as far as his sitting room. She removed her shoes and lay down on the sofa with a light blanket she'd retrieved from an unused guest room. Not that she expected to get much sleep, but she knew she should at least rest.

But she wanted to be as close as possible should there be any changes in his condition.

Please, Heavenly Father, let any changes in his condition be for the better and not the worse.

Seth found himself being pulled reluctantly from his sleep. His head was pounding and there was an irritating raspy noise coming from somewhere nearby that he just wanted to make stop. He pried his eyes open with difficulty, only to find himself in a darkened room. The sole source of light came from a lamp on the bedside table. But it was enough light for him to identify the source of that irritating noise. On the left side of his bed was a large overstuffed chair occupied by an elderly woman who looked vaguely familiar. She sat with her head lolled back, sound asleep and snoring loudly.

What in the world was she doing in his room?

He tried to sit up but his body wouldn't cooperate. His

movement, however, drew a response from his right. A soft hand took hold of his and a sweet face came into view hovering above him. "Hush now," she said softly. "Lay back and I'll sing you another song."

Another song? When—

Then she put action to words and her soft, lilting voice somehow canceled out the grating sound of the other woman's snoring. He closed his eyes, strangely comforted by the touch of her hands and soothed by the sound of her voice. He tried to hold on tight, afraid if he let her go she would disappear. But it was no use. The pull of the nothingness was too strong for him to resist.

Seth grimaced in irritation. He'd been somewhere... He couldn't quite remember where, but it had been pleasant and tranquil. He'd been listening to singing that seemed meant just for him. He liked it there, yet something was trying to draw him away.

It was the light burning against his lids. Yes, that was it. If he could just block out that light, he could return to that tranquil place.

He tried turning his head but it was no use. His peace had been disturbed—he couldn't hear the singing any longer, couldn't even remember exactly what it had sounded like.

Wait...tranquil place? That didn't make sense. He was in a hotel in Texas.

He must have been dreaming, but why was he having so much trouble waking up? Both his mind and body seemed unaccountably sluggish, caught somewhere between waking and sleeping.

A wisp of a memory—two women in his darkened room, one sleeping, one ministering to him. Had they been real?

He finally managed to pry open his eyes and glanced blearily at his surroundings. It was daylight now and he was alone. Had he imagined it then?

But the padded chair was still there beside his bed, so some part of what he remembered must have happened. He attempted to focus, to clear his head and try to make sense of what had happened. Based on the light streaming in from the windows the day appeared to be well underway. What was he doing still abed?

He tried to sit up and the room began to spin. Good grief, he felt as weak as an infant. Additional bits and pieces of memory came tumbling back in a confusing kaleidoscope of images. Him feeling light-headed. Someone singing to him. The sense of being on fire and being drenched at the same time. A blinding headache. Holding tight to a gentle-yet-strong hand as if it was a lifeline.

His door opened and Miss Fulton came bustling in carrying a tray containing a bowl and glass.

She gave him a dazzling smile. "Well now, you look a lot better today."

Today? How long had he been in this bed?

"I must say, you gave us quite a scare."

He felt at a distinct disadvantage and he didn't like it. "What day is it?" Had that gravelly voice come from him?

"It's almost noon on Tuesday. We found you with a fever yesterday morning. It finally broke in the wee hours this morning and you've been sleeping soundly ever since."

He'd lost a day and a half! Had she been watching over him all that time? Studying her closer, he saw circles under her eyes and a weariness behind her cheery demeanor. "I'm sorry if I put you through any trouble."

She brushed aside his apology. "It's Mrs. Peavy you need to be thanking. She spent last night here keeping an eye on you and I've been checking in on you off and on since."

So he *hadn't* imagined the snoring woman last night. Which meant he probably hadn't imagined the other woman, either.

"And the hotel?"

"Don't you worry—I have it covered."

"Have it covered how?"

"I asked Mr. Scruggs to come in a couple hours earlier and stay an hour later every day until you're up and about again. Then I hired some temporary help and between him and Ruby, they're keeping an eye on the front desk when I can't be there."

"You what?" How could she leave the front desk in the hands of such untrained staff?

"Now don't go getting all worked up, you need to take it easy." Her tone was that of an adult speaking to a wayward child. "Both of them have strict instructions to come get me if they run in to anything they can't handle. They are basically just babysitting the desk. Everything is fine."

She set the tray on the bedside table and he was suddenly aware of just how hungry he was. He attempted to sit up and she immediately began fussing over him, rearranging the pillows to support his back and neck.

Her sudden closeness rattled him.

He was unused to such ministrations and wasn't certain how to react. It did feel rather nice, though.

When Miss Fulton finally stepped back, he actually missed her closeness. Which was highly inappropriate. It must be his illness.

She reached into her apron pocket. "By the way, a letter arrived for you this morning. If you're not up to reading it yet, I can set it on the bedside table for you to look at later."

He accepted the missive, relieved to have something else to focus on. Then he noted it was from Jamie and changed his mind. This was something he'd prefer to read in private. He set it on the table. "I think I'll save it for later."

She nodded. "Of course. But if it's just that you're not up to reading it, I'd be happy to read it to you."

"It can wait. Right now whatever you have in that bowl is making me anxious to get a taste."

"It's chicken-and-vegetable broth along with a slice of some fresh baked bread." She said that as if it was a grand meal. "Would you like me to feed you?"

He frowned. "I'm quite capable of feeding myself, thank you."

Not appearing to take offense, she picked up the tray and handed it to him. "Very well. Unless there's something else you need from me, I'll leave you to your meal. I'll check back in on you a little later to retrieve the tray and dishes."

Seth gingerly balanced the tray on his lap then lifted his spoon. "Don't bother. I'll take care of it when I'm done."

Her hands fisted at her hips. "Most definitely not. Dr. Pratt said the best thing for you was to get lots of rest. You are not to get out of bed until he says it's okay. Understand?"

"Then you'd better send for him so he can do just that. I don't intend to stay in bed a moment longer than I have to."

She rolled her eyes, then nodded. "I'll send someone right now to ask him to stop by."

Seth jabbed his spoon in the bowl of soup as he

watched her walk away. He had a feeling there were some things about the past day and a half she hadn't told him. Had he done something inappropriate or foolish?

And why couldn't he get the soft strains of a sweetly sung hymn out of his head?

Whatever had happened, perhaps it was better he not push to find out.

After he set aside his bowl, Seth leaned over to retrieve his letter, then paused when he saw an unfamiliar book laying there. He picked it up and checked out the title. *Journey to the Center of the Earth* by Jules Verne. How had this gotten in here? Had one of his nurses read this as she kept vigil over him?

Something about this book teased at his memory but he couldn't recall ever reading it before. The effort to remember made his head throb so he finally gave up and set it down.

Retrieving Jamie's letter, he leaned back against his pillow and opened it. As usual, his eight-year-old nephew had scrawled a page of information about his classes and activities since they'd last met. Then the boy asked about what Seth was doing and about the place he was currently located. He'd been excited when he learned Seth was going to Texas—apparently the boy had some highly romanticized notions that everything in this part of the world was similar to what he'd once seen in a Wild West show. And once again his letter closed with broad hints about how much he disliked living at a boarding school and how he wished he could live with Seth instead.

As usual, Jamie's obvious yearning to have some semblance of a family life elicited a twinge of guilt. But Seth fought it off with memories of how much easier the boy had it than Seth himself had at that age. Jamie was in a fancy, comfortable boarding school, not a stark orphanage like the one Seth had grown up in. He had a nice room, hearty meals and was attending a school that not only challenged him to learn the basics, but also gave him opportunities in the arts, music and sports.

Yes sir, Jamie had a good life. And just as soon as Seth could finalize the Michelson deal, he would have a place to settle down in, a permanent home that he could bring Jamie to live in as well. Seth was determined that the boy would have all the security and advantages he himself had never had.

Which meant this time apart was necessary, even beneficial, with regard to their future.

So why did he still feel this niggling twinge of guilt?

Chapter Eight

Once Abigail had sent for Dr. Pratt, she took a seat behind the front desk, suddenly exhausted.

Even though Mrs. Peavy had spent the night, Abigail hadn't slept well, getting up to check on the patient often. Around one in the morning she'd found Mrs. Peavy had fallen asleep and Abigail hadn't been able to bring herself to wake the elderly woman. So she'd pulled up a chair to the other side of his bed and kept vigil. A few hours later she discovered his fever had broken and she'd managed to get a couple of hours sleep. Mrs. Peavy had awakened her when it was time for her to leave.

Wanting to keep busy, Abigail opened the accounting ledgers. She carefully recorded the extra hours each staff member was putting in during this emergency, so that when payday came they would be prepared. She also made note of Darby's hours in the ledger as well.

Then she pulled out her personal notebook and added another question to the list she had for Mr. Reynolds—how was the staff to be paid? She assumed Judge Madison had set up an account for that purpose, but she figured she should learn the particulars. After all, she needed to understand all aspects of running the establishment if she was to become hotel manager.

Her thoughts drifted to that letter he'd received. It had appeared the handwriting was that of a child. Mr. Reynolds had said he didn't have any family, so who was writing to him?

Dr. Pratt arrived and paused a minute to speak to her. "I understand our patient is doing better this morning."

She nodded. "His fever's gone and he's sitting up and eating. But the patient is *im*patient to resume his normal activities."

The physician smiled. "It's a common side effect of recovery. I'll have a look at him."

She waved toward the owner's suite. "You know the way."

She didn't have a lot of time to dwell on what the doctor might be discovering in his examination. Mr. and Mrs. Jamison, the couple in room three, had decided to check out a day early. Then Walter Hendricks came to her with a problem they were having with the quality of the last hardware order he'd placed.

By the time she'd taken care of both those issues, Dr. Pratt had returned to the lobby.

"How's he doing?"

"Mr. Reynolds is much improved but not completely back to full strength. He is determined to get out of bed and resume his normal activity, but hopefully I convinced him he should take it easy for the next day or two. It's important he take it slow until he's had a chance to fully recover."

"Thank you, Dr. Pratt, I'll do what I can to encourage him to follow your orders." But she had her doubts about whether Mr. Reynolds intended to pay attention to the physician, much less her. That man seemed to have an overabundance of stubbornness and outright male pride.

Probably a side effect of having to work harder at everything due to his leg injury. She still mentally cringed when she remembered the sight of those awful scars.

How had he come by them? It must have taken such courage and determination to survive whatever had caused them.

She supposed she could forgive him a little pigheadedness after all.

Seth finished dressing and grabbed his cane. His conversation with Dr. Pratt had been illuminating. Apparently Miss Fulton had been the one to check on him and she'd found him in the throes of a fever. And even though Mrs. Peavy had been here last night, he was certain Miss Fulton had as well.

It seemed he was in her debt. Whether he wanted to be or not.

He entered the lobby, irritated to find himself leaning on his cane more than he liked. Apparently he wasn't quite as recovered as he'd thought. When he saw Miss Fulton behind the front desk dealing with a guest, he remained in the shadows for a moment, watching her at work.

He recognized the guest as Craig McPherson, a rather hard-to-please gentleman who'd checked in Sunday afternoon. He couldn't hear the conversation, but when he saw the man make a sweeping gesture and raise his voice, Seth started forward. Then he stopped.

Far from looking alarmed, Miss Fulton was responding with composure and a disarming smile. He couldn't hear her words, but McPherson blinked, quieted, then nodded.

Once the man walked away, Seth moved forward again.

She finally glanced up and saw him. A radiant smile lit her face for a split second and he blinked. When was the last time he'd seen someone so genuinely pleased to see him?

Then she gave him a stern look. "I hope you don't plan to do any work today. Dr. Pratt explicitly said that you were to take it easy for a few days."

He waved aside her objections. "I'm fine. And I don't want to do anything to delay the work schedule."

"The work will go on whether you're available to supervise it for the next few days or not."

Did she really think the work required no supervision whatsoever?

But he had something else to deal with first. He cleared his throat. "It seems I owe you a thank-you. Dr. Pratt informed me that it was you who discovered me in a fevered state and sent for him."

She blushed and waved a hand dismissively. "You're welcome, but there's no need to feel indebted. We're business partners and as such should look out for each other. I'm just glad I was able to help."

"Still, I do apologize for leaving you to tend to matters here by yourself." He nodded toward the stairs. "What was Mr. McPherson complaining about?"

"Apparently he'd planned to sleep late today and he found the noise from the construction to be intrusive."

Seth frowned. "I explained in great detail that there would be construction going on during his stay and that that was why he would be receiving a discount from our normal rate."

She smiled. "And I did the same yesterday. I think the

poor man is just lonely and unhappy and wants someone to listen to him."

That particular explanation was not one he would have come up with. "You seem to have settled him down."

"I merely apologized once more for the noise, expressed our appreciation that he had agreed to stay with us during this time and told him we would be happy to provide him with a free slice of pie to go with his meal this evening."

"Pie? That's all it took?"

"I told you, I think he just wants to have someone listen to his complaints and take him seriously."

Could she be right? Whether she was or not, she'd certainly taken care of the problem with minimal effort and the guest had gone away satisfied.

His hands grew shaky as his strength ebbed and it took effort for him to remain steady on his feet. Perhaps he should have rested a bit longer before trying to get up after all.

She studied him a moment, then indicated the door to her left. "If you would join me in the office, I'd like to go through the accounts with you. I have a few questions."

Why had she been going through the books? Was she looking for something in particular? Did she even understand what she was looking at? "Questions?"

"I need to speak to you about what sort of budget we have for staffing needs."

The change in subject confused him even more. Was she hoping to earn a salary herself? "Is there something in particular you have in mind?"

She led the way into the small office, leaving him to follow. He was grateful her back was to him so she didn't notice how pronounced his limp had become.

"For one thing," she said, "I've had everyone working

extra hours yesterday and today. And I hired someone to help out while things were…so unsettled. I'd like to extend that for a day or two, just until we're ready to set some kind of routine again."

Apparently she had truly taken charge in his absence. "We can cover that," he replied.

To his chagrin, she took the seat behind the desk, leaving him to take the guest chair, which he dropped into with more relief than he cared to admit.

"In fact, I'd also like to suggest we permanently hire the young man who's been helping out. At least for the duration of the renovation."

"To do what?"

"Primarily to assist guests with luggage, run errands and such. But when he's not busy with that, we could train him to watch the desk from time to time so things are covered when we need to do other things."

It was what he himself had planned to do, but he was particular about the kind of person they needed. "Tell me about this young man."

She leaned forward, her crossed arms resting on the desk. "He's sixteen and is the oldest of five boys. And his family could really use the money."

"But what kind of skills and character does he have?"

"Darby's a fine young man. Perhaps he doesn't have the sharpest of intellects, but he's pleasant, steady, a hard worker and is scrupulously honest."

"High praise indeed. And how do you know this? Is he a relative? A close friend?"

She leaned back and met his gaze without blinking. "Neither. I know this because he helps at Daisy's restaurant occasionally so I've worked with him before."

He still wasn't convinced. "Why don't you ask him

to come in and I'll speak to him. If I agree with your assessment, we can hire him on a trial basis."

Her expression indicated she'd noted his lack of enthusiasm, but she merely nodded. "Of course. Don't worry, you won't be disappointed."

Seth decided it was time to move to something else. "Was there anything else about the books we need to discuss?"

"Actually, I need to know what sort of budget I'll be working with for purchasing the furnishings. Did Judge Madison discuss that with you already, or should I write to him for the information?"

"I have the overall budget for the project." He hesitated a moment. "Perhaps it would be best if you come to me when you're ready to make any purchases and we can discuss whether or not it makes economic sense."

She sat up straighter. "And of course you'll come to me so we may discuss the particulars of purchases related to the construction." There was more than a little challenge in her tone.

"I don't see—"

"You can't have it both ways, Mr. Reynolds. Either we are working together on *every* aspect, or we each direct our own tasks and merely touch base on overlapping areas to make certain we're moving in harmony."

The woman was definitely determined. "Miss Fulton, do you know anything at all about managing a working budget? And I don't mean a household budget."

"As a matter of fact, I do. My brother is an excellent businessman, but he isn't fond of balancing his books. So once a week for the past four years I've performed that task for both the newspaper and the restaurant. And so far we've managed quite nicely."

Despite himself, Seth was impressed. "Very well. I'll

gather my notes on the budget and identify what piece of that you have to work with. However, I'd like us to meet at least once a week to go over the numbers, for *both* pieces of this project, just to make certain we're staying on track."

She gave a quick nod. "Acceptable. I trust you to divide the funds fairly. And you can trust me to be responsible with my purchases."

Seth, who still had visions of a lobby decorated with overblown images of cabbage roses, felt less optimistic.

"Oh, that reminds me," she said quickly. "While we're discussing budget, we should probably talk about what we want to do for the upcoming holidays."

"What do you mean?"

"Well, we represent one of the major town businesses so it's expected we'll participate, as I'm sure the judge would agree. The town Thanksgiving Festival should be easy. Mr. Crandall usually donated some food—a large ham or roast and all the trimmings—as well as some money toward prizes for the competitions."

"We should be able to do that."

"Christmas, though, will be a little different this year."

Since he didn't know what it had been like for Turnabout in the past, he had no idea what that meant. But before he could comment she was already explaining.

"We don't normally do a community festival for Christmas since folks prefer a more intimate family gathering. There's a children's pageant on Christmas Eve, though, and lots of festive decorations around town."

"Sounds pleasant."

"Oh, it is. But this year, there are plans to make it extra special. Since this is the last Christmas of the nineteenth century, the town council proposed we do something memorable. First, all the folks in town are encouraged to decorate the exteriors of their homes and businesses. Then the Saturday before Christmas, the town will put on a Christmas parade. And at the end of the parade they will award a prize to the home and the business deemed the best decorated. Then there will be hayrides and fireworks." Her smile seemed to double in size. "Doesn't that sound absolutely grand?"

"I'm sure it will all be quite nice, but where does the hotel come in to all this?"

"We'll want to decorate the building, of course. Wouldn't it be fabulous if we could win the competition? Not only would it draw attention to the hotel just as we're preparing to open the new wing, but it would also be a nice surprise for the judge."

Seth didn't see it as quite the benefit she did, but he also didn't see a problem with it. "I agree we should participate—the judge always likes to be a contributing member of any community he becomes part of. But I think expecting to win is a bit overambitious. For one thing, it would require a focus that would take away from our other work."

"I always say that any job worth doing deserves your best effort."

"And I always say, best to stay focused on what matters most."

He hid a smile as she rolled her eyes. Then he spread his hands in a do-what-you-will gesture. "You're in charge of the decorative aspects of the renovation. If you think you can add this to your workload and not fall behind on anything else, then I have no objections."

"Don't worry, I'm up to the challenge."

He didn't doubt that for a minute. "Once you've decided on a theme, I *would* like to have a chance to go over it with you before you actually implement it."

"Absolutely—I welcome your input." She clasped her hands in front of her. "Oh, this is going to be such fun!" Then she stood. "Now, I have some things to take care of. Why don't you stay here and I'll send for Darby. You can go ahead and speak to him today and satisfy yourself as to his qualifications. I'd like to make him an official member of the staff as soon as possible."

Secretly relieved not to have to get up out of his chair just yet, Seth nodded and leaned back while Miss Fulton bustled off.

It seemed, against all his expectations, Miss Fulton had really stepped up and done a good job of keeping things going in his absence.

What else had he gotten wrong where she was concerned?

Abigail shook her head as she left the office. She'd seen the way the man's hands had started shaking earlier, had seen the stubborn set of his jaw as he tried to ignore the sign of weakness. If she hadn't invited him to join her in the office, would he have stood there until he fell?

It seemed Everett wasn't the only stubborn male of her acquaintance. Was it a trait shared by every male, or just the ones in her life?

Pushing those philosophical questions aside, she asked Ruby to find Darby for her, then went back to her place behind the front desk. There was still work to be done and for now it was up to her to get it done.

She supposed, just to humor the refuse-to-slow-down partner of hers, she'd ask Mr. Hendricks to come by in a little bit to give Mr. Reynolds an update.

She doubted the man would accept anything she told him about the work progress as valid.

Men!

Chapter Nine

Just as Abigail hoped, things went much smoother with Darby on the staff. The boy—young man, really—was eager to please and did everything he was instructed to with a gratifying eagerness.

By Wednesday morning Mr. Reynolds appeared to have recovered completely—or at least he wasn't admitting to it if he hadn't. He was definitely back to his stiff, standoffish self, though Abigail did think she sensed an ever-so-slight unbending during odd moments when he thought no one was looking.

Both she and Mr. Reynolds took turns teaching Darby various aspects of the desk-clerk job. Although Mr. Reynolds seemed to reserve judgment, Abigail was very happy with the young man's work. He was cautioned to send for one of them if he should run in to the slightest issue, but so far had seemed capable of handling most things that came up.

With Mr. Reynolds focused once more on overseeing the construction and remodeling, and Darby handling the desk-clerk job, Abigail finally felt free to begin the research she needed to do for her part of the project.

So after lunch on Wednesday, she grabbed some of the catalogs she'd collected and happily dived in.

"What in the world are you doing poring over catalogs in the back corner of the dining room? Doesn't the hotel have an office?"

Abigail looked up, smiling as she saw Constance approach.

"It does, but Mr. Reynolds and I have to share it." She stretched her neck to try to ease some of the kinks she hadn't felt until now. How long had she been at this?

Constance took a seat. "And you don't want to share with him?"

Abigail grinned. "It's not a matter of wanting to. With his blueprints and schedules spread out everywhere, not to mention an ever-growing pile of paperwork, it's just easier for me to work in here."

"That doesn't sound like sharing to me."

Abigail felt a strange urge to defend him. "I don't mind. And most of the day it's pretty quiet in here."

"And how is Mr. Reynolds doing? Since you're out here I assume he's back to work."

"He appears to have completely recovered with no lingering effects."

"How's your part of the project coming?"

"I'm really enjoying the challenge. And I think I'm going to actually be good at this."

"Of course you will. I always said you had a good eye for such things."

"I just want to make certain I do the judge proud."

"He wouldn't have put you in charge of this if he hadn't trusted you could do it." Constance tapped the catalog. "So show me what you're thinking of ordering."

"I thought you'd never ask."

Abigail spent the next twenty minutes happily discussing her plans with her best friend.

"I've also been talking to Hazel down at the dress shop about what kinds of fabric will be best to use for the drapes, upholstery, cushions and such."

"Good idea."

"And I don't plan to stop there. It seems to me I should take advantage of all the folks in town who know anything about art or wood or anything else decorative in nature. I want to make certain I educate myself as much as possible on the nuances of what to look for in the products I need to acquire."

Constance gave her a speculative look. "Have you discussed any of this with Mr. Reynolds yet?"

Abigail shook her head. "I want to make certain I have a solid plan first." She impatiently tucked a stray hair behind her ear. "I need to convince him I have the skills and good sense it takes to make a proper hotel manager."

"He strikes me as a sensible man. I can't imagine him not agreeing to this."

Unfortunately, Abigail could. The man seemed predisposed to challenge her at every turn. But that just made her all the more determined to prove herself to him.

But there was another component of the renovation she had on her mind as well. And tomorrow morning she planned to confront him about it.

On Thursday morning Abigail sought out Mr. Reynolds as soon as she arrived at the hotel. She found him in the office, studying the newspaper.

He looked up when she entered and waved her to the guest chair. "I see you made use of the interview you conducted."

Abigail smiled. Everett had printed her interview of

Mr. Reynolds on the front page of this morning's *Turn-about Gazette*. "Do you like it?"

He raised a brow. "I don't recall giving you quite so much detail when we spoke, but there are no inaccuracies that I could spot."

At least he didn't seem upset.

"Is there something I can do for you?"

His question reminded her of her reason for being there. "If you have a moment, I'd like to discuss where we might set up my library."

He set aside the newspaper. "I'm listening."

"The guest parlor is rarely used now that the number of guests we're taking in has been curtailed, and it's ideally located for the library."

He crossed his arms and leaned back. "That space is set aside for our guests who wish to entertain. It would be another step back in service if we no longer made it available to them."

She was prepared for that particular objection. "Yes, but a new, larger parlor has been allocated in the new wing. Once that room is ready, this one will no longer be needed. I think Mr. Crandall had the current parlor earmarked for a first-floor guest room to be held in reserve for emergencies."

Mr. Reynolds nodded. "A sound policy in case of over-bookings or unexpected issues with one of the regular rooms."

She refused to give in without a fight. "But not something altogether necessary, especially right now while we have other rooms that are sitting empty. And I know the current parlor is larger than what I need for my library at the moment, but there's not another space as well suited. The parlor is on the first floor. It's near the front entrance but out of the way of the reception desk. And

I can see into it quite well when I'm working the front desk." There, she'd presented a well-reasoned, dispassionate case. Surely he couldn't find anything to argue with on that point.

Seth didn't know whether to be more amused or affronted by her determination. "It appears you've given this quite a bit of thought."

She smiled confidently. "I have. Surely you agree, it's the only space that makes sense."

He'd been giving it some thought as well. "Actually, there's another option."

"There is?"

He spread his hands. "We could simply convert this office to your library."

She looked around thoughtfully. "There's no doubt this would work. It's not as big as the parlor but it's still more than double the size of the space I currently have." She met his gaze again. "But if we turned this into the library, what would we use as an office?"

"The guest parlor." He noted with satisfaction the way her eyes widened.

"So you agree we don't need that space as a spare guest room, you just don't see it as a library."

He gave a short nod. "Correct."

"I do see your point. It would be nice to have a larger office, one we could both use without getting in each other's way." She gave a decisive nod. "I accept."

Her quick capitulation surprised him. He hadn't expected it to be quite so simple. "You're okay with having the smaller space for your library?"

She waved a hand dismissively. "Of course. As I said, this space will do quite well. And the south-facing window lets in lots of light. In fact, this will make a perfectly marvelous library."

He could find no hint of reluctance in her demeanor.

She tapped her chin with her index finger. "The only real difficulty I see is where the door is located. One has to practically step behind the front desk to get to it. That wasn't a problem while this remained an office. But it could be intrusive once we turn this into a library."

Miss Fulton's ability to see bigger issues when studying problems continued to surprise him. Before he could form a response, she brightened.

"Oh, I know. What if we close the opening to the registration counter on this end and have the access on the other end made more prominent? I think that would be an easy change, we'd just need to find a way to make it look intentional and not an afterthought."

She turned to him again. "I imagine Mr. Hendricks would have some ideas." She gave him a bright smile. "Would you like me to speak to him about it or would you prefer to do it?"

Seth was somewhat bemused by the speed at which her thoughts moved. "I'll take care of it."

"Very well. I'll work with Darby to start rearranging furniture. He can work on it as he has time."

Seth tried to take control of the conversation again. "Hold on. We should wait until the new parlor is complete before we find a new use for the current one. Our guests' needs come first. Mr. Hendricks assures me that's only three to four weeks away."

She waved aside his concern as if it was inconsequential. "We've already curtailed our services during construction, and informed our guests that certain amenities are temporarily suspended. This just becomes another."

Then her eyes widened as if she'd suddenly received

inspiration. "In the meantime, since we no longer have a full complement of guests to feed, we can shut off a portion of the dining room to serve as a temporary parlor for any guests who would have need of one. In fact, we can use the privacy screens from our unused guest rooms to do it so there won't be any delay on that account. And carving that space out of the dining room will have the added benefit of keeping it from looking so empty at mealtime."

Again she'd come up with an unorthodox solution to a logistical problem. "That could work," he said thoughtfully.

"Of course it will." She flashed a brilliant smile. "Transforming the parlor into an office was a marvelous idea."

It sounded almost as if she was trying to give him a pat on the head.

But she was still chatting away. "The new office will be large enough to hold two desks so we can both work at the same time if we need to, rather than taking turns."

That was the second time she'd made reference to both of them working in the office. Had she felt excluded before? He supposed he had considered it his personal domain, allowing him first claim on it. Miss Fulton had seemed content to restrict her use to the times he was occupied elsewhere.

Apparently she hadn't been as content as he'd thought.

How would it be sharing the space with the talkative Miss Fulton? Would he be able to get any work done?

And was he actually looking forward to finding out?

Abigail sought out Darby as soon as she left the office, and explained what needed to be done.

"First, we'll need to clear the west end of the dining

room," she instructed after she'd explained the new purpose for each of the rooms. "We can store the extra tables and chairs in some of the unused guest rooms. And while you're at it, gather the privacy screens from those same rooms. We'll use them to partition off the section of the dining room we're converting into our temporary guest parlor."

"Yes, ma'am."

She tapped her chin. "You can do some of this on your own, but you're definitely going to need some help with the bulky and heavier pieces. When school lets out, why don't you get your brother, Odie, to help? I'll pay him four bits for the afternoon and he can take his meal in the dining room for free."

"Yes, ma'am!"

Darby went right to work and under her occasional direction, he spent the rest of the day moving furnishings around from one room to another.

While Darby worked on the changes needed in the dining room, Abigail returned to the office and began to organize and box up the files, correspondence, blueprints and other papers in preparation for the move across the lobby. Mr. Reynolds had disappeared—he was probably working with the Hendrickses again—and she felt a little uncertain about going through his things. But it wasn't as if she'd be reading his mail or prying into his personal business.

Taking a deep breath, she grabbed a box and began carefully packing up the items from the top of the desk. As she worked, an item on the corner of his desk caught her eye. It was an envelope addressed to a Jamie Shaw in care of the Bridgerton Academy for Boys.

Was Jamie Shaw the youth who'd written to Mr. Reynolds? And who was he to the man?

Of course he could also be an adult—a headmaster or instructor at the school. But, remembering the youthful handwriting on the letter he'd received, she didn't think so.

Abigail placed the letter in the box and went back to clearing the top of the desk. But she couldn't stop thinking of Jamie Shaw. Whoever he was, she felt an immediate sympathy for and kinship with him. She knew how lonely living at a boarding school could be. She hoped this Jamie was having a better time of it than she'd had.

Would it be too forward of her to ask Mr. Reynolds about him? He would likely tell her it was none of her business. But fear of being rebuffed had never stopped her before.

Unfortunately, Abigail didn't have an opportunity to broach the subject with him right away. The two of them kept missing each other as she worked with Darby to get all three rooms set up just right. Even when they paused for lunch, Constance came by to chat.

By late afternoon everything was done. The new guest parlor had been partitioned off and furnished with a number of pieces from the original parlor. Abigail stood at the entrance and looked around, pleased to see that it had turned out just as she'd imagined. The only problem the guests who used this temporary parlor might encounter would be noise carrying over from the dining room.

She turned to Darby and his brother. "Great job, boys." She reached into her pocket. "Odie, here's the money I promised you for your help. Darby, you'll have a little extra in your pay this week as well."

With a smile and another thank-you, she sent the boys on their way.

Next she made a quick stop in what had been the office and, as expected, found it empty. A good sweeping and cleaning was all it lacked to be ready for her to begin setting up her library. With it empty like this, she could really appreciate how much space she would have. Already she was mentally picturing how she would arrange her bookshelves and the other touches she would add to make it a more inviting space.

Closing the door, she headed for the one-time parlor that had been transformed into the office. Stepping inside, she gave a little sigh of satisfaction. The room now contained two desks—though the one Abigail had allocated to herself was a smallish writing desk that had been part of the original furnishings of the parlor. No matter, it was more than she'd had before and it meant she would no longer have to share Mr. Reynolds's desk.

There was also the bonus of a nice-sized worktable that she'd had moved in here from one of the storerooms. Now they would have a proper place to lay out work plans, blueprints and furniture catalogs when the need arose.

She'd also told Darby to leave a couple of the more worn but comfortable chairs and a settee when he was moving the furniture. Those pieces gave the room the cozy, welcoming feel she'd hoped for. And the bookcases and cabinets that had been transferred from the office were now, thanks to her, polished and the contents better organized.

She couldn't wait for Mr. Reynolds to see it. Would he appreciate all the little extra touches she'd added? Abigail envisioned many a productive hour, working side by side with him. This would make them more effective business partners.

Perhaps it would lead to stronger mutual appreciation and respect?

"I must say, it looks good."

Abigail started guiltily at the sound of his voice. Thank goodness she'd had her back to the door. Getting herself under control, she turned to see Mr. Reynolds looking around, his expression reflecting approval.

"I'm glad you like it."

"We will certainly have more room to work in here." He nodded toward her desk. "And I see you found a work place of your own."

"No more need to share," she agreed. Then she waved a hand. "All the papers and such from the top of your desk are in those boxes, waiting for you to arrange as you see fit."

He moved toward the desk. "Sorry to have left you to deal with this on your own. But I can see I left it in good hands."

She smiled, warmed by his praise. "Darby did most of the actual work, I just pointed to what needed to be moved where."

That earned her a smile. "The skill of a good supervisor."

"And a good hotel manager."

He made a noncommittal sound and continued toward his desk without meeting her gaze.

Should she let it go? No indeed. "Don't you agree that a good hotel manager should have strong supervisory skills?"

He finally turned, meeting her gaze. "Of course. Along with a number of other skills."

"Such as?"

"Good people skills. The ability to anticipate needs of both the business and the customers. The ability to face unexpected problems without panicking. The ability to deal with staffing issues."

"And how do you think I fare in those areas?"

"To be honest, Miss Fulton, I haven't observed you in action enough to be able to evaluate. But I do know that there is one area that you are lacking."

She tried to brace herself. "And that is?"

"Experience."

"Everyone has to start somewhere."

"True. But one rarely starts at the top."

"Well, I still have two months to gain that experience, don't I?"

He merely rolled his eyes at that. "Thank you again for getting things set up today. But if you'll excuse me, I want to get my papers organized and filed properly."

Apparently she was dismissed. With a flounce, Abigail turned and left the room.

It was already past five o'clock so she headed home. As she marched down the sidewalk she tried to get her temper under control. The man could be so infuriating!

But she supposed he had a point. He *hadn't* had enough time to observe her in action, and without any experience to back her up, how was he to know if she could handle such an important job on her own? She would just have to do her best over the coming weeks to prove to him that she was capable.

But what would it take?

That night, when she said her prayers, she turned it over to God.

Heavenly Father, help me prove myself. I'm not asking for any major disasters to come our way, just some opportunities to show what I can do. But in this and all things, Your will be done.

Now if she could just have enough faith to leave it in God's hands.

Chapter Ten

Seth stared at the closed door. He'd seen the disappointment in her eyes and it had made him feel like a bully kicking a puppy.

She obviously had her eye on the hotel-manager job. He should have told her outright he already had someone else in mind for the job, but he'd been too cowardly to completely extinguish her hope.

He didn't know which was worse—killing all hope from the outset, or letting her have her hope and then disappointing her when he eventually hired someone else.

Perhaps, before the time came to make the decision, she would have changed her mind or done something to show she wasn't right for the job.

But the nagging suspicion that he'd be proven wrong about that kept him from sleeping well that night.

Despite how irritating the woman could be, he couldn't help but admire her spirit and optimism.

When Seth entered the office on Friday morning it was obvious Miss Fulton had already been there. Fresh flowers, arranged in a china vase, perched proudly on the worktable. An ormolu clock sat on her desk. A small framed sketch of a dandelion sat on the table near the settee.

On the fireplace mantel, he spied another sketch, this one of a frog on a lily pad.

She had certainly made herself at home. It appeared she was trying to take their new office and turn it back into a parlor.

Ah well, he supposed he could live with a few feminine touches, so long as she didn't go overboard with it.

The more important question was, did this display mean she was no longer upset?

Still wondering, he stepped into the lobby to find her talking to Larry and Darby. Larry appeared to be on his way out and Darby stood behind the counter, elbows resting next to the guest register.

Both men, who'd been informally chatting with Miss Fulton, came to attention when they caught sight of him. Normally he would have been pleased by the reaction, seeing it as a sign of respect. So why didn't he feel that same sense of satisfaction this time?

Miss Fulton turned to greet him and she, at least, looked pleased to see him. "Good morning." The smile accompanying her greeting drew one from him in return.

"Good morning. I noticed you added a few personal touches to the office."

"I hope you don't mind. I thought it needed a little warmth."

"It's your office, too." He waved a hand toward the dining room. "I was just going for some breakfast. Care to join me?"

As they took their seats at one of the tables, Seth was relieved to see she had returned to her sunny-mannered self. Was it not in her nature to hold a grudge? Or was she still convinced she could sway him to her side?

Once Della took their orders, Seth moved to a topic that seemed safe. "When do you plan to set up your library?"

Her expression grew animated. "Soon. I want to free up the space in Daisy's restaurant as soon as possible. She'll be so excited to be able to accommodate more customers." She tucked a stray hair behind her ear. "Did you speak to Mr. Hendricks about what we want to do with the front desk?"

"I did. And he doesn't think it will take much. He told me he should be able to get to it sometime in the next few days."

"Good. I won't open it to the public until that's all squared away. Which shouldn't be a problem since it will take me some time to get everything organized once I move the books from the restaurant."

Della brought out their orders and conversation ceased while they were served.

Once Della departed, Seth picked up his fork. "Will you need some help moving your books?"

She shrugged. "I'll worry about that when the time comes."

"I wasn't going to offer my own services," Seth said dryly. "but if you would like to ask Darby to help you, I can cover the front desk while he's otherwise occupied."

"Thank you. I may just take you up on that."

It galled him that he was useless to help in a situation like this. The best he could hope for was to succeed well enough at business that he could hire folks to handle manual labor for him.

Even though Mr. Reynolds's expression remained impassive, Abigail sensed he was frustrated. It must rankle for a young and otherwise healthy man such as himself to be limited by his injury.

And it was strange she could pick up on his feelings this way.

When they'd finished their meal, Abigail dabbed her lips and then put aside her napkin. "I've made some decisions on the decor of the lobby and dining areas," she told Mr. Reynolds. "As we discussed, I'm prepared to go over them with you when you have a moment."

A flash of surprise crossed his face, as if he hadn't expected her to follow through on his request to be consulted. But he recovered quickly. "If you like, we can do it now."

She stood. "My things are in the office."

He stood as well and swept a hand in the general direction of the office. "Lead the way."

When they entered the office, Mr. Reynolds moved toward his desk. "Let's get to it."

Abigail moved instead to the worktable. "I think I can show you better over here." She rested a hand on the stack of catalogs she'd placed there earlier and waited for him to join her. "Right now I'm focusing primarily on the public areas of the hotel—the lobby, restaurant and guest parlor."

He came up beside her, studying her materials. For a moment Abigail was thrown off-kilter by his closeness. It was as if her senses were suddenly heightened. She could feel the warmth of his presence, hear the sound of his breathing, smell the hint of coffee that clung to him.

"Walk me through what I'm looking at."

His words broke the spell and she quickly tried to pull her thoughts together. "As I said before, I want to play off of the rose in the hotel's name, but using it as a sort of subtle motif rather than going overboard."

She held out her hand. "Here are swatches of the fabric I plan to use for the front drapes."

He took the cloth she held out, fingering them as he studied the pattern and colors.

His expression didn't give away any of his thoughts.

Feeling the need to fill in the silence, she explained further. "As you can see, there are two separate pieces. One is very lightweight and almost sheer." She touched it lightly, loving the pale pink shade that was shot through with green sprigs. Did he like it?

"This second fabric is much more solid without feeling overly heavy. The maroon shade plays off the sheer print beautifully. When you layer them together, the effect is stunning."

"And where do you plan to use these?"

"They'll be fashioned into drapes for the lobby. When we want to let lots of daylight into the area, we can simply pull back the heavier layer. When we want to have more privacy or block out the view, we pull it closed."

He nodded, still not expressing either approval or disapproval.

She lifted another piece of fabric. "The chairs and settee in the lobby are still good solid pieces. And I really like the rosettes carved into the arms and back. But the cushions are worn and faded. So, rather than replacing them altogether, I plan to simply reupholster the pieces in this fabric."

This one was a soft but heavy fabric with ivory and green stripes. The green was an exact match for the green shade in the curtain fabric. Would he pick up on that?

He rubbed the fabric between his thumb and fingers, studying it from several angles.

Finally she decided the direct approach was best. "Well, what do you think?"

"I think it's a good start."

Not the enthusiastic response she'd hoped for, but at least it wasn't negative.

"What else have you selected?"

She opened one of the catalogs. "For the guest parlor we'll need brand-new pieces. I'm thinking something along these lines." She turned the page and pointed. "Similar to this but less elaborate."

He studied the chair she'd pointed to and nodded. "Certainly less expensive."

She grinned acknowledgement but then changed the subject slightly. "While we're discussing the parlor, I had an idea of something different we could do to better utilize the space."

His face took on a wary, long-suffering expression. "I'm listening."

She took a deep breath, determined to do this right. "What if we divided the room in half so that if two of our guests required the use of a parlor at the same time we could accommodate both of them?"

"That's all well and good if we should need two smaller rooms, but the point of building a new parlor was to have a more spacious area to offer our guests." He waved a hand irritably. "Besides which, that part of the construction is nearly complete and it would take additional money to change it now. Not to mention add more time to the project."

"I'm not saying that we need to reconstruct the room," she explained, "and I agree that there may be guests who would wish to reserve the entire space. But I think we can have it both ways."

"Miss Fulton, it's obvious you don't understand much about construction. It's much too late in the process to add new rooms now."

How dare he talk down to her that way? "That's not what I'm suggesting." She tucked a stray lock of hair behind her ear. "Please let me finish explaining before you rush to dismiss the idea."

His lips tightened, but he nodded for her to continue.

"I once saw a picture of a large ballroom that could be divided into two rooms by the use of a set of folding panels. These weren't just any ordinary panels or privacy screens, mind you. Each panel was beautifully engraved so they were nearly a piece of art. And they were tall enough to almost reach the ceiling, insuring not only privacy, but also reducing the amount of sound from the other side. They were hinged together in a manner that allowed them to collapse against each other and be folded away when not in use."

She came to her point. "We could build something similar, using wood etched with elegant floral carvings to fit the rest of the decor, so that the parlor could be divided into two rooms should the need arise, yet still open up into one large space when required for a large group."

He rubbed his chin, nodding slowly. "I've seen something similar myself. It might just work."

Resisting the urge to crow in triumph, she tried to keep her expression businesslike. "If you agree, I could furnish it in such a way that the pieces could be functionally divided between the two spaces when the divider is in place. And the only change that need be made to the room itself that would require construction would be to move the door and add a second one."

Before he could raise other objections, she added, "From what Mr. Hendricks said yesterday, however, they're not so far along that it would cause a problem."

He raised a brow. "You've already talked to Mr. Hendricks about this? Were you that confident I would agree to this?"

She held his gaze without blinking. "I merely wanted to make certain it could be done with minimal impact before I bothered you with the idea." She raised a brow. "What do you think? Do you agree it's worth pursuing?"

"Let me speak to Walter Hendricks and have him work out firm details, then we'll talk again."

She supposed that would have to do for now.

Would there ever come a day when he would stop feeling the need to double-check everything she had to say?

Because even though she knew she wasn't as experienced as he was, hadn't she earned some measure of trust by now?

Chapter Eleven

Seth gave his head a mental shake. Who was this young woman who could speak of motifs and better space utilization in one breath and pretty fabrics in the next? He'd expected to see frills and furbelows. Instead she brought him innovative ideas about room configurations and elegant furnishings. Perhaps Judge Madison had selected her to do this job for more reason than just friendship.

"Which brings me to an important point," she said, pulling his thoughts back to the present.

Was she not through with her recommendations then? "And what point is that?"

"Rather than purchasing everything out of catalogs and having the pieces shipped here, I want to use local craftsmen to provide as many of the needed furnishings as possible."

Local craftsmen? Did she have any idea how to separate issues of quality from those of friendship?

But she was already expanding her statement. "Hazel Gleason, the seamstress over at the dress shop, can make the drapes. Chance Dawson is an excellent woodworker and he can carve the panels for the dividers. Mr. Hendricks and his sons, of course, can build the dividers themselves. There are a couple of local folks who are very good artists who could create pieces—sketches and watercolors—for us to hang on the walls. With the right frames—which Chance can fashion—they'll look exceptional."

She waved a hand enthusiastically. "Judge Madison's granddaughter is a talented photographer and some of her photographs can be strategically placed around the hotel to provide decorative touches."

Time to insert a touch of reality into this discussion. "Miss Fulton, using local merchants for perishable goods such as meal ingredients and fresh flowers makes good economic sense. And I'm sure there are some local craftsmen who are quite talented in their own way, but if you're going to succeed as a businesswoman, you need to learn to put personal feelings behind you and make objective decisions."

She narrowed her eyes. "Perhaps to some extent. But I disagree that one must remove *all* personal feelings from decision making. Personal feelings and personal relationships *are* important, especially if they lead to choices that benefit everyone. I would never recommend anyone whose work I didn't think was of the quality we're looking for, because I don't want to let Judge Madison down in any way."

He decided she'd have to learn the hard way. "I have some strong reservations about this direction you're headed in." He straightened and nodded. "But that being said, Judge Madison did put you in charge of the decor so I won't try to stand in your way."

Her countenance cleared and she gave him a sunny smile. "I appreciate that. As for the direction I'm taking, aside from which craftsmen I'm using, if there is any other aspect of how I'm choosing to furnish and decorate that you have concerns over, I would welcome discussion on the matter. After all, it's been some time since I was in any sort of fine establishment."

Some time? "So you've traveled outside of Turnabout?"

She grinned. "Oh my, yes. In fact, I only moved to Texas six years ago when my brother put down roots here."

"Oh, of course. You came with him from Philadelphia." Strange to think he might have passed her on the street at some point.

But she shook her head. "I've never actually lived in Philadelphia. I attended a boarding school in Boston for most of my life."

Ah, so that explained her polish. Still, six years ago she would have been quite young. "Most of your life?"

She nodded. "My mother passed away when I was five, leaving me with our stepfather and Everett. Everett was eleven years older than me and had already moved out of our home—he and our stepfather didn't get along. Anyway, he made sure I was well taken care of, even though he couldn't look after me himself. He sacrificed quite a lot to make certain I had a good upbringing."

As he himself was doing for Jamie. It seemed he and Everett Fulton had similar outlooks on bachelors raising youngsters. And it also appeared the experience hadn't harmed her any. Just one more indication he was doing right by his nephew.

As if she'd read his thoughts, she continued. "I love my brother dearly and I know he loves me. And I truly appreciate his good intentions and all he sacrificed to make sure I was in a place that was comfortable and safe. He always assured me he would have a place for me with him when I graduated."

She paused and he sensed there was something she wasn't saying, some *but* that she was mentally tagging onto that statement.

When she kept silent, he tried a gentle nudge. "And your brother did finally send for you when he settled here."

She winced guiltily. "Strictly speaking, Everett didn't send for me."

He frowned. "What do you mean?"

Her gaze slid from his and she began fiddling with the narrow strip of lace on her collar, something he'd noticed she did when she was nervous.

"I was fifteen when I learned Everett had moved to Texas," she explained. "By that time I'd grown tired of waiting for him to send for me. I figured ten years cooped up in that one place was long enough. It was one thing when he was in Philadelphia, where I might have the opportunity for him to visit from time to time. But with him half the country away, I knew I would be fortunate to even get a visit at Christmastime."

She shrugged but he didn't for one minute believe the gesture was casual.

"Naturally Everett didn't see it that way at all. To give him his due, he was trying to establish himself here and start up a newspaper—he hardly had time to bother with having a younger sister underfoot. But I couldn't see past my own desperation to get away from Miss Haversham's. The place had begun to feel like a prison, no matter how velvet-lined." She gave a crooked smile. "I was a bit melodramatic as an adolescent."

He hid his own smile. Did she really think she'd left that trait behind?

She took a deep breath. "So I made the decision that it was time for me to take my fate into my own hands and I set wheels in motion to run away from school and travel here."

Had he heard her correctly? He straightened, no longer amused. "On your own?"

"Not initially," she said quickly. "I arranged to have a chaperone accompany me. But she got ill halfway into our journey and I had to leave her behind and make the rest of the trip on my own."

Did she have any concept of what a terrible chance she'd taken? He shuddered to think of the things that could have befallen an innocent fifteen-year-old girl making such a journey on her own. "That was a very foolhardy thing to do. Do you have any idea what could have happened to you?"

She met his gaze, her expression defensive. "You sound just like Everett."

"My sympathies are solidly with your brother." No doubt she'd shaved several years off the unfortunate man's life.

"Then I suppose you won't be surprised to hear he threatened to send me right back."

"Since you're still here, it appears you managed to change his mind."

She lifted her chin. "I told Everett if he sent me back, I would just run away again."

His sympathy for her brother doubled.

"So he compromised and told me I could stay for a visit. But then he married Daisy, and she helped me convince him that it was better for both me and him if I stayed." She spread her hands triumphantly. "And there you have it."

"Why were you so determined not to go back?"

Her expression sobered and her gaze slid away from

his. "A person is always happiest when surrounded by family, not strangers."

"It depends on the family." The words escaped him before he could call them back.

He could tell by the look on her face he'd startled her. Mentally scrambling for something else to say in order to stave off her questions, Seth remembered the other half of her statement. "Didn't you say you'd been at that school for ten years? Surely you made a number of friends in that time?" He couldn't imagine the always cheery, talk-to-anyone Miss Fulton *not* making friends wherever she went.

She shrugged and began fiddling with her collar again. "Perhaps *strangers* is the wrong word. But I never did get really close to anyone there, certainly not close enough to consider them family."

Had she been different as a child?

"The thing was, Everett wanted me to stay at Miss Haversham's mainly because he had some foolish notion that only by having me mix with the elite of society and finishing my education there could I be happy." She shrugged. "He was wrong. It's not being in a particular social circle that makes a person happy. It's being with the people you love."

Ha! There was no guarantee that being with loved ones would make you happy, either, Seth thought.

That only worked if they loved you back.

Abigail worried that she'd said too much, had revealed things better left buried. It was time to change the subject. "If you don't mind me borrowing Darby for an hour or two tomorrow, I'd like to go ahead and move the library. As I said earlier, I want to free up the space in the restaurant as soon as possible." She would worry about organizing things on this end later.

Mr. Reynolds nodded. "Since the library will in essence become part of the hotel, I don't view that as a personal project so much as an extension of the renovations."

She was pleasantly surprised by his statement. "Thank you. I'll make certain it does become a valuable service for the guests here. And don't worry about the work schedule, I'll make sure we only tend to it during the hotel's slower times."

"I trust your judgment in that area."

The casually offered praise lightened her mood considerably.

"By the way," he added, "I thought you should know that I think your selection of Darby was a good one. The lad is a good fit for what we need right now."

Yet more praise. Was the man finally ready to admit she had good business sense?

She decided to press while he was in a friendly mood. "I'm glad you feel that way. I'm hoping he can come on as a permanent desk clerk once we are ready to make staffing decisions."

"Please don't make him any promises. Once we near completion we'll hire a hotel manager and he will be the one making those decisions, with our input of course."

"Or she."

He let out a breath. "Miss Fulton, as I said before, the job of hotel manager is best suited for someone with experience in managing people—employees as well as guests. And someone who can also handle any problems that come up, be it with the facility or the merchants we do business with or the town's officials."

She was determined to make him see her as a realistic candidate. "I understand, but I still think I'm up to the challenge. And you did say you'd keep an open mind. Am I to understand that's no longer true?"

Mr. Reynolds hesitated a moment. "Actually, there's a gentleman back in Philadelphia who has the right kind of experience and who I feel would be perfect for this job. And while it's obvious you have potential, so far you've done nothing to make me think you'd be a better candidate. And I believe we owe it to Judge Madison to hire the best person for the job—don't you?"

It was not what she wanted to hear. Still, she refused to give up hope. "Of course. But the decision isn't actually made yet, so I still have time to prove myself, don't I?"

He held her gaze without speaking for a long moment. Then he finally shrugged. "There's always the chance that something could change."

She nodded in satisfaction, grabbing tightly to that one little kernel of hope. "Then there's time yet for me to change your mind."

"Miss Fulton—"

She didn't let him finish whatever negative thing he was about to say. "All I want is a fair chance."

She only hoped she could prove herself equal to the challenge.

Seth gave himself a mental shake. He should have come right out and told her the job of hotel manager was already taken. But he hadn't been able to completely dash her hopes, even though that day would be coming soon.

He had to admit, she was proving her worthiness for the position more and more each day. And she was also getting under his skin in a way no one ever had before.

Was it possible he was actually attracted to her? That thought was troubling on a number of levels, the main one being that there was no way he could allow himself to act on that attraction.

He'd seen the flinch in her expression when he mentioned he had someone else in mind for the job, but to do her justice, she hadn't crumpled or backed down. In spite of himself, he felt a grudging admiration for her determination.

If things were different—

No! He wouldn't allow himself to finish that thought. Things weren't different. Life wasn't fair—that was a lie believed by children and wide-eyed idealists.

He hadn't been either for a very long time.

Chapter Twelve

On Saturday Seth found himself eating breakfast and lunch alone. In the week that he'd been here, he'd gotten used to sharing his meals with Miss Fulton, using the time to discuss the progress they were making with the hotel and for her to chatter on about her plans.

Though he'd first thought her cheery prattling an intrusion into his private time, somehow he'd become accustomed to their mealtime conversations to the extent that he now missed it. So after lunch he wandered over to the space they'd allocated for her library. To his surprise, he saw what appeared to be the entire contents of her library scattered about the room.

"I see all of your books have been moved over." Is that what had kept her from joining him for breakfast and lunch? Or had she merely used it as an excuse to ignore him after yesterday's discussion?

"Yes." She looked around, her pleasure evident. "Daisy's already added three more tables to her establishment so it's working out well all the way around."

"But your books are just stacked on the floor." He was pleased to see she seemed as friendly as ever.

"I know." She appeared entirely unconcerned by the

lack of order. "I'll organize them as I have time. Since I had more books than the space allowed for, many of the books were shelved two deep. I have more space here but not additional bookcases so I'll need to improvise at first. I'm thinking about using some of the tables we just took out of the dining room as makeshift bookshelves for now." She shot a questioning look his way, as if uncertain he'd agree.

"I don't see a problem with that. When do you plan to open it up to the public?"

"Not until I get everything organized. But the word is already getting around that I've moved the books here and if anyone really wants to get a book I won't turn them away."

He rubbed his jaw, studying the chaos around them. "Once you're set, you might think about training Darby on what to do in case a patron comes along while you're busy elsewhere."

She graced him with a dazzling smile. "What a splendid idea. I'll talk to him about it today."

She gave him a conspiratorial smile. "But for right now, I snitched a bite to eat at Daisy's earlier but I'm hungry again. I think I'm going to head to the dining room and order a piece of Della's apple pie and a cup of coffee. Care to join me?"

Feeling that all was right with the world again, Seth swept a hand out for her to precede him. "Lead the way."

He refused to dwell on just why his day felt suddenly brighter.

After lunch on Sunday, Seth returned to the hotel. Strange to think this was only the second time he'd joined the group for their Sunday gathering and already he felt a genuine sense of camaraderie with them.

When he'd first entered the restaurant this afternoon, he'd immediately noticed how much bigger the space felt without the library anchoring one end of the room. To his way of thinking, though, what the restaurant had gained in additional customer tables, it had lost in atmosphere. It felt to him as if the restaurant had lost something that had made it special, had set it apart from other restaurants he'd frequented.

Then again, the restaurant's loss was now the hotel's gain.

He entered the hotel lobby feeling restless. He needed something to do, something to occupy both his mind and his hands.

He nodded to Darby, who was seated behind the front counter. "What's that you have there?"

Darby lifted the book he'd been reading. "It's one of Mr. Twain's books, *A Connecticut Yankee in King Arthur's Court*. Miss Abigail said I could borrow any book from her library to read when we're not busy." He gave Seth an encouraging look. "I reckon she'd let you do the same. There's some mighty fine stories in her collection."

"I'm sure there are." Reading didn't interest him at the moment—it was too passive an activity for his mood.

Miss Fulton really was very good with the staff, though. She managed to keep them on task but personally content at the same time. He still didn't agree with her philosophy of being friends as well as management to them, but she seemed able to pull it off—or at least had so far.

He was afraid one day, though, she'd have to choose between the two roles. How she handled things then would prove if she truly did have what it took to become a hotel manager. Not that anything she did would sway him. The job had to go to Michelson.

His future depended on it, hers did not.

Seth restlessly made his way to the new wing, walking through the entire area, floor by floor, room by room, making mental notes of things he wanted to ask Walter Hendricks about when the builder showed up with his sons the next day.

They were making progress but there was still much to be done.

He spotted the pile of lumber scraps left over from the prior day's work, noting how much waste there was and judging it acceptable. One piece in particular caught his eye. It was a nice-sized piece, rectangular in shape and fairly smooth. Why had it been tossed aside? He picked it up and turned it over and discovered a crack on one side that hadn't been visible on the other. Hendricks had been right to discard it—the piece wouldn't have held up for construction purposes. Still, he remembered how his father, a cabinet maker, had told him to always look for ways to find the beauty in the broken pieces, how one should never be too quick to discard something simply because it didn't fit the purpose of the moment.

He carried the damaged board to the worktable, studying it, remembering the way his father had created such beautiful things from wood.

And an idea took shape…

Abigail entered the hotel lobby Monday morning eager to get started on a new week of progress. Darby was already behind the front desk and she offered him a cheery greeting. But what caught her attention was something mounted above the library door. It was a wooden sign, rectangular in shape with rounded corners. It had been painted a soft rose color and outlined in green and gold. In the center, in bold gilt lettering, were the words *Abi-*

gail's Library. The colors were a perfect complement for the decor she was planning and the lettering was beautifully rendered.

What a thoughtful thing for Mr. Hendricks to do. She hadn't realized he even knew about her library. Then again, perhaps it had been Calvin. He borrowed books occasionally.

She turned to Darby. "Do you know where Mr. Hendricks is? I want to thank him for the sign."

"I think he's up on the second floor of the new wing. But I believe it's Mr. Reynolds you're going to want to be thanking."

"Mr. Reynolds?" She turned to study the sign, more enchanted than before by the perfection of the colors, the exactness of the lines, the crispness of the lettering. It was truly the most beautiful sign she'd ever seen.

"Yes, ma'am. I saw him give that sign to Mr. Hendricks this morning and tell him exactly where to hang it. He was right picky about making sure it was hung just right. I got the idea he painted it himself, too."

He'd done this for her? "Thank you, Darby, that's good to know."

Abigail headed for the office, a feeling of buoyancy lightening her steps. She found Mr. Reynolds bent over the worktable, studying a set of blueprints.

She paused on the threshold, suddenly shy. A moment later he looked up and gave her a polite smile. Had Darby been mistaken about his making the sign? Or had she read too much in to his gesture?

"Good morning, Miss Fulton. Is there something I can do for you?"

She realized she still stood at the threshold, staring at him. Crossing to the worktable, she smiled. "Good morning. I understand I have you to thank for that sign over my library door. It's quite lovely."

He looked slightly uncomfortable and waved a hand dismissively. "Think nothing of it. I found a nice piece of scrap lumber and thought this would be a good way to have a practical look at the color scheme you selected."

"Oh." Not exactly flattering. Then she rallied. "Well, whatever the reason, it was a thoughtful gesture. Thank you."

He nodded and then turned back to the blueprint.

"Is there a problem with the plans?" Abigail moved closer.

"Not a problem, exactly." He waved a hand over the blueprints. "The plans, as they stand now, include the addition of a dumbwaiter that goes from the kitchen to the upper floors."

She nodded, trying to make sense of the drawing. "Mr. Crandall told me about that. He was quite proud of the addition, seeing it as a better way to get the food to those folks who want to take their meals in their rooms."

Then she frowned. "Surely you aren't thinking about doing away with it?"

"No. In fact, Mr. Hendricks has already started work on it." He rubbed his chin. "I've just been trying to figure out if we could do the same thing on a much larger scale."

"Larger scale?"

"I think it would be a great benefit if we could include an elevator in the new wing. I'm just trying to figure out if it could be done without impacting the project schedule."

"An elevator? What a marvelous idea."

He nodded. "It would make transporting heavy trunks to the upper floors easier. Not to mention be a benefit to those guests who have trouble negotiating stairs, such as the elderly and infirm."

Her mind went immediately to his limp. No wonder he'd come up with the idea—he could so easily empathize with those who'd get the most use from it. Not that he hadn't managed the stairs quite well since he'd arrived.

She frowned, wishing she was better able to decipher the plans he was studying so critically. "But if it wasn't in the original design, is there even space for it?"

He nodded and pointed to a section on the blueprint. "See here? If we do away with this storage room on the first floor, and shorten the corridors here, and build the walls out slightly on the second and third floors, I think we can squeeze in a nice-sized elevator."

That seemed a lot of *if*s. "And the budget?"

"It will require extra funds, but I think if I explain to Judge Madison what I want to do, he'll be open to covering the costs. He likes to install practical, modern touches in his properties when possible."

"Then it sounds as if this is something you really should do. It could provide major benefits to our guests and staff. And it would give the hotel the added cachet of being the first building in Turnabout to include an elevator."

He frowned. "As I said, there's the matter of the schedule to consider."

"I'm sure, even if it adds a few extra weeks to the schedule, Judge Madison will understand."

Mr. Reynolds stiffened slightly. "Actually, the Christmas deadline is important to me personally."

"Oh?" Why would that be? Did he have important Christmas plans? Someone back in Philadelphia he wanted to spend the holiday with?

When he didn't elaborate further, she tried to tamp

down her curiosity and move on. "Well then, we'll just have to make certain we put in the extra effort to ensure it all gets done on time."

He raised a brow. "We?"

"Of course. I'm part of this team, too, remember?" Then she paused. "Have you spoken to Mr. Hendricks about this yet?"

He shook his head. "I've only just figured out how we might be able to make it work in the current design."

"Do you expect Mr. Hendricks to install the elevator? That might be outside his expertise."

He rolled up the plans. "I've had elevators installed on other projects I've worked on. The company who supplies the materials and engineering usually provides experts to do the installation as well."

"Then it seems to me you should speak to Mr. Hendricks right away to get his opinion on the impact to his construction progress. That way you can gauge the impact on your work schedule."

"Actually, the first thing I need to do is to contact the elevator company. It takes time to get the necessary equipment, materials and workmen lined up."

He set aside the plans and moved to his desk. "So if you'll excuse me I'll get busy drafting the telegram."

"Of course." She hesitated a moment, then spoke up again. "If you don't mind, though, I do have a favor to ask."

He paused and turned to face her. "And what might that be?"

"Sometime, when you have a moment, would you teach me how to read those blueprints?"

His brow furrowed. "Whatever for?"

"So I'll understand what I'm looking at the next time we have a discussion like this."

He studied her curiously for a moment, then nodded. "Of course. Perhaps after lunch, if that fits your schedule?"

"Yes, thank you." And before he could change her mind, she grabbed her victory and left the room.

The next few days found the two of them settling into a routine of sorts. To Abigail's relief, Mr. Reynolds seemed to accept that she was competent enough to do the job the judge had assigned her.

She measured walls, floors and windows so that she could plan the furnishings accordingly. Determined to make as few mistakes as possible, she took the measurements multiple times. Finally Mr. Reynolds showed her how to set up scale drawings to make it easier for her to play with different configurations.

Abigail also got in the habit of meeting with the staff every morning when she came in, making sure they understood their priorities for the day, listening to any problems or concerns they wanted to bring up and encouraging them to make suggestions on how to improve service. After all, she figured if she wanted to earn the job of hotel manager, it was important that she get the staff's perspective on the inner workings of the hotel as well.

But no matter what else she had going on, Abigail tried to join Mr. Reynolds for lunch and breakfast whenever possible. She found it to be the best time to speak to him when he wasn't distracted by other things requiring his attention. She always tried to share how things were progressing with her responsibilities and attempted to draw him out, sometimes with great difficulty, on how he fared with his.

On Wednesday, as they sat down to lunch, Abigail felt

quite pleased with her progress. "I've had a very productive couple of days."

"Have you now?"

She didn't let his lack of enthusiasm dissuade her from elaborating. "Yes indeed. I talked to all the local folks who might be able to provide some of the furnishings and most have agreed."

"Is there anything you're *not* having crafted locally?"

"Of course. There are furniture pieces and other special items that will need to be ordered. I'm digging through catalogs now to identify what will work best."

Then she changed the subject. "Have you made any decisions on the elevator project yet?"

He nodded. "We're going forward with it. Hendricks thinks the required modifications won't cause more than a few days change to the schedule. Judge Madison has approved additional funding to cover it. And the elevator company is sending an engineer over to take a look at the layout and draw up the engineering plans."

"Well then, I'd say things are definitely moving along." Would he have mentioned any of this to her before the engineer showed up if she hadn't asked?

She glanced down at her plate. "Pork roast, potatoes and peas. This is the same dish Della served three days ago."

"It is. But I don't see that as a problem, especially right now when we're informing our guests that we're providing limited services."

"Still, I think we can do better. We also want to make certain we're prepared when we return to full service. So I think I'll work with Della to update our menu offerings."

"What did you have in mind?"

"I'd like to work on creating a few special dishes we

can promote as signature items like some of the fancier establishments do. First, though, I'll need to find out what Della's strengths are and play on those. And perhaps teach her a new trick or two."

"And you think you're the one to teach her those new tricks?"

"I've learned a thing or two working with Daisy the past several years."

"Do you really think that's the best use of her and your time right now?"

"Actually, I think now is the perfect time. We have a limited number of guests so she can experiment freely and if things go wrong, we'll be able to come up with a replacement offering quickly." Not giving him time to object, she continued, "Are there any particular dishes you'd like to see added?"

He waved a hand dismissively. "Since you've taken charge of this project, I'll leave it entirely in your hands."

She nodded acknowledgment. "So tell me how the rest of your work has been going. Anything happening that could impact your schedule?"

He picked up his knife to cut into his slice of roast. "Everything is proceeding as it should."

That certainly wasn't very informative. "I hear you've been actually rolling up your sleeves and pitching in from time to time. I thought perhaps you were concerned Mr. Hendricks and his sons weren't working fast enough."

He shifted slightly, as if uncomfortable with her question. "Not at all. As it happens, my own father was a woodworker, though he made furniture rather than buildings." He shrugged. "I still like to feel a hammer in my hand occasionally."

Inordinately pleased that he'd shared a personal glimpse with her, Abigail decided perhaps she was beginning to make progress in cutting through his guard after all.

Which made her more determined than ever to keep working at it.

Chapter Thirteen

After the church service Sunday morning, Seth again waited for Miss Fulton to join him before making his exit. It seemed the polite thing to do. As folks filed past him he received several smiles and greetings, some from folks he'd met, some from those who were still strangers to him. He had to admit, small towns did have their own kind of charm.

They made their way out the door, pausing to greet Reverend Harper. Just as they stepped off the church steps, a small child jostled past Miss Fulton, knocking her slightly off balance. He reached out a hand to steady her, leaning heavily on his cane to protect his own balance.

Her eyes widened at the contact and he felt a small jolt of awareness as well. Not at all appropriate for any number of reasons.

"Are you okay?" he asked, carefully keeping his voice steady.

She nodded and straightened, her gaze still staring at him like a startled fawn. Then she blinked and looked down, brushing at her skirt. "I'm so sorry. I didn't—"

He gave her a crooked grin, hoping to put her at ease.

"No need for apologies. It's not often I find myself to be the second clumsiest one in the room."

She glanced back up at that, her startled look quickly changing to amusement. Then she tilted her chin haughtily. "Such an ungentlemanly comment, sir. And for your information, we are not in a room, so you can't lay claim to that honor yet."

As they set off down the sidewalk, Seth wondered at what had just happened. He hadn't teased anyone in quite some time, not since before his accident. But somehow it had felt right with her.

And he couldn't decide if that was good thing or not.

"I have to say, I find the news that you're planning to install an elevator in the hotel mighty exciting."

Seth smiled at Miss Fulton's sister-in-law as she reached to clear away one of the many platters on the table. He was also very aware that Miss Fulton herself stood across the table, where she, too, was gathering up dirty dishes.

"I've never seen an elevator before," Mrs. Fulton continued, "much less ridden in one."

Seth made a deprecating gesture. "It's Judge Madison you should thank for this—I'm just following his direction. He likes to add whatever modern conveniences make sense while we're undergoing construction and renovation."

Mrs. Fulton shook her head as she added another dish to the stack in her arms. "Don't go getting all modest. Abigail told me how the elevator was your idea and how hard you worked to find space for it in the construction plans."

Abigail—Miss Fulton—spoke of him? He cast an involuntary glance her way and noticed she was very studiously *not* looking at him.

The woman at his elbow reclaimed his attention. "You've been here in Turnabout what—about two weeks now?"

"That's right."

"Have you had an opportunity to see much of the area in that time?"

Seth gave her a polite smile as he shook his head. "I'm afraid I've been much too busy to do any sightseeing."

"Well, you're not too busy now and it's a beautiful day for a carriage ride." She turned to Abigail. "And you should go along as a guide. You haven't had much chance to get out lately, either."

Miss Fulton appeared flustered. "I need to help with the kitchen cleanup."

Was she protesting out of politeness or did she not want to ride out with him?

But it seemed her sister-in-law was not going to take no for an answer. "Don't be silly. There's plenty of help here—in fact we'll likely be stepping over each other when we get back to the kitchen."

"Well, if you're sure…" Miss Fulton eyed him diffidently. "And if Mr. Reynolds would like to have a guide…"

Politeness demanded he accept. "It sounds like a pleasant outing. And I'd be pleased to have you join me."

"There now, that's settled then." Mrs. Fulton's tone carried a suspicious hint of smug satisfaction. "Get along with you and enjoy yourselves."

As they stepped out on the sidewalk, Miss Fulton gave him a sideways look. "I hope you don't mind Daisy's pushiness. She means well."

"Not at all. She was correct—it's a pleasant day for a ride." And the company was nice as well.

They strolled toward the livery in silence for a while, until Miss Fulton finally spoke again. "You know, once that elevator is installed, we'll probably get a bunch of local folks who'll want to ride in it just for the novelty of it."

He smiled. "We can probably accommodate them, as long as it doesn't interfere with our normal operations. The novelty will wear out quickly, I imagine."

Twenty minutes later, Seth was driving the buggy out of the livery. He was quite pleased that he'd managed to hand her up and then climb up to his seat with relative grace—or at least no noticeable troubles.

"You were recruited to be my guide, so where shall we go?" he asked.

She pointed forward. "Turn the carriage left on Schoolhouse Road. It leads out of town and through some lovely countryside."

He obliged and they rode in silence for a while.

As they left the town behind them, he decided it was time he picked a topic of discussion. "You know, the climate here takes a little getting used to. Back in Philadelphia, you'd likely need a coat and scarf for a ride like this."

She nodded. "I remember from my time in Boston. We don't get quite the same dramatic foliage colors here. But I'll take the milder weather any day." She cut him a curious look. "Back in Philadelphia, do you live in the city or out in the countryside?"

"I have a small apartment in the city." Not that he spent much time there.

"Then you must find life here very different from what you're used to."

He grimaced. "An understatement. The streets there have nearly as many automobiles as carriages. And the use of electricity and telephones is widespread. You can find almost anything you need or want in a nearby shop without having to order from a catalog. And there are any number of museums, libraries, galleries, theaters and opera houses if you are a fan of the fine arts."

"I remember. And sometimes I do miss the theater and museums aspect. But not enough to want to leave here."

"So you enjoy theater?"

"Absolutely. A theater performance can be so exhilarating, so emotional."

"Do you have a favorite play?"

"I once saw *Hamlet* performed—that was quite moving." She grinned. "You look surprised."

"I suppose I expected you to lean toward something less somber, something lighter in tone."

She tossed her head. "Oh, I enjoy those as well. *The Taming of the Shrew* and *H.M.S. Pinafore* are also favorites. But *Hamlet* spoke to me on a level the others didn't."

Curious. But before he could think of a response, she suddenly pointed to her left. "Look!"

Seth obediently looked where she'd pointed and pulled the buggy to a stop. Strutting across an open meadow was a large turkey.

She took his arm, her gaze still focused on the bird. "Isn't he magnificent?" she whispered.

Seth looked from the bird to the girl seated beside him. He could feel the warmth of her touch through his sleeve. Her face was flushed and her eyes were wide and shining with pleasure. Magnificent. Yes, it was the perfect word.

Then he gave his head a mental shake and turned back to study the fowl. "Now that's a sight you wouldn't see in the city."

"I've seen deer and foxes and other wildlife out here before. But this is the first time I've seen a turkey in the wild."

The bird disappeared into the tree line and she turned back to him. "This meadow is one of my favorite spots. In the spring you can pick blackberries to your heart's content. And there's a creek just past those trees over yonder that you can wade in."

She turned impulsively. "Would you like to get out and walk?" Then her expression shifted. "I'm sorry. Perhaps that was insensitive of me."

He didn't want sympathy from her. "No need to apologize. It's true that I have trouble with uneven ground, but if I'm careful it shouldn't be a problem."

He set the brake and tied off the reins, then he carefully dismounted. Pain shot up his bad leg when he inadvertently let it take too much of his weight. He'd overcompensated trying to prove he was "normal." But he recovered quickly. Once he had his balance under control, Seth retrieved his cane from under the seat, then went around to assist Abigail. When her feet were firmly on the ground he found he had to force himself to release her.

But she immediately smiled and linked her arm with his. Was it for her own support or was she trying to assist him? Or was she as eager to retain that physical connection as he was?

Whatever the case, he found he enjoyed the contact—perhaps a little too much.

Abigail stopped periodically to pick some late blooming wildflowers, a yellow bloom he didn't recognize but that she called tickseed. She kept up a steady patter of conversation, exclaiming over the flowers, pointing out pecan trees that she scrutinized and assured him would be dropping their fruit "any day now." She only occasionally made statements or asked questions that required a response from him, but he didn't mind. He was beginning to enjoy listening to her ramble.

She finally quieted and seemed lost in thought. After a moment, she cut him a sideways look. "Do you mind if I ask a personal question?"

His guard immediately came up. "That depends on the question."

She nodded. "Fair enough. What happened? To your leg I mean."

Seth stiffened, her question dampening his enjoyment of the outing.

She gave his arm a light squeeze and met his gaze with a steady one of her own. "Feel free to tell me it's none of my business if you don't want to talk about it. I truly won't take offense."

He held his peace for a moment, not sure he wanted to share such personal information. Finally he nodded. "There was a fire when I was a child. A beam fell on my leg."

Again she squeezed his arm, but this time it was more supportive in nature. "Oh, I'm so sorry. That must have been awful for you."

He'd lost so much that night—freedom of motion was only a part of it. But he wasn't ready to go in to that, not even with her. Perhaps especially with her.

So he merely shrugged. "I was actually quite fortunate. The doctor who examined me right after it happened didn't think I would ever walk again."

"How old were you?"

"Seven."

Her free hand went to her throat. "So young!"

The last thing he wanted from her was pity. "Miss Fulton—"

"I would take it as great favor if you would call me Abigail."

Her request caught him by surprise.

She must have sensed his hesitation because, though she did a good job of keeping her expression steady, the color climbed up her neck and into her cheeks.

"I hope you don't think it impertinent of me to make such a suggestion, but we *are* business associates after all, and we see each other every day. It just seems silly to stand on ceremony in this manner."

He cleared his throat. "Not impertinent, just unexpected." He realized that he'd already begun to call her Abigail in his thoughts. And to refuse her, after she'd gathered up her courage to make the request, would be ungentlemanly. So he gave a short bow. "I would be pleased to call you by your given name if you will extend me the same courtesy."

She gave him a brilliant smile, as if he'd just handed her a precious gift, and Seth found himself responding in kind.

And that scared him.

What was he doing? First the teasing earlier and now this. A personal relationship with her was out of the question. He was not the kind of man that a woman like Abigail needed. And she was going to hate him when she realized the deck had been stacked against her on the hotel-manager job from the very beginning.

That thought was enough to sober him completely.

He straightened. "I think it's time we head back," he said abruptly.

Her expression changed from buoyant happiness to bewilderment. "I— Of course."

He held his arm out so she could hold it for support, but he made no attempt to be more than dutiful.

They turned and headed back to the buggy without speaking. He kept his gaze focused straight ahead, but he could still sense her hurt and confusion.

He resisted the urge to console her.

It was best this way. For both of them.

No matter how much he wished things could be different.

Chapter Fourteen

Abigail walked back to the buggy at Seth's side, her mind a jumble of disjointed emotions. It was as if she'd been walking through a lovely garden and suddenly had a thick swarm of gnats fly into her face. They'd been getting along so well, or at least she'd thought he was enjoying himself, too. What had happened to stir up that particular swarm of gnats, to turn him all stiff and closed off again? Was it because she'd asked about his leg? Or because she'd asked him to call her Abigail? Had he decided she was being too forward after all?

Or was it something else altogether?

When they reached the wagon, he helped her up, but his touch was impersonal, lacking the warmth of their earlier contact.

She made a couple of attempts to engage him in conversation on the ride home, but while his demeanor remained pleasant, it was also impersonal, and he limited himself to brief responses. It was almost a relief when he pulled the buggy to a stop in front of the restaurant.

Abigail quickly dismounted from the buggy. She couldn't bear the thought of his polite but oh-so-impersonal touch.

"Thank you for an enjoyable outing," he said politely.

"You're quite welcome." She managed to keep her tone equally polite. Then she stepped away from the buggy. "Well then, I guess I'll see you at the hotel in the morning."

With a nod, he set the horses in motion once more.

Abigail wasn't ready to go inside and face Daisy's curiosity, so she turned in the opposite direction of the livery and headed out at a fast walk. Perhaps some exercise and time alone to think and to pray would help clear her head.

Seth walked back to the hotel from the livery, making sure to go up Main Street rather than Second so he wouldn't risk encountering Abigail. He was definitely out of sorts.

His leg ached from the jolt it had gotten and the walk they'd taken through the meadow. But he'd dealt with those aches and pains before and likely would again.

No, what had him so rattled was the image of the hurt look on Abigail's face, and the knowledge that he was responsible for placing it there.

There was no doubt in his mind that putting some distance between them had been necessary. They were business associates and that was all they would ever be. He should never have done anything to make her think different.

Still, perhaps he could have been gentler with her.

Not that she could have intended anything more than a warmer friendship. He realized that now that he'd had some distance from the situation. Her overtures may have even been driven by sympathy. After all, she'd made her request to use given names after she'd heard the story of his leg injury.

It had just been wishful thinking on his part that had seen things leading to something more. For one thing, a vibrant young woman like Abigail would never be happy shackled to half a man, such as himself.

And that was the crux of the problem—wishful thinking. It did him no good to wish for something he couldn't have. He thought he'd come to terms with that a long time ago.

But then Abigail had happened.

And now nothing was the same.

Chapter Fifteen

Abigail felt her frustrations rise as the next several days provided more of the same. She wasn't certain exactly what had happened out there in the meadow on Sunday, but if he didn't want to be more than friends, then so be it. Sure it stung, but she'd get beyond it. Why couldn't Seth?

Whenever she crossed paths with him he was polite, but nothing more. And while she made an extra effort on a few occasions to seek out his opinion on some matter of decor, he seemed to be making a conscious effort to avoid her as much as possible.

It was infuriating and more than a little hurtful.

By Wednesday she'd had enough.

She waited until he went into the office, gave him a minute to get settled in, then followed him inside and shut the door behind her.

He looked up and must have seen something in her demeanor because his expression turned wary.

"We need to talk," she said as she approached his desk.

He stared at her with a what-is-she-up-to look on his face, then leaned back. "If this is another discussion concerning which finish to select for the chair rail, there's no need. Those matters are your concern. I have my own job to attend to."

Had he forgotten he'd requested she consult with him? But that wasn't what she wanted to focus on right now. "No, the discussion I want to have is of a more personal nature."

A little tic near the corner of his mouth pulsed as he crossed his arms. "I'm listening."

"I'm not sure exactly what bee you have in your bonnet right now, but whatever it is you need to speak your mind so we can get past it. If I did something to upset you, say so and let's work it out."

"Miss Fulton—"

"There, that's exactly what I mean. I thought we'd gotten past the *Miss Fulton* and *Mr. Reynolds* stage. Something's obviously changed and I don't aim to leave this room until you tell me what it is."

She waited, holding his gaze while he tried to intimidate her with the force of his stare. Finally he let out a breath and uncrossed his arms. "You're right." He waved a hand. "Do you mind if I speak frankly?"

He looked so serious that she almost backed down. But it was too late for that. So she tilted up her chin. "It's what I came in here looking for."

He gave a short nod. "As I've said before, finishing this job by Christmas is very important to me. I just don't want to do anything to interfere with our ability to work together professionally and get this job done. Our relationship needs to remain on a purely business level. And Sunday afternoon, things seemed to be moving past that."

The heat rose in her cheeks as she took his meaning. To be honest, she *had* been flirting with him, but she'd thought—

No matter, she'd obviously thought wrong. "I understand. But just because things are businesslike, it doesn't mean we can't also be friends."

He smiled at that. "I apologize if I misread your feelings. And I'd be honored to call you my friend. As long as it doesn't interfere with our ability to work together."

Abigail wasn't altogether sure he *had* misread her intent. Not that she'd ever admit as much. If being friends was all he wanted, then she supposed she'd have to be satisfied with that.

After Abigail made her exit, Seth picked up his pencil again, intending to get back to work. But instead, he stared at the closed door, tapping his pencil against the pad.

Abigail was one of the most intriguing women he'd ever met. She had looked so strong and determined when she'd confronted him just now. And even when he'd gone on the attack, when he'd seen the hurt and vulnerability cloud her expression, she'd still not let it defeat her. Instead, she'd faced him down and even managed to put a positive light on his demands.

How did she do that?

It had been all he could do to keep his seat, to not march over to her and take her in his arms.

Not that she'd have welcomed such an action on his part. She wanted his friendship, nothing deeper.

And that was for the best. After all, he had a deadline to meet and he couldn't afford distractions.

No matter how tempting that distraction might be.

On Thursday morning, Abigail stepped out of her library just as Zeke Tarn entered the lobby from the front entrance. He was clutching a piece of paper in his hands.

As soon as Abigail's gaze met his, he held up the note. "I have a telegram here for Mr. Reynolds."

"He's up on the second floor looking over the work that's being done. I can show you the way."

But Zeke shook his head. "Do you mind if I leave it with you? Lionel is shorthanded today and wanted me to hurry right back."

"Of course." She glanced at the grandfather clock. It was nearly time to deliver refreshments to the Hendricksses. She could take care of both deliveries at the same time.

Retrieving a tray from the kitchen that she loaded with lemonade and cookies, Abigail let the sound of hammering lead her to the area where the men were working today.

When she stepped into the as yet doorless room, she halted in her tracks. Seth was lending a hand today. She knew he often did, but this was the first time she'd actually witnessed him at work. He had his back to her at the moment, and was bent over a worktable, sawing on a board.

His coat and vest were off and his sleeves were rolled up to just above his elbows. His shirt stretched tight across his back as he worked and the hair that had fallen across his forehead was plastered there by the sweat from his exertion. The muscles in his arms flexed with each push-and-pull motion.

Seeing the normally well-tailored businessman in this light was a revelation. Abigail felt rooted to the spot, unable to look away.

"Oh, hello, Abigail. That lemonade for us?"

At Calvin's question, Seth halted his work and his gaze shot to hers.

Had he caught her staring? Abigail tried to ignore the

heat rising in her cheeks as she quickly shifted her gaze to Calvin. "It is," she answered brightly. "And Della sent along a few cookies, too."

She set the tray atop a crate and fussed with it a moment as she collected herself. By the time she plucked the telegram from her skirt pocket and turned, the three Hendricks men were crowded around.

But Seth still stood near the worktable. He'd set aside the saw, however, and was rolling down his sleeves. His gaze was locked on her with an unreadable expression. She only hoped hers was equally unreadable.

Pasting a businesslike smile on her face as she moved toward him, Abigail held out the folded piece of paper. "This telegram came for you."

His expression shifted to a concerned frown and he grabbed his cane and moved forward to take it from her.

She watched as he read the missive. From the way his jaw tightened it didn't appear to be good news.

Was it a problem with this project? Or something more personal?

He finally looked up and met her gaze. "There's something I need to tell you." The normally unflappable Seth Reynolds looked rattled.

What in the world had happened?

Chapter Sixteen

A few moments later Seth allowed Abigail to precede him into the office. She took a seat on the settee, but he was too distracted to sit still. Instead he paced across the room, his cane rapping against the floor with satisfying thumps.

How much should he tell her? Where to start?

With the bare basics, of course. "The telegram is from Judge Madison. It concerns my nephew, Jamie."

"You have a nephew? But—" Then she waved a hand dismissively and leaned forward, her anxiety evident. "Has something happened to him? Is he all right?"

No doubt she recalled his response to her question about family that first day. He hadn't lied to her, but he acknowledged that he had misled her. "He's my ward and he's fine. The problem is that his dormitory at the boarding school he attends has been shut down temporarily. So he's being escorted here until other arrangements can be made."

She leaned back, a frown on her face. "You enrolled him in a boarding school?"

There was a censorious note in her voice and he remembered she'd spent time in a similar institution as well. He wondered again what her time there had been like.

Her forehead creased. "But, I don't understand. It's not an ideal circumstance, of course, but it's not so terrible." Then she tilted her head in question. "How old is he?"

"Eight."

"Are you worried he'll be in the way? Because I can help you keep an eye on him." She waved a hand. "I help Daisy and my brother with their children all the time."

"Yes. No." Seth rubbed the back of his neck, trying to focus his thoughts. "I mean, that's not my main concern."

"So what *is* your main concern?"

That was a good question. "My relationship with Jamie is…complicated."

Some emotion flashed across her expression then but for once he couldn't read it.

"In what way?" she asked.

Seth tried to find the right words. Then he dropped into his desk chair and set his clasped hands on the desk in front of him. "Jamie is my sister Sally's son. Sally and I lost our parents at a young age and subsequently became separated. We grew up apart from each other and never reconnected in any meaningful way." He straightened a sheaf of papers. "I didn't even know she'd married or that she had a child until Jamie was dropped in my lap a year ago with the information that Sally and her husband were deceased and I was Jamie's only blood relative."

She stood and crossed the room. "How terrible." This time she was easy to read. Her expression was full of sympathy.

Was it on his behalf? Or on Jamie's? Knowing her, it was both.

Then she reached across the desk and touched his hand lightly. He immediately felt his pulse jump.

She gave him a soft, approving smile. "At least Jamie had you to turn to, someone who could understand what he'd lost. I'm sure that was a great comfort to him."

Seth's conscience twinged at that. Had he done everything he could to help Jamie through this difficult time? Truth was, he wasn't so sure.

Then she removed her hand and gave him a probing look. Strange that he felt the loss of that touch so keenly.

"Would it be wrong to assume that you registered Jamie in that boarding school shortly after he *dropped in your lap*?"

He tried to keep the defensiveness from his tone. "I was in the middle of an out-of-town project when it happened. Of course I took time off to acquaint myself with him. I also spent quite a bit of time researching facilities to find the one that would afford him the very best care."

"The kind of care you didn't feel you could provide yourself?"

He didn't like the note of accusation in her tone. "I'm a twenty-nine-year-old bachelor with absolutely no idea how to take care of a kid. Sending him to Bridgerton Academy was the best thing I could have done for Jamie."

"I imagine part of the reason your relationship is complicated is because the two of you haven't had much opportunity to get acquainted. But now that he's going to be here with you, you have a chance to fix that."

He didn't feel very optimistic on that score.

Fortunately she didn't wait for a response. "When is he scheduled to arrive?"

He waved a hand toward the telegram. "According to Judge Madison they should be here tomorrow." The man certainly hadn't given him much notice. Had that been deliberate, or had things really happened that quickly?

"Oh dear, that doesn't give us much time to prepare."

He focused on Abigail again. "What is there to prepare?" And had she really meant the *us* part?

"Lots of things." She placed a finger on her chin. "Naturally you'll want him to have the other room in your suite." Her gaze was no longer focused on him. Instead it seemed focused inward. "I'll have Ruby get it ready today. Then, of course, you'll want to have the kitchen prepare something special so he feels properly welcomed." She met his gaze again. "Do you know what his favorite meal is?"

"I'm afraid not. But surely that's not—"

"Never mind, I'll have Della prepare a special dessert, that will have to suffice." She focused on him again. "I assume he'll be accompanied by an escort?"

"Of course. Judge Madison mentioned a Mrs. Carmichael he hired." Perhaps he could convince the woman to stay on as a governess or some such.

"Then we should make certain we have a room ready for Mrs. Carmichael as well."

"I thought all three available rooms were booked."

"Yes, but we can make an exception and open up one of the other ones. It won't be ideal but we'll have to make do." She fiddled with her collar. "And I'd be happy to accompany you to meet his train. Unless you prefer to meet him alone."

"Your presence would be most welcome, thank you." And it would also delay the moment when he and Jamie would be alone together. Whatever would he and the boy find to talk about?

Not for the first time he wished he shared some of Abigail's easy way with people.

The next morning, as Abigail accompanied Seth to meet the ten-o'clock train, she found herself eager to meet

Jamie. In fact, she'd thought of little else since she'd left Seth in the office yesterday.

She felt a kinship with him already, based on the fact that she'd also been exiled to boarding school at a young age. Of course, his experiences might be quite different from hers. He could have made lots of friends, feel completely at home and be perfectly happy to stay there as long as his uncle would allow him to. After all, he was a different person than she had been, and his circumstances were certainly *very* different.

But if he was unhappy being relegated to that Bridgerton Academy place, she was certainly ready to sympathize and do what she could to make his lot easier.

Seth was quiet, which wasn't unusual. On the other hand, though he gave no outward sign of it, she had the distinct impression that the normally unflappable man at her side was feeling nervous about the upcoming reunion with his nephew. She couldn't help but wonder why. Did he actually not get along with the boy? Or was it that he just didn't know how to relate to his nephew?

Regardless, the man needed to relax. The poor boy was probably anxious about being uprooted once again, not to mention being sent halfway across the country. Seth needed to put aside his own anxieties—whatever they might be—and make certain his nephew felt welcome here.

Perhaps talking would help him relax. "Tell me about Jamie."

His gaze shot to hers as if he'd forgotten she was there. "What do you want to know?"

"Anything. Everything. What are his likes and dislikes? Is he shy or exuberant? What is his favorite color? His favorite subject in school?"

His brow furrowed. "I would say he is more subdued

than exuberant. As for school, according to his letters he enjoys mathematics and geography."

"What else?"

"I'm afraid I really don't know him very well. As I said, he's only been with me a little over a year and we haven't spent much time together in that time."

She gave him her best bracing smile. "We'll just have to see about remedying that while he's here."

Seth didn't seem as taken with the idea as she was. He brushed at something on his sleeve. "We're not here on vacation. There's a job to be done and a deadline to be met, and Jamie's presence doesn't change that."

There he went mentioning that deadline again. Why was it so important to him? "Not even you can work *all* the time. There'll be time enough in the evenings for the two of you to get better acquainted."

He seemed poised to argue the point, but the sound of a train whistle in the distance caught their attention. People on the platform and inside the depot began to stir in anticipation of the train's arrival.

The train pulled into the station with a flourish of noise and smoke and ash. In gentlemanly fashion, Seth escorted her back away from the tracks and stepped slightly in front of her to shield her from stray ash that might blow their way.

As soon as the train stopped, they stepped forward, though Abigail could tell she was more eager than Seth was.

"There he is." Seth pointed to a woman and boy exiting from the third car up.

The boy spotted them at the same time. "Uncle Seth!" he called out as a grin lit his face.

Abigail let out a little sigh of relief. Jamie apparently liked his uncle.

The boy pulled his hand free from the woman's and raced over to where they stood, stopping just short of throwing himself at Seth.

Abigail bit her tongue to keep from demanding Seth hug the boy.

Instead, Seth patted his nephew awkwardly on the shoulder. "Hello, Jamie. It's good to see you."

The woman whose hand Jamie had been holding, a stiff, tired-looking woman with steel-gray hair and a plump figure, approached at a slower pace, stopping when she was next to Jamie. "Mr. Reynolds, I presume."

He gave a slight bow. "And you must be Mrs. Carmichael. You have my sincere gratitude for delivering Jamie safely to me."

She nodded. "Of course. That's what I was paid for."

Seth appeared taken aback by the woman's very matter-of-fact response so Abigail quickly stepped forward and extended her hand to the woman. "Hello, Mrs. Carmichael. My name is Abigail Fulton and I'm Mr. Reynolds's business partner. Welcome to Turnabout. I trust your trip wasn't unduly difficult."

She patted her sensible black felt hat. "I will admit to being a bit travel-weary."

"We have a nice room waiting for you at the hotel where you can rest and freshen up. And if you're hungry, our kitchen can provide you with an excellent meal." She turned to Jamie with a conspiratorial smile. "And I do believe Mrs. Long has prepared a peach cobbler for dessert."

Jamie gave her an answering smile. "I like peach cobbler."

"Me too. It's one of my favorites."

Once the pleasantries were complete, Seth reached for the carpetbag Mrs. Carmichael carried. "Allow me."

She eyed his cane and hesitated.

Abigail saw the woman's hesitation and Seth's answering stiffness.

He kept his hand out and Mrs. Carmichael finally handed over her bag.

"Are there any other bags to take care of?" he asked.

"That one is all I have. However, young Jamie here has a couple of trunks in the baggage compartment."

Abigail quickly spoke up. "Why don't I make arrangements for the trunks to be delivered to the hotel while Mr. Reynolds gets reacquainted with his nephew? It won't take me but a moment."

As promised, it didn't take long to make the arrangements, but she returned to find the three standing there without speaking.

She stepped up and took Jamie's hand. "Come on, you and I can lead the way."

The boy only hesitated a heartbeat before nodding.

As they proceeded down the sidewalk he looked around, as if trying to take in everything at once. "Am I really in Texas now?" he finally asked.

She smiled at the note of awe in his voice. "That you are."

"Then where are all the cowboys?"

Abigail swallowed a grin. "You'll find most of the folks around here are farmers and merchants, not cowboys."

"Oh."

She grinned sympathetically at the disappointment in his tone. "Let me guess, you've seen a Wild West show?"

He nodded. "Momma and Poppa took me once, before…" He swallowed. "Before Uncle Seth became my guardian."

Her heart softened further. "Well, I'm afraid Turnabout doesn't have much in common with one of those shows. But don't worry, you'll find lots of other things to like about our town."

He cocked his head her way, staring with big, curious eyes. "Like what?"

"Well, there's a sweet shop where you can get some of the best candy you've ever tasted. And there are some creeks and ponds where you can go fishing. Oh, and if you like wooden toys, we have a man right here in town who makes some great ones."

"Really?"

"Absolutely. And there are lots of other things for you to explore and do."

He gave her arm a swing. "I think I'm going to like it here. Even if you don't have any cowboys."

While Abigail and Jamie walked ahead, Seth took the opportunity to have a word with Mrs. Carmichael. "Judge Madison didn't provide many details in his telegram, other than that Jamie's dormitory had been closed and that he would need to stay here with me for a while."

The woman nodded as she reached into her handbag. "I understand there was a fire of some sort. I don't really know any of the details, other than that no one was seriously injured, praise God. However, the building will need some serious work before it is habitable again."

She handed Seth the letter she'd retrieved from her purse. "Judge Madison said I was to give you this. I imagine it answers most of your questions."

Seth accepted the missive and slipped it into his jacket pocket. "As Miss Fulton said, we have a room ready for you. Perhaps once you've had an opportunity to rest up from your trip, we can discuss your plans."

She gave him a surprised look. "Plans? My only plans

that you need to be concerned with is that I'll be leaving on tomorrow's train."

Seth felt his hopes of keeping her on as a governess begin to shrivel, but he tried anyway. "Is there some way I can convince you to stay on a little longer while Jamie gets settled in?"

"I'm afraid not. I already have another job waiting for me."

Seth tried not to panic. "I need someone to take care of Jamie while he's here. Do you have any recommendations?"

"Why, I figured you would handle that, sir." Then she waved a hand at the pair walking ahead of them. "With the help of your lady friend there, perhaps."

Seth swallowed. Abigail had offered to help but he couldn't expect her to take on the role of full-time nanny. Could he?

When they arrived at the hotel, Abigail took charge before he could say anything. She released Jamie's hand and touched him lightly on the shoulder. "You go on with your uncle—he'll show you where your room is. I'll help Mrs. Carmichael get settled in."

Seth decided it was easier to follow her lead than not, so he led Jamie to their suite. "That's my room," he said, pointing to the right as they stepped in the sitting room. "Yours is this way." He turned to the left.

Jamie stepped inside his room, moving to the center and slowly looking over the space. Seth remained in the doorway, not sure what to say next, but feeling as if he should say something welcoming.

"I trust you'll enjoy your stay while you're here. If there's anything you need, let me know and I'll try to provide it."

Jamie nodded. "I like it here already. Miss Abigail seems nice."

So Jamie had fallen under her spell already, had he? "She is." Before things could grow awkward, Seth straightened and cleared his throat. "I have something I need to take care of. I want you to wait here until your trunks are delivered. Rest up if you like. I'll be back to fetch you when it's time for lunch."

The boy nodded. Standing there he looked so small and vulnerable that Seth felt like a wretch for leaving.

"Uncle Seth?"

"Yes?" Seth braced himself for whatever it was the boy had to say to him.

"Thank you for letting me come here to be with you. I promise I won't be any trouble."

Seth felt as if the boy had sucked all the air out of him. He gave a short nod then made his exit.

He stepped out of the suite, then leaned back against the door for a moment. He wasn't sure he could do this. The boy deserved someone who could be a proper parent.

Someone who knew how to give him the tenderness and affection a child needed.

Someone who wasn't him.

Chapter Seventeen

Once he was back in the office, Seth opened the judge's letter. It was singularly lacking in details or apologies. Apparently Jamie's dormitory would be closed through the end of the year and the judge thought the best place for the boy in the interim was with Seth. Seth wasn't at all certain he agreed with that decision, but it was too late for that now.

Though Seth admired Judge Madison a great deal, and owed him for the opportunity he'd given him to make something of his life, Seth also knew the man could be craftily manipulative, in a benevolent sort of way. He'd probably thought putting him and Jamie together for a couple of months would be a good thing, whether Seth agreed or not.

What in the world was he going to do now?

Before he'd come up with an answer to that question, the office door opened and he looked up to see Abigail stepping inside. "Mrs. Carmichael is settled in her room. And Jamie?"

"The same. Thank you for accompanying me this morning."

"You're welcome. Did you find out how long they'll be with us?"

"*He*, not *they*. It appears Mrs. Carmichael is leaving tomorrow. Jamie, on the other hand, is stuck here for a while, perhaps until the end of the year."

"I see."

Her expression was thoughtful, assessing, and he sensed that perhaps she saw a little too much.

Then she smiled. "That will certainly give the two of you time to get to know each other better."

"I have work to do here." He hoped he'd kept the defensiveness from his tone.

"That seems to be a constant refrain with you."

He frowned at her censorious tone.

"Perhaps Jamie can tag along for at least part of the day. I'm sure he would enjoy learning a little about what it is you do," Abigail said.

"I don't have a lot of spare time to keep up with a child or answer his questions." Seth mentally winced at the petulant tone in his voice. "Besides, a construction site can be a dangerous place for a child."

She gave him a knowing look. "You're right, of course. It would be irresponsible to allow him to go in the construction areas without someone to keep a close eye on him. If you're worried you might get distracted, Jamie is welcome to spend part of his time with me. And, of course, we ought to see about enrolling him in the local school. I could take care of it for you, if you like."

He latched on to that idea like a lifeline. "School, of course. That would be a big help, thank you." In fact it was a very good idea. Being in school would keep Jamie occupied elsewhere for a good part of the day.

"Do you mind if I ask you a personal question?"

His first instinct was to say yes, he minded a lot. There

were too many secrets he'd prefer to keep buried. But refusing seemed churlish. "Ask away."

"Why did you feel it necessary to send Jamie to a boarding school in the first place?"

He supposed, as personal questions went, that wasn't as bad as it could have been. Still, it put him on the defensive, which he didn't like. "I did it *for* Jamie. The work I do for Judge Madison requires that I travel, often for months at a time." He spread his hands. "Like this job, for instance. And when I'm on the job, it requires a lot of focus. That's no life for a young child."

She seemed less than satisfied with his answer. "This boarding school you sent Jamie to…"

She hesitated just a moment. Then she waved a hand. "I assume it costs you quite a bit of money to keep him enrolled there."

That was something he didn't have to feel defensive about. "It does. But the cost is beside the point. I want to make certain Jamie has the finest care possible."

"Admirable. Yet couldn't you take that same money and hire a nanny or tutor with excellent credentials to travel with you, providing quality care for Jamie while at the same time allowing him to have the family connection—which in this case means connection to you— that all children need?"

Who did Abigail think she was? How dare this snippet of a woman-child try to lecture him about what was best for his nephew? "Not that I need to explain myself to you," he said with what he considered admirable restraint, "but there are other factors at play here that you're not privy to. Besides, this will all be moot soon. I have plans to start a business of my own. When I do, I'll be able to quit traveling and provide a proper home for Jamie."

She raised a brow at that revelation. "It's a lofty goal.

Just make certain you don't wait too long. Because to a child, having a sense of being wanted, of belonging somewhere, is much more important than promises of someday."

She was coming very close to stepping over a line. Then something in her expression caught his attention. He suddenly remembered that she had attended a boarding school herself. Was all this passion based on her own experience growing up? Had she felt some lack in her own life during her time in such an institution?

He suddenly wanted to know the answer to those questions, to find out just what her hurts were and help make them better.

She stood and her action broke into his thoughts. What was wrong with him? Hadn't he told himself less than a week ago that he had to keep his distance?

"If you'll excuse me," she said, her tone stiff, "I have some matters to attend to. When it's time for school to let out for the day I'll take Jamie to meet Miss Bruder, the teacher whose class he'll be in, and talk to her about getting him enrolled."

Seth watched her go and knew he'd not come off in the best light during their conversation. She obviously expected more from him where Jamie was concerned, perhaps she even thought he didn't care for the boy.

That wasn't true. He felt keenly for Jamie and wanted to make certain his nephew didn't suffer the same fate he himself had. That was one reason it was so important he do whatever it took to close the Michelson deal—even if it meant having to thwart Abigail's desire to be hotel manager.

Surely, when it came down to it, she'd understand that he was doing this not only for himself, but for Jamie as well.

Wouldn't she?

* * *

Abigail stepped into her library and closed the door, wanting to be alone for a moment. Seth Reynolds could be so frustrating! The man seemed to be blind when it came to the needs of his nephew. Jamie was obviously starved for affection and was looking to his uncle to fulfill that need.

And whether he would admit it or not, Seth needed Jamie just as much as Jamie needed Seth. All this talk of someday meant nothing when it came to easing loneliness. Abigail should know—she'd lived on someday promises for many, many years. They were cold comfort when you cried yourself to sleep at night alone.

But this was not about her. She had to find a way to get through to Seth, to show him there was nothing to fear and so very much to gain by keeping Jamie close.

Perhaps showing him by example was the best way. And there was no time like the present.

She took a deep breath as she stepped back into the lobby, just in time to see Kenny Glenn from the train depot delivering Jamie's trunks.

"Where would you like these, Miss Abigail?"

"Just follow me."

She found Jamie sitting on the sofa in the parlor of his and Seth's suite, looking just a bit lost.

"Hello, Jamie. Are you getting settled in okay?"

"Yes, ma'am."

She grimaced. "Oh, dear, let's have none of the *ma'am* stuff please."

"What shall I call you?"

"How does Miss Abigail sound?"

He smiled and nodded. "Yes, ma— I mean, yes, Miss Abigail."

"That's better. Now let's show Kenny where to set your things, shall we?"

Once the deliveryman had deposited the luggage and left, Abigail turned back to Jamie. "Now that that's taken care of, what do you say we go down to the dining room for an early lunch?"

"Uncle Seth told me to wait here for him."

"Then we'll stop by the office to let him know you're with me."

A few moments later she was ushering the boy into the office. "I just wanted to let you know—Jamie's trunks have been delivered and he's with me," she said when Seth looked up. "We're on our way to the dining room to eat lunch."

"It's only eleven o'clock."

She shrugged. "There's nothing that says lunch must be eaten at noon." She gave Jamie a conspiratorial nudge. "Besides, we're hungry now, aren't we?"

When the boy nodded, she glanced back to Seth. "You're welcome to join us if you'd like."

He hesitated a moment, then pushed away from the desk. "Very well."

She felt a little spark of satisfaction, but hid it behind a nod. Then she turned back to Jamie. "Let's see what sort of meal Mrs. Long has prepared to go with her peach cobbler, shall we?"

A few minutes later, the three of them were seated around one of the tables in the hotel dining room and Abigail realized it would be up to her to get the conversation moving.

"So Jamie, if you had to pick your absolute favorite meal, what would it be?"

The boy thought for a moment. "Pot roast with potatoes, carrots and corn on the cob."

"Oh, that does sound delicious—I like corn on the cob, too. But my favorite meal has to be the rabbit stew cooked by Daisy—that's my brother's wife. I've tried to duplicate it but no one makes it quite as good as she does." Then she turned to Seth. "Your turn, if you could have any meal you wanted, what would it be?"

"Clam chowder, the way my mother used to make it."

Hearing a personal reference from the usually guarded Mr. Reynolds caught Abigail by surprise. So he hadn't closed himself back off entirely. Was that due to Jamie's arrival?

She nodded. "Childhood memories—they certainly add a dash of something special to the taste of a meal." Then she leaned in, as if telling them a secret. "Just think, if we had a meal with all of our favorite foods represented, what a grand feast it would be."

Seth listened to Jamie and Abigail expound over this make-believe feast for the next several minutes with only half an ear. He was surprised by his own statement about the clam chowder. He hadn't thought of his mother's cooking in a long time, but when Abigail had asked the question the answer had just popped up.

He knew what Abigail was doing, of course. Getting him and Jamie to talk about themselves so they would be able to relate to each other better. It wasn't a bad plan, he just wasn't certain how much good it would do.

One thing was certain—his interactions with Jamie came easier when Abigail was there to smooth the way. Jamie was more relaxed than he'd ever seen him. She even had him laughing at one point, something Seth had never seen him do.

Later, when they'd finished their meal, Abigail turned to him. "What do you have planned for this afternoon?"

"I need to look in on the construction and see how everything is going. I also want to recheck some of my measurements for the elevator area."

She nodded thoughtfully. "I'm going to be in the office looking through furniture catalogs. I received notice this morning that one of the sets of chairs I ordered last week is no longer available so I'll have to find a replacement." She turned to Jamie. "If you'd like to join me, I have paper and pencils. You can draw or write whatever you like."

He gave her a wide grin. "So you mean I don't have to go back to my room?"

Seth mentally winced. That was exactly what he'd had in mind for the boy.

"No, of course not," Abigail assured him. Then she turned back to Seth. "I plan to head over to the school with Jamie a little before three o'clock to get him enrolled. If you'd like to join us so you can meet his teacher, you're most welcome to do so."

It sounded almost like a command. What had happened to her offer to take care of it for him? But he could hardly say no, especially with the look she was giving him. "Of course."

With a satisfied nod, Abigail stood and held her hand out to Jamie. He watched them go, marveling again at the ease with which she interacted with his nephew after knowing him less than half a day.

Would he ever be able to establish that kind of relationship with his nephew?

Chapter Eighteen

Abigail escorted Seth and Jamie into the schoolroom as soon as she'd seen the last of the children leave. She'd wanted to make certain they weren't interrupting anything.

"Miss Bruder, this is Mr. Seth Reynolds, and his nephew, Jamie. Mr. Reynolds would like to enroll Jamie in your class."

The teacher gave Seth a smile then focused on Jamie. "Hi there, Jamie. I'm very pleased to meet you. How old are you?"

"Eight."

"Wonderful." The teacher nodded approvingly, as if being eight was a great accomplishment. "And have you attended school before?"

"Yes, ma'am."

Seth spoke up quickly. "He's been at the Bridgerton Academy for Boys for the past year or so."

She couldn't detect any defensiveness in his tone, but Abigail had the feeling he'd wanted to make a point.

The schoolteacher gave him a quick smile then addressed Jamie again. "Then I'm sure you're ready to join right in with the rest of the class."

She turned back to Abigail and Seth. "Why don't you give me and Jamie a moment to get acquainted? Abigail, perhaps you can show Mr. Reynolds around."

"Of course." Not that there was much to see.

She led him toward the back of the room. "You and Jamie will find school here is different from what he experienced in boarding school. For one thing, there are just two classrooms. Miss Bruder here teaches the younger children up to age ten. The older children go into Mitch Parker's class in the next room."

She smiled. "But Turnabout is growing and the classes have begun to get a bit crowded. At the last town-council meeting there was talk of adding another classroom and hiring another teacher."

"That's good to hear. A growing town is good for the hotel business as well."

Always the businessman.

Then he glanced to the opposite corner of the room. "I see there's a piano here—does that mean they teach music to the students in this class?"

He sounded surprised. "Yes, but not during regular class hours. Verity Cooper, the church's choir director, provides lessons after school three days a week for any student, young or old, who has an interest."

"I wonder if I should enroll Jamie in that program as well."

Pleased that he was showing an interest in Jamie's future, she gave him an approving smile. "Certainly, if he has an interest in learning. If not, there's also a children's choir he can join. It would be an excellent way for him to make friends with some of the other children."

"I agree. In fact, I should probably speak to Miss Bruder about it today while I'm here."

"Why don't we wait to see if Jamie is interested first?"

He nodded. Then he eyed her speculatively. "Do you play?"

"Music was a mandatory part of the curriculum at Miss Haversham's School for Young Ladies. So, yes, I took piano lessons. I was never more than mediocre, though. And I haven't touched a keyboard since I moved here."

She noticed he was studying the instrument with a faraway look. Had he even heard her answer to his question?

"My mother played the piano." His voice was thoughtful, as if he was talking to himself rather than her. "I always liked listening to her play. She tried to teach me and Sally how to play as well, but I wasn't interested. I wish now I'd paid closer attention."

There was an unexpected poignant quality to his expression that both touched and intrigued her. What had he been like as a child?

"We all do—or don't do—things as children we regret as adults," she said softly. "It's nothing to feel guilty about."

He met her gaze, and she thought she detected a touch of self-consciousness there. Then he straightened and cleared his throat. "Yes, well, I think Miss Bruder is signaling for us to return." And he retraced their steps to the front of the room without waiting for her response.

Seth wanted to go back in time and unsay that confidence. Dwelling on the past served no purpose other than to revive bitter feelings. And vulnerability was something he didn't wear well.

He tried to push aside those uncomfortable thoughts as they neared the teacher.

Miss Bruder placed a hand on his nephew's shoulder. "Jamie seems to be a fine young man. I think he'll do well here."

The teacher spoke of looking forward to having Jamie in class on Monday morning and of a homework assignment that would acquaint him with what the class was currently working on.

But Seth had trouble focusing fully on her words.

What was wrong with him? It wasn't like him to blurt out personal information. In fact, he was usually strict about keeping such information private. When he was in Abigail's presence, that all seemed to go out the window. And it wasn't as if she pushed him for the information, or at least not overtly.

He pulled his thoughts back to the present when he realized Miss Bruder was collecting her things.

"And don't worry about not knowing anyone, Jamie. I'll partner you with Noah Wilder for the first few days. He's about your age and I think the two of you will get along."

He noticed Jamie looked relaxed. That was a good sign.

Then the schoolteacher turned to him. "And don't worry, Mr. Reynolds, we'll take good care of Jamie."

"Thank you, ma'am. I'm sure you will."

Once back at the hotel, Seth escaped to the office and allowed Abigail to watch Jamie the rest of the afternoon. It was cowardly of him, but he wasn't quite ready to take on the role of day-to-day caretaker just yet.

Chapter Nineteen

⟨⟩

After Abigail departed for the day, Seth invited Mrs. Carmichael to join them for dinner, a meal he managed to draw out for nearly an hour.

Once they finished their meal, Seth sent Jamie to get ready for bed. After saying an awkward good-night, Seth stood in the sitting room that separated their bedchambers and watched Jamie trudge off to his room.

Should he have gone with him and tucked him in, listened to his prayers? It was something his mother had always done for him and Sally before the fire, and he could still remember the way it had made him feel, as if all was right with the world.

But he wasn't this boy's parent, and he was sure Jamie hadn't received such coddling in boarding school this past year.

Still, he couldn't help but think Abigail would have expected it of him.

He sat in the sitting room for the next hour, reading an architectural journal. But he didn't take in much of what was on the pages. He found himself listening for any sounds that might come from Jamie's room.

Later, when he went to bed, his mind unexpectedly

turned to those long, lonely nights he'd spent at the orphanage and how miserable he'd been.

Which was ridiculous because this suite was no orphanage, and Jamie was likely sound asleep after the long day he'd had. Still, a little after midnight he tossed his covers aside and padded over to Jamie's door. Easing it open, he saw the still form of his nephew curled under the covers, his face turned away from the door. Was the boy sleeping or just pretending to be? Seth quietly moved farther into the room until he could hear the soft, even breathing that signaled a peaceful sleeper.

Feeling foolish for having worried needlessly, he started to leave when something caught his eye. The blanket Jamie was snuggled under—unless his eyes were playing tricks on him—wasn't the one that had been on his bed earlier. Where had it come from?

Had Jamie brought it with him?

He studied the sleeping boy a while longer, seeing hints of his own father in the shape of Jamie's nose, reminders of Sally in the wave of his hair.

He left the room, closing the door behind him, and padded back to his own room. Jamie was his blood kin, the only one he had left. Why didn't he feel closer to him?

Perhaps Abigail had been right; he needed to try harder.

Then he grimaced. There was no perhaps about it— he owed it to Jamie, and perhaps to himself as well, to try harder.

As he crossed the room, Seth made another admission to himself. Abigail was almost always right when it came to dealing with people.

Abigail rose the next morning, refreshed and eager to face the day.

Truth be told, she'd felt a little apprehensive when she

left yesterday. She wasn't certain who she'd most worried about—the uncle or the nephew. How had the two of them gotten on last night?

Abigail arrived just as Seth and Jamie entered the lobby from the direction of their suite. Looking at them now, it appeared her worry had been for nothing. If the pair didn't exactly look cozy together, at least they didn't look tense.

She'd been right, all they needed was time to get to know each other better.

"Good morning, you two. Jamie, it appears you survived your first night here in good spirits."

"We're just going in to breakfast." Seth swept a hand toward the dining room. "Please, join us."

As they approached the table, Seth stepped forward and pulled out a chair for her. His hand grazed her arm as she took her seat and she shivered slightly at the contact. Had that touch been deliberate or accidental?

Della came up just then to take her order, providing a welcome distraction. "I'll have a cup of tea while we wait on the food," she said. Perhaps that would settle her down properly.

Seth retrieved his napkin as he sat. He wasn't sure himself if he'd brushed her arm accidentally or on purpose. In either case, how could such a simple contact spark such feelings?

But, watching her speak to Mrs. Long and smile at Jamie, it was apparent the reaction was completely one-sided.

Which was a good thing. Wasn't it?

Then she turned and spoke to him, forcing him to push aside those thoughts.

"Where is Mrs. Carmichael this morning?"

"She asked to have her breakfast sent up to her room. Darby is going up in about an hour to help her get her baggage to the train station."

Seth wondered if the woman was avoiding them or just resting up. Either way, it didn't matter. It was time for him to get used to being fully responsible for his nephew.

Her tea arrived and she dropped in two sugar cubes. "How was your first night here in Turnabout?" she asked Jamie as she stirred the sweetened liquid.

The boy gave her the same "It was fine" response he'd given him earlier.

Abigail, however, didn't seem ready to leave it at that. "That's good to hear. Because, you know, I always have trouble getting to sleep my first few nights at a new place."

"You do?"

She paused to take a sip before responding. "I think it's because the night sounds are different from place to place. Did you notice?"

He nodded, shifting in his seat. "But I wasn't scared or anything."

The way he said that gave Seth the impression that he had felt just the opposite.

She propped her elbows on the table with the cup between her hands up near her face, as if immersing herself in its aroma. "I remember when I first moved here, how unsettling it was. The dogs barking. Having a room to myself, which meant I didn't hear my roommate's breathing. The creaks that are different from the ones I was used to." She smiled. "That sort of thing."

Jamie nodded, obviously hanging onto her every word.

Seth, too, was interested to see where she was going with this.

"But I got used to it in no time. And it helped that I

had one of my mother's shawls with me. It was something to bring part of my old home to my new home. I still have it." She tilted her head slightly "Do you have something like that?"

He nodded. "A lap quilt my momma made for us to use when we went on sleigh rides."

So that's what had been on his bed last night. How in the world had Abigail known about that? Or had she?

"How wonderful. So you have a little piece of home with you wherever you go, too."

Seth felt as if he was more outsider than participant in this discussion. How did Abigail manage to earn Jamie's confidence and get him to open up to her so easily? The boy was as comfortable with her as if they were old friends.

"I like being here," Jamie said. "Even if you don't have cowboys."

"I'm glad," Abigail said. "And you'll like it even more once you get the chance to explore a little bit."

She sat up straighter. "Speaking of which, do the two of you have plans for today?"

Seth cleared his throat. "I need to check on the materials that were supposed to come in yesterday but didn't. And I also need to go through the invoices and review the progress to schedule." Even to his own ears it sounded dry and uninteresting. Not that he would have noticed that a month ago.

She rolled her eyes. "So, it's to be a normal Saturday for you."

Was she poking fun at him?

Then she turned to Jamie. "What about you?"

"Uncle Seth says I can sit in his office with him or stay in our suite and prepare for class on Monday."

She made a face. "Neither of those sound like much

fun. I tell you what. I'm planning to run a few errands around town this morning. Would you like to join me? It'll give you a chance to see more of Turnabout and perhaps meet some of the townsfolk."

She'd never made him an offer like that.

Jamie sat up straighter. "Yes, ma'am." Then he glanced toward his uncle. "If that's okay?"

Seth nodded. At least Jamie would be taken care of for part of the morning. "Of course. Just make certain you mind Miss Fulton and don't get in her way."

"Yes, sir."

"I'm sure he'll be fine."

Fifteen minutes later he watched the two of them exit the hotel, hand in hand. Was that a twinge of jealousy he felt, a tug to join them in their outing?

Whatever it was, he needed to push it aside and maintain focus on the all-important Christmas deadline.

There would be plenty of time later for him and Jamie to get to know each other better.

Chapter Twenty

Abigail's first stop was the dress shop. Her wallpaper samples had finally arrived and she wanted to hold them up to her fabric choices to make certain everything was going to go together as well as she'd envisioned it.

As soon as they walked in the dress shop, she saw Hazel's adopted daughter, Maggie, was there, playing on the floor with both a dog and a cat.

Sending a smile of greeting Hazel's way, Abigail took a moment to introduce Jamie to Maggie, then left the two children to get acquainted while she turned to her business with Hazel.

Ten minutes later, she and Jamie were back out on the sidewalk. "Maggie is lucky," Jamie said as they left. "She has both a cat and a dog."

Abigail took his hand. "Have you ever had any pets?"

The boy shook his head forlornly. "No, ma'am. But I always wanted a dog."

What would Seth think if she found a pet for Jamie? She grimaced as she thought of his probable reaction. She probably shouldn't test those particulars waters. "Perhaps someday you'll get your wish." Then she gave his hand a squeeze. "But for now, I need to stop by the restaurant."

She gave him a conspiratorial smile. "And perhaps we can talk Daisy in to giving us a slice of her special pecan pie."

"I like pie," he said eagerly, his previous disappointment apparently forgotten.

She ruffled his hair. "Then by all means, let's get some pie."

Seth looked up when his office door opened. Jamie and Abigail entered, though Abigail had paused at the threshold.

"We're back," she said unnecessarily. "I need to check on some things in the kitchen so I'll leave Jamie with you."

She turned to the boy with a smile. "Thank you for keeping me company this morning."

Jamie returned her smile, obviously enamored with the never-too-busy-to-play Abigail. "I had fun."

She squeezed his shoulder, waved goodbye to Seth, then exited, closing the door behind her.

Which left him alone with Jamie. He leaned back in his chair. He probably should try to make conversation before going back to his work. "How did your walk through town go?"

"It was fun," Jamie repeated as he came around to the side of the desk. The boy's tone was enthusiastic and his expression animated. "We stopped at lots of places. I got to play with a cat and a dog. And we went to Miss Abigail's friend's restaurant and I had pecan pie. And there was a photography studio where the lady showed me how her camera works. Oh, and we went to a shop where they sell lots of different kinds of candy." He held out a parchment-wrapped confection. "We brought you a piece of maple taffy."

Seth accepted the slightly sticky gift, oddly touched. "Thank you."

"And Miss Abigail took me by the stable so I could pet one of the horses." His nephew eyed him hopefully. "Do you think I could learn to ride a horse while I'm here?"

"Perhaps."

The answer, vague though it was, seemed to please the boy.

"It certainly sounds as if you've seen quite a bit of the town." More than he himself had.

"What did *you* do this morning, Uncle Seth?"

Jamie's question caught him off guard. Was the boy really interested or just being polite? "I checked with the builders this morning and helped with some of the work. For the last hour I've been checking material inventories and trying to figure out how we can get things done faster."

"Wouldn't that mean hiring more workmen?"

It was a reasonable question, especially coming from an eight-year-old. "It might. But having additional workers doesn't always make things go faster."

"Why not?"

The boy seemed genuinely interested, so Seth took the time to answer seriously. "Well, if you're working in small spaces, then having extra people might actually slow things down because they would get in each other's way. Or if the work needs to be done sequentially—that means in a certain order—then having extra workers might mean some folks are just sitting around while they wait for earlier jobs to get done."

Jamie seemed to think about that a moment, then slowly nodded. "Like when Momma used to make bread. She couldn't put it in the oven until the dough had risen, no matter how much you wanted to hurry it so you could have a piece."

"That's a very good analogy." Apparently the boy had a good head on his shoulders. Seth glanced at the clock, then stood impulsively. "Mrs. Long will have lunch ready for us in about thirty minutes. In the meantime, would you like to see what the builders are working on?"

Jamie nodded enthusiastically. "Yes, sir!"

Seth put his hand on his nephew's shoulder as they exited the room and was gratified when the boy looked up at him with shining eyes. He was also the tiniest bit worried that Jamie might want something that he wouldn't be able to live up to.

When lunchtime rolled around, Seth tracked down Abigail in the nearly complete guest parlor and invited her to join him and Jamie in the dining room.

"So how did you two gentlemen spend your time since I left you?" she asked as they took their seats.

Jamie answered before Seth could. "Uncle Seth took me to see the workmen. And I got to help hammer a board in place."

Seth hid a smile at the note of pride in Jamie's voice.

"That sounds impressive." Abigail shot him an approving glance that brought a different kind of smile to his face.

Then she turned back to Jamie. "Your uncle must trust you very much to let you help that way."

Jamie's chest poked out proudly as he nodded.

She leaned forward, laying her clasped hands on the table. "Is construction something you're interested in doing when you grow up?"

"Building things is fun. But what I really want to do is be a blacksmith, like my dad."

Strange, Seth hadn't known that. In fact he'd never taken the time to learn anything about Jamie's father. He would have guessed Sally would have married a gentleman of means.

Uncomfortable with the implications of both those thoughts, he was relieved when Della came by to take their orders.

When she departed, he decided to change the subject and turned to Abigail. "How is your library coming along?"

"There's still work to be done, but I've gone ahead and opened it up to the public again."

"You have a library?" Jamie asked this as if that was a very odd thing.

"I do. Do you like to read?"

He shrugged. "Sometimes. But it's more fun to have someone read to me."

Abigail grinned. "That can be fun sometimes, too. But what I really like is to curl up in a comfy chair, all by myself, open a book and just sink into the story."

Seth had a sudden, clear image of how she'd look totally engrossed and it was a picture that appealed to him a great deal.

Jamie, however, had more trouble with the imagery. "What do you mean?"

"Well, when you're reading a really good book, the world around you just sorts of disappears and suddenly it's as if you're living in the world the book is set in. You can see the images the writer is painting for you and the people in the book feel as real to you as the people you pass on the street. If something happens to one of them, it's as if something happened to a friend."

She smiled and spread her hands. "That's what I mean about sinking into a book."

"Oh." Jamie pondered her explanation for a moment, then nodded. "That sounds nice."

Della brought out their meals, heaping bowls of a savory beef stew along with a fresh loaf of a crusty yeast bread.

They said grace and then dug in.

"What kind of books do you like?" Abigail asked Jamie.

"I like adventure stories."

Abigail leaned back, her eyes widening. "Me, too."

Jamie frowned. "But you're a girl."

Seth hid a smile, anticipating what was coming.

She didn't disappoint. "What?" There was a heavy note of disbelief in her voice. "You don't think girls like adventures?"

The boy wrinkled his nose. "Girls usually like tea parties and silly stuff."

She pointed her fork at him. "Tea parties are not silly, young man." Then she lifted her chin. "I dare say you'd be surprised by how many girls like adventure stories. And I'm a librarian, so I should know."

Giving in to her logic, Jamie nodded. "So what are some of your favorites?"

"I've always enjoyed Mark Twain and Jules Verne myself."

"I know who Mark Twain is—he wrote about that jumping frog. But who is Jules Verne?"

Abigail leaned back in her seat, her expressive face reflecting a melodramatic air of shock that had Seth rolling his eyes.

"You don't know Jules Verne?" she asked "The man who wrote *Around the World in Eighty Days*, *Twenty Thousand Leagues Under the Sea*, *Journey to the Center of the Earth* and more?"

Jamie shook his head. "But those all sound like grand adventure stories."

"They are. But he's not the only author to write of grand adventures. I remember when I was just a little older than you I read a book about a man who sailed away to faraway places and encountered all sorts of exotic animals—now there's a story to capture your imagination"

"I haven't read anything like that one, either."

"Well, we'll just have to remedy that. I'm planning to do a little organizing in my library this afternoon. Would you like to help me? I can point out some really good books to you while we work."

"Yes, ma'am."

Seth decided Abigail had found her true calling as a librarian. She'd managed to not only capture Jamie's interest, but also have him champing at the bit to get hold of one of her books. In fact, she'd come close to convincing him he needed to dive into one of those adventure stories himself.

Then Jamie turned to him. "You want to come with us, Uncle Seth?"

For a moment Seth was tempted. Just having Jamie invite him was enough to make him want to say yes. But there was work to be done and he had to keep his eyes on that deadline.

He shook his head, his regret genuine. "I'm afraid I have too many other things to take care of this afternoon. But thank you for the invitation."

Abigail was disappointed at Seth's response. He was getting better in his interactions with his nephew but he still had a long way to go.

During the rest of the meal, she continued to draw out both of them as much as possible. It was her belief that the more they knew about each other, the easier it would be to make those personal connections. And she knew that if she left it up to Seth to ask the right questions in the right way, it might never happen.

After the meal, Abigail led Jamie to the library. "Today I'm working on organizing the biographies," she said as they stepped inside.

"What are biographies?"

"They are the stories of real people's lives." She lifted a slim book with a dark blue cover. "For instance, this one is about the life of George Washington, our country's first president." Then she picked up a gilt-edged book. "And this one is about Jean Laffite, the pirate."

Jamie's eyes widened. "A real-life pirate?"

She smiled, not surprised by which book he'd focused on. "Absolutely." She held it out to him.

"Do you think I could read this one?"

"Of course. But why don't you start with something a little simpler and work your way up to this one."

They worked for about fifteen minutes with Jamie handing books to Abigail, and Abigail shelving them in their proper places. Finally she called a temporary halt.

"I need to figure out how I want to organize this next group." She waved to a nearby table. "That's where I have most of the adventure stories right now. Feel free to look through them and see if anything interests you."

After that, Jamie spent as much time thumbing through books as helping her shelve them. As they worked, she drew him out about books he'd read in the past, discussing what aspects he liked and didn't like about them.

Seth had said he didn't have much time for pleasure reading. Did the man take time for *any* kind of pleasure in his life? He worked so hard, which he apparently saw as a virtue. But that wasn't necessarily a positive thing, not if taken to the extreme. And it wasn't a good example to be setting for Jamie.

Could she help him learn to strike a little balance in his life, for Jamie's sake if not for his own?

One thing was certain, it was most definitely worth a try.

Chapter Twenty-One

Near midafternoon, Seth stepped into the library to ask Abigail a question about one of the furniture invoices. To be honest, though, he was curious about how things were going.

But the sight that met his eyes stopped him on the threshold. Abigail and Jamie sat on the floor looking very much at home. Abigail held an open book in her lap, and she was reading from it with great dramatic flair, her arms gesticulating broadly and her voice taking on aspects of the characters. Jamie leaned against her, raptly listening to her every word.

It was such a mother-child moment, he didn't want to intrude.

In the middle of one particularly dramatic flourish, Abigail glanced up and spied him standing there. Rather than being embarrassed at being found in such an unladylike position, she smiled brightly up at him. "Hello. I'm sharing my love of *The Swiss Family Robinson* with Jamie. Have you ever read it?"

"No, I haven't." There hadn't been much reading material at the orphanage, except for bible tracts and schoolbooks. When he'd gone out on his own, he'd focused on learning what he could to make his way and hadn't had time for leisure reading.

She shook her head. "My goodness, you must read it. Unless you don't care for grand adventure stories."

Was that a challenge?

"It's really good, Uncle Seth. There's a shipwreck and everything."

"Is that so?"

"We're only one chapter in, so you haven't missed too much." Abigail's smile broadened as if she'd just thought of something wonderful. She made as if to stand and Seth stepped forward to give her a hand, careful to keep a steadying hand on his cane.

She smiled her thanks. "In fact, this is perfect. You can read parts of it at night together as a bedtime story." She held out the book. "Here, you can take it with you."

"But what about you?" Jamie sounded disappointed that she was passing the reading time off to Seth.

"Oh, I've read it a number of times. And you and I can discuss what you've read each day and share our favorite parts."

She moved to a nearby bookshelf. After a moment she reached over and plucked out a book, then turned and handed it to Jamie with a smile. "In the meantime, I think this one you can enjoy all on your own."

Seth read the title on the cover and smiled. *Aesop's Fables*. A good choice.

Jamie immediately sat back down on the floor and began thumbing through the pages.

Then Abigail turned to him. "Did you come here because you needed something, or were you just checking in on us?"

It took him a moment to remember the invoice. He quickly retrieved it from his pocket. "Yes. I had a question about this statement. Do you have a minute to go over it with me?"

"Of course." She led the way to her library desk. After a moment of studying the invoice, she looked up with a frown. "This is for some baking pans for the kitchen. What was your concern?"

"I just wondered if you authorized the expenditure. It seems unusual to be purchasing pans when we have fewer-than-normal guests to feed."

"Of course I authorized it—in fact, I initiated it. I told you I would be working with Della on some new recipes for our menu. These pans are needed to properly prepare some new desserts we're trying out."

"Very well. Just checking."

She studied him and he thought he detected the faintest hint of amusement in her eyes. It had been an admittedly thin excuse to come in here, but he wasn't about to admit that now.

He retrieved the invoice, then moved toward the door with what dignity he could muster. "Sorry to have interrupted your story time," he said. "I'll let you get back to it. I have to get back to my own work."

"It wasn't any trouble," Abigail said. "Feel free to return any time. Whether you have something for me to look at or not."

Yes, there was a definite ring of amusement in her voice.

Chapter Twenty-Two

That evening, after Jamie had prepared for bed, he brought *The Swiss Family Robinson* to Seth. "Can we read it now?"

"Of course." Seth had taken the time this afternoon to read the first chapter for himself so he'd be caught up with Jamie.

He'd been surprised by how entertaining he'd found it and had begun to understand what Abigail had meant by sinking into a book. Perhaps, once he had this Michelson property business squared away, he'd give himself permission to spend some time reading strictly for pleasure. Maybe even share some reading time with Jamie.

Once Jamie had said his prayers and settled under the covers, Seth sat on the edge of the bed and opened the book. Before he started reading though, he lightly touched the coverlet. "Is this the blanket your mother made you?"

Jamie nodded, watching Seth warily. Was he worried Seth would belittle it in some way?

"It's nice" was all he said as he opened the book.

The boy relaxed, smoothing the blanket with a motion that was almost a caress.

Before long Seth was as engrossed in the tale as his nephew, so much so that he had to force himself to stop when he reached the end of the chapter.

When he finally closed the book, Jamie gave a disappointed sigh. "Do we have to wait until tomorrow night to read more of the story?"

Seth smiled indulgently as he set the book on the bedside table. "I'm afraid so. But in the meantime, you can try to guess what happens next. As Miss Abigail said, make yourself part of that world."

Jamie nodded on a yawn. "Wouldn't it be fun if it was true?"

Seth raised a brow. "You think it would be fun to be shipwrecked on a remote island?"

"Maybe. If it was an island like the one in the book."

"Such things are fun to imagine, but I'd guess they're not fun to live out." Seth stood and gave Jamie an awkward pat. "Good night." He turned down the lamp, then headed for the door, wondering if this urge to protect and teach, to make things better, was what being a parent felt like.

Perhaps he could make this work with Jamie after all.

On Sunday, Seth and Jamie attended the service then accepted Abigail's invitation to join the lunch gathering once again. Jamie was introduced to the other children and was quickly pulled into their activities. Seth watched as his nephew was soon busily engaged in play.

"Warms your heart to see him so happy and carefree, doesn't it?"

He turned to see Abigail at his elbow. "A rather sentimental way of looking at it."

"Perhaps, but true nonetheless." And with a saucy toss of her head, she headed for the kitchen.

Amused rather than put off by her teasing, Seth turned to help the men set up the tables.

When everything was in place and they sat down to the meal, Jamie was grinning with a carefree genuineness that Seth hadn't seen in him before. Perhaps the time the boy was spending here in Turnabout really would be good for him, would allow him to move on from the grief he felt over his parents' death.

There was still a stiff sort of awkwardness between the two of them, but so far it hadn't been too bad and it seemed to be getting better. Once Jamie started school tomorrow, things were bound to go even smoother.

Later, after the front area of the restaurant had been set back to rights, Seth went in search of Jamie. He frowned when he realized his nephew wasn't out back with the other boys. Where had he gotten off to? Regina's son, Jack, indicated he'd seen Jamie headed into the kitchen.

Had Jamie gone in search of Abigail for something?

When Seth stepped inside, he found most of the women gathered there cleaning up after the meal. Jamie was stooped down next to the Fulton's black-and-white dog, petting him and talking low.

When he spotted Seth, Jamie scrambled to his feet but he kept a hand on the dog's head. "His name is Kip," he told Seth. "And look, he has one blue eye and one brown eye. Isn't that something?"

"It certainly is." The shaggy-looking dog also had a torn ear and a few scars. Not exactly a perfect specimen.

"He's real friendly, too. And he can fetch sticks and balls. Kip is just about the best dog I've ever seen."

Abigail, washing dishes nearby, smiled. "Kip's pretty special all right. Daisy considers him one of the family."

Jamie glanced hopefully up at Seth. "Do you think maybe we could get a dog of our own someday?"

"Perhaps. When we have a place of our own."

"Don't we have a place of our own now?"

Before he could stop himself, Seth cast a quick glance Abigail's way and saw the sympathetic look she gave his nephew.

Straightening, he turned back to Jamie. "No. This is just a temporary assignment. In a few months I'll be working another job in another city and you'll be back in boarding school. Which means neither of us will be able to take care of a pet."

Jamie's hopeful expression turned to disappointment. He stood, his shoulders drooping dejectedly. "Yes, sir."

Seth wouldn't let himself look Abigail's way—no doubt he would see disapproval in her eyes.

But he couldn't—wouldn't—take it back. It was important that Jamie understand this was a temporary situation. If the boy was allowed to get his hopes up, it would only lead to a much bigger letdown when he faced the truth.

It was bad enough he was letting Abigail believe there was hope when there was none, he couldn't do it to Jamie too.

On Monday morning Abigail hurried down the sidewalk. She was hoping to arrive at the hotel before Jamie left for his first day of school in Turnabout, but she was running late. She'd been helping Daisy feed the children breakfast and Danielle had dumped a bowl of oatmeal in her lap, forcing her to change clothes.

Her thoughts turned to what had happened yesterday. She'd been saddened more than she could say by Seth's lack of sensitivity in his response to his nephew's request for a pet. She'd thought earlier that he was making such progress with Jamie.

Why did he have to look at everything from the standpoint of how it fit into his business plan? Didn't he know there was so much more to life?

One day he'd figure it all out.

She just hoped it wasn't too late.

Abigail finally made it to the hotel and rushed inside to find Seth standing rather irresolutely in the lobby. Apparently she'd missed Jamie's send off.

"Did Jamie get off to school all right this morning?" she asked.

Seth stiffened. "I'd planned to walk him there since it was his first day, but Jack Barr came by and Jamie wanted to walk with him."

Did she detect a disgruntled note in his voice? The man really was developing a soft spot for his nephew. There was hope for him yet.

"Don't worry. Between the friends he made yesterday and Miss Bruder, I'm sure he will be well taken care of."

She decided to change the subject. "What are your plans for today?"

"Walter Hendricks needs to make changes to one of his orders from the sawmill. I figured I'd take care of it for him so he and his sons can keep working." Then he raised a brow. "Would you like to join me?"

She could tell the invitation had been offered on impulse, but that made it all the more intriguing. Already he seemed to be thinking better of it.

"That would be lovely," she said before he could take back the offer. Then, afraid he'd take her eagerness amiss, she quickly elaborated. "I mean, it's such a beautiful day, it would be a shame to spend it all indoors."

He nodded, already looking back down at his papers. "I plan to head out in about thirty minutes."

"Perfect. That'll give me time to check in with the staff and make certain everyone is set for the day."

As she left the office, Abigail felt surprisingly light-spirited. And why wouldn't she with a nice ride in the beautiful sunshine to look forward to?

Seth clicked the reins, feeling relaxed for a change. It was a nice, sunny day, he was riding in an open carriage and he had a pretty girl by his side.

A girl who was an associate and pleasant company, nothing more.

"Have you heard back from Mr. Doyle?" she asked, breaking the comfortable silence.

Eldon Doyle was the engineer whom the elevator company had sent to look over the structure.

Seth nodded. "They expect to be back with the materials the week after Thanksgiving."

"How does that fit into your schedule?"

"It makes it a little tighter than I'd like, but we should still be able to meet the deadline."

Then she folded her hands in her lap and cut him a hopeful glance. "Are you ready to discuss the hotel-manager position yet?"

Now was the time to tell her that he'd promised the job to someone else. But he hesitated and she spoke up first.

"Never mind," she blurted out hastily. "I'm sorry, I shouldn't have put you on the spot that way. After all, it's only been a few weeks and there's still time yet to make a decision. I'm just happy you're willing to keep an open mind on the subject."

Seth covered his guilty conscience with a change of subject. "How are things going with your plans for Christmas decorations?"

She gave a deep sigh. "I still haven't settled on a theme yet."

"Is it because you have too many ideas or not enough?"

She grinned at him. "A little of both I'm afraid."

"You're going to have to explain that one to me. How can it be both?"

"Well, I'm not having any trouble with ideas—ideas related to Christmas themes are easy to come up with. And that's part of the problem. Every idea I think of is something I'm certain a half-dozen other folks will have come up with as well. I want something unique, something that will stand out, and I'm afraid ideas like that are proving difficult to find."

"I see. Well, why don't you tell me some of the ideas you've already discarded and maybe we can find a way to put an interesting or unique spin on one of them."

The resulting discussion took them all the way to the sawmill and back. And though they came up with some absurd and nonsensical spins on some of her ideas, in the end she declared herself no closer to having a usable idea than she had been before.

Abigail sat in her library after lunch, cataloging and shelving that last shipment of books Judge Madison had sent her all those weeks ago.

She was thinking as much about her outing with Seth that morning as she was the books, though. She'd had a really good time. He'd been talkative and friendly and had really listened to what she had to say. He'd even made her laugh a few times with his absurd ideas of how to twist some traditional holiday themes. Christmas cowboys instead of shepherds, indeed. Jamie would probably love that one.

Perhaps, while Seth was still in an agreeable mood,

she should approach him with another concern that had been niggling at her.

She popped up and headed for the office before she could lose her courage.

"Do you have a moment to discuss a matter of business?"

He leaned back in his chair. "Of course. Did you run in to a problem with the furnishings?"

"Not at all. Things are moving along according to plan there. This concerns the hotel itself."

He frowned. "I'm listening."

"We turned away another customer today, and that doesn't sit right with me when we have rooms sitting empty."

He relaxed, nodding agreement. "It's not ideal, but there's nothing we can do about it until the construction is complete."

"Turning away business is not only costing us in missed income and plain old goodwill from the folks we refuse, but in some cases we're also placing a true hardship on folks who have nowhere else to go."

"I thought the boardinghouse was accommodating the guests we had to turn away."

"Miss Ortolon can only accommodate so many."

He folded his arms. "What do you suggest? I assume you have a plan of some sort."

"Right now we only have three rooms open—those farthest from the construction. But there are four other rooms that, other than the noise, are perfectly fine. The other three need to remain closed but let's open those four back up at a reduced rate with the understanding that the occupants acknowledge there will be a lot of daytime racket to put up with. Many of the guests will be happy to agree to that for the chance to have a comfortable place to sleep at night."

He rubbed his chin. "If we do this, it'll mean additional work for everyone. And probably more guest complaints to deal with."

"I thought of that. But since we'll be hiring additional staff in four to six weeks anyway, perhaps we could hire one additional person now. A woman who could work part-time as kitchen help and part-time as maid."

She watched him think through what she'd suggested.

"I can also pitch in occasionally if things get tight," she added.

He finally nodded. "It sounds like you've given this a lot of thought. I don't suppose you already have someone in mind for us to hire."

She ignored the hint of sarcasm in his tone. "As a matter of fact, I do. I think Cora Schmidt would be perfect. She's young, healthy and eager to find work. She's also a widow who's struggling to put food on the table for herself and her mother."

"Ask her to come in tomorrow and I'll talk to her."

Seth felt the full force of Abigail's smile. If he wasn't careful, he would find she'd turned the hotel into a refuge for widows and orphans.

Perhaps it was his turn to ask a personal question.

"Tell me, why is getting the job of hotel manager so important to you? It's a rather unusual ambition for a young lady, isn't it?"

She raised a brow. "So you share Jamie's opinions that girls just like tea parties and silly stuff?"

"Not at all. I said it was unusual, not silly. I'm just curious about your particular reasons."

She reached up and fingered her collar. "Getting the

job of hotel manager would not only provide me with a salary, but it also comes with living quarters. Which would come in very handy for me since it's time I moved out of my brother's home and set out on my own." She tilted up her chin. "Besides, I think I'd be good at it."

Seth chose to focus on the part of her statement that made him the least uncomfortable. "Your brother asked you to move out?" Even though he didn't know Everett Fulton well, and had reason to distrust him based on that scandal he'd been involved in back in Philadelphia, he could tell the man was very fond of his little sister. He just couldn't see him kicking Abigail out.

"Not yet."

"So what makes you think he will?"

"With a new baby on the way, his family is growing and the living quarters are getting a bit cramped. They need more room, which means I need to move out." She tucked a strand of hair behind her ear, dropping her gaze away from his. "I don't want to put him and Daisy in the position of either having to kick me out or suffering in silence."

"So you're just *assuming* they want you to move out, you haven't actually discussed it with them." More than likely she was making mountains out of molehills here.

She glared at him. "Didn't you hear a word I just said?"

"I did. I still think you're reading too much into the situation. Your brother is not going to just throw you out."

Her lips thinned and her eyes took on a bitter light. "He did once before when he put me in that boarding school."

Seth felt that blow as if it had been aimed at him. He knew exactly how her brother must have felt. "You were five years old and he likely didn't know what to do with a kid. You're not a kid anymore."

That unsettling bitterness he'd sensed in her disappeared, replaced by a guilty flush. "Yes, of course. I didn't really mean that." Then she lifted her chin defiantly. "Still, my moving out is undeniably the best thing for everyone, so my decision stands. And this time it'll be *my* decision to leave, not his."

A very telling choice of words. "So you're saying your whole future hinges on you getting the job of hotel manager."

"Not entirely. That's just my best option. But one way or the other, I'm moving out of their home before their baby comes."

"One way or the other—what does that mean?" He had an alarming vision of her running away again, the way she had once before.

"There's another job that will be coming available around Christmas, one that would also provide a place for me to live."

So she had an alternative. He was guiltily relieved he wasn't going to completely ruin her plans of independence. "And what might this other job be?"

"It's working for Mrs. Ortolon at the boardinghouse."

That didn't sound so terrible. Not as prestigious as being a hotel manager perhaps, but not everyone could start at the top. "I would think all of your experience at the hotel would come in quite handy at a boardinghouse."

She gave him a suspicious look. "Are you saying I won't be getting the hotel-manager job?"

"I'm saying you need to stop pretending it will be the end of your world if you don't. You don't know for sure that your brother wants you gone. And you just said yourself that you have another option in the boarding-house job."

"Well, whatever the case, I'm not giving up on this

one just yet. Not until you tell me I have absolutely no chance of getting it."

As she flounced out of the office, he rubbed the back of his neck, trying to convince himself he had no need to feel guilty. After all, he'd never promised her the manager job—in fact, he'd done just the opposite. It wasn't his fault she continued to hold on to this irrational hope.

As for her reasons, should he talk to Everett, let the man know what his sister was feeling? If the positions were reversed, he was sure he'd want to know.

Then again, did he want to get in the middle of what was really none of his business? Abigail was his partner, not Everett. To go behind her back in such a way felt like the worst sort of betrayal, even if it was for her own good.

He had enough to deal with knowing he couldn't give her the job she wanted.

Best to let well enough alone for now.

Wednesday morning, James Hendricks, the youngest of the Hendricks boys, came racing through the hotel lobby. "There's been an accident—Pa's hurt. I'm going get Doc Pratt." And with that he raced out the door.

"Oh, my goodness." Abigail turned to Darby. "Have Ruby get some cloths and fresh water ready in case they're needed. I'll let Mr. Reynolds know."

She was already headed to the office as she spoke.

Pushing through the door, she gave Seth the news. "There's been some kind of accident—Mr. Hendricks is hurt."

He was out of his seat before she finished talking. "How badly?"

"I don't know. That's all James said as he ran out to fetch the doctor."

Without another word, he headed out the door, and

Abigail was right behind him. They climbed the stairs in the new wing together. While Seth couldn't exactly race up them, she was surprised at the pace he managed.

They found Walter sitting on the floor, leaning against a barrel. Calvin was bent over him, examining his left arm. The young man's gaze shot up when Seth and Abigail approached, but his expression fell as soon as he recognized them.

"I thought you were Doc Pratt."

"I'm sure he'll be here soon," Seth said as he crossed the room. "What happened?"

"Pa was sharpening the saw blade and the thing slipped, slicing his hand."

Abigail saw the hand in question had been wrapped with a cloth of some sort that was now soaked with blood. Walter Hendricks looked pale and shaken.

"Mr. Reynolds, I'm sorry, sir. It was careless of me, I know. I just—"

Seth cut off his apologies. "Let's not worry about that right now. First we need to get your hand taken care of."

Ruby showed up with the rags and pitcher of water and let out a little screech.

"So much blood. Oh, my, I can't look."

Abigail took the supplies from the woman, blocking her view. "Thank you, Ruby, I'll take those. You just go on back downstairs."

Dr. Pratt arrived a few minutes later and cleared the room of all but Calvin.

As they headed back down the stairs, Abigail touched Seth's arm briefly. "I'll have Ruby make up one of the unused rooms in case it's needed."

Twenty minutes later Dr. Pratt met them in the lobby. "Walter's boys are taking him home. He's going to be okay but I don't want him using that hand for another four or five days. Understand?" The question was aimed at Seth.

Seth nodded. "Yes, sir."

Walter and his boys joined them. Walter was obviously shaken and quite pale but he was walking unaided. "I'm sorry about this, Mr. Reynolds. But my boys will be able to keep working while I'm recuperating. Calvin has a good head on his shoulders and can direct James."

"You just rest up so you can come back when you're fit." Seth rubbed the back of his neck. "In the meantime, is there someone you can recommend who could help out while you're recuperating?"

"Simon Tucker might be able to lend a hand. He works with Hank Chandler over at the sawmill. Of course, there's any number of men around here who can swing a hammer, but they'd need some supervision and that would take away from the time these two can do their job."

"I'll check with Mr. Tucker this afternoon."

As it turned out, Simon Tucker could only commit to work half days, but Seth figured it was better than nothing. He would pitch in himself as much as he could, work in the office until it was time to get Jamie off to school, then spend as many hours as he could spare working with the builders until Jamie returned home.

On Friday afternoon, Jamie approached him, his expression earnest. "Can I help, Uncle Seth? I'm a good worker."

Seth was touched by the boy's concern, and treated the offer with the gravity it deserved. "I know you are, Jamie. But you have another job to do that's just as important."

"I do?"

"Absolutely. Your job is to do your homework, keep up with your studies and be the best student you can be."

The boy frowned. "That's not a job."

"Of course it is. It's what will build you into the man you will be someday. And I won't be able to do my job if I'm worried that you're not doing yours. So you see, by taking care of your schoolwork, you're helping me focus on my own work. Can I count on you to do that?"

"Yes, sir."

Seth put a hand on the boy's shoulder. "Thank you. You make me proud."

The glow of pride that statement put on Jamie's face was a fine sight to see.

By Saturday, Walter Hendricks could no longer stay away. He showed up at the job, and though Calvin kept telling him he was just there to observe and give direction, Seth saw the man wielding a hammer with his good hand on more than one occasion.

They might make the Christmas deadline after all.

Chapter Twenty-Three

As the three of them sat down for lunch in the hotel dining room on Saturday morning, Jamie turned to Abigail. "The other kids at school were talking about a Thanksgiving Festival. What's that?"

She gave him a reminiscent grin. "Every year, on Thanksgiving Day, the town has a festival to celebrate the day as a community. There's a group meal that all the ladies of the town contribute to, lots of games and competitions and there's even a dance. It's lots of fun."

"Miss Bruder says the children's choir will be doing some singing."

Abigail nodded. "That's right—they usually do a program of some sort that morning. Will you be participating?"

"I suppose so."

She nodded decisively. "Then I intend to stand in the front row so I can have a good view."

"Speaking of holidays," Seth said, "have you figured out how you're going to decorate the hotel for Christmas yet?"

Abigail shook her head and turned to Jamie. "Perhaps you can help." She cut her gaze Seth's way with a sly grin. "Your uncle tried but he wasn't very good at it."

Seth rolled his eyes but otherwise didn't contradict her.

"What do you need help with?"

"Don't worry, it's nothing difficult. In fact it's going to be fun. I'm in charge of decorating the outside of the hotel for Christmas."

The boy wrinkled his nose. "Christmas is a long time away."

She nodded. "It is. But we're not going to actually start decorating for a while yet. I just need to start planning for it. Which means I need to come up with a theme."

Jamie swallowed the bite he'd been chewing. "What's a theme?"

"It's an idea you use to build your plan around. For instance we could say the theme is the three wise men, or the Christmas star or Christmas trees. And then we would know what kind of decorations we want to use."

"Oh." He seemed to give it some thought. "Those all sound like good themes. I especially like the Christmas-star one."

"Yes. But I'd rather come up with something that gets me excited, something no one else is going to think of." She speared a carrot with her fork. "There's going to be a prize for the business that does the best job of decorating."

The boy sat up straighter. "What kind of prize?"

"A plaque that we can hang in the lobby saying we had the best decorations. And even better than that, a beautiful, very special silver star to hang on our tree." She pointed her fork, carrot and all, at him. "It's on display at the town hall. If you like I can take you by to show you."

Jamie nodded enthusiastically. Then he cocked his

head to one side. "So, do you know what your theme is going to be yet?"

"Not yet. If you think of any good ones, let me know."

"Yes, ma'am."

Seeing an opening for more getting-to-know-each-other conversation, Abigail lowered her fork. "So tell me, what's your favorite thing about Christmas?"

"I used to think it was the presents. But that was when I was just a kid and didn't know better."

Abigail hid a smile at Jamie's attempt at maturity. "And now that you're older?"

"Now I know that spending it together with my family is the best thing." He looked down at his plate and dragged his fork through his vegetables. "When my parents were still alive, on Christmas Eve night we'd sit in front of the fireplace and I'd climb up in Momma's lap while Poppa would get the Bible and read the Christmas story. Then we'd sing some Christmas carols while drinking hot cocoa with peppermint sticks for stirrers."

His fork stilled. "Christmas morning we would get up and go to Christmas service together. Afterward we'd come home and open presents, then sit down to a feast Momma had prepared for us."

Abigail lightly touched his wrist. "Those sound like perfectly lovely memories."

Jamie nodded, his eyes moist with unshed tears.

Seth listened to Jamie's story and realized it was a memory his sister had been a part of. Whatever had turned her away from him, at least she'd been able to give her son a loving home.

Not for the first time he wondered what had hardened her heart against him when they'd once been so close. Was it due to his infirmity? Was it because she'd risen above him socially and didn't want any reminders of her origins? Neither of those sounded like the sweet little sister he remembered, but something had obviously changed her.

"What about you—do you have some favorite child-hood memories of Christmas?"

It took a moment for Seth to realize Abigail's question had been directed at him. He lifted his glass to take a drink, giving him a moment to collect his thoughts.

Thinking back to the time when his family was still untouched by tragedy was a bittersweet thing.

"My mother loved Christmas. She did her best to make it as festive as possible for me and my sister. She would bake the most delicious pies. Cherry with walnuts was my father's favorite so she always made sure she had one of those, no matter what else she baked."

"I like those, too," Jamie said softly, "especially the way Momma made them."

So, despite her privileged upbringing, Sally had learned to bake.

"What else?" Abigail asked.

"The house would be decorated with lots of evergreen and ribbon and paper ornaments, most of which we made ourselves. I remember there was one special ornament we always placed at the top of our tree—it was an angel with a china face and real feathers on the wings. Mother said it had belonged to her mother, and she always treated it like it was made of gold." That ornament had been destroyed in the fire along with all the other trappings of his childhood.

Shaking off that thought, he continued. "And then on Christmas Eve, before they tucked us in, Father would read the Christmas story from the Bible with me and Sally seated on either side of him."

Jamie was watching him with wide eyes. "That was my mother. She used to tell me those same stories about how Christmas was when she was a little girl."

Seth cleared his throat. "More recently, if I'm in town, I spend the day with Judge Madison. He has a Christmas gathering in his home for friends. If I'm out of town, however, working on a project, like I will be this year, I usually have a quiet day, with perhaps a fine meal, at whatever hotel I'm staying at."

"That sounds lonely."

He wasn't looking for pity. "Not at all. It's a nice quiet time to reflect on accomplishments from the year that's winding down and to set goals for the coming year."

"And to reflect on the message and true meaning of the season, of course."

"Of course."

She gave him an it's-going-to-be-all-right smile. "And now that you have Jamie in your life, you two can start building a whole new set of lovely memories."

Seth wasn't quite sure how to respond to that, but Jamie spoke up. "Last year, Uncle Seth picked me up at school early in the morning and we went to church service together. Then we went to lunch at a nice restaurant and he gave me a new winter coat as a Christmas present. After that we went for a walk in the snow and then he brought me back to school."

This time Jamie's recitation of the day was devoid of emotion. Had the day really been so dull?

Perhaps this year he'd put more effort into seeing things from Jamie's point of view.

Ready to turn the spotlight away from himself, he faced Abigail. "Your turn—how do *you* normally spend Christmas?"

She didn't hesitate even a heartbeat. "The best thing

about those Christmases I was at boarding school was that Everett came to spend time with me. We would try to cram as much as we could into those visits to make up for the months of being apart."

He could see how much that had meant to her.

"He used to take me to the theater and museums and on long walks in the park, weather permitting," she continued. "We weren't allowed to have Christmas trees in the dormitories, but Everett always bought me a small potted plant that we decorated together, just like it was a tree. And on Christmas day itself we would go to service, then exchange gifts and afterward we would play word games."

"And now?"

"Now I get to spend the day with Daisy and Everett and their children. We still do a lot of the same things, only now we have a real tree to decorate, and a home-cooked meal to feast on. It's all very warm and merry."

She sat up straighter, her face taking on a glow of excitement. "You know, I think I may have my theme after all."

"What is it?" Jamie asked eagerly.

"Making memories."

Seth felt as confused as Jamie looked. "How would you turn that into any kind of decoration?"

"I'm not sure yet."

Apparently that little detail didn't have her the least bit concerned.

"It'll take some thought for sure," she said airily, "but the more I think about it, the better I like it. I said I was looking for an idea that got me excited and this one definitely does that."

"Can I help?" Jamie asked.

She grinned at him. "I'm counting on it."

Seth had no doubt whatsoever that she'd make it work and that it would be spectacular. The intriguing Miss Fulton would settle for nothing less.

Later that afternoon, Abigail and Jamie merrily burst into the office. "We've figured it out," Jamie announced.

"Have you now?"

"We have indeed," Abigail proclaimed. "I knew between us, Jamie and I would come up with something fabulous."

"Out with it, then. What is this amazing, fabulous idea?"

"Stars."

"Stars? I thought your theme was to be making memories."

"It is. But the stars are going to be how we display them."

"We're going to have a paper nativity scene in the front window," Jamie explained. "And hanging over it will be a sky full of stars, and on each one, someone will have written their best Christmas memory."

Seth nodded, mentally visualizing what they were describing. "It will definitely be unique. But how will you get people to participate?"

"Oh, that part will be easy. I'll start with the children. Miss Bruder and Mr. Parker can pass stars out to their classes for me. I'll also ask people I know. That'll give me lots to start with." She shrugged. "After that I'll spread the word that anyone who wants to participate can."

"This is going to be the best Christmas decoration ever," Jamie said happily.

"That'll be for the contest judges to decide," Abigail cautioned. "But it will certainly be the most fun to put together."

Apparently as far as Abigail was concerned, that was a reward in and of itself.

Now that she'd decided on a theme, Abigail threw herself into preparations for the Christmas decorations with a vengeance. Anytime she wasn't busy working with one of the craftsmen on the furnishing for the hotel, she was planning her decorations.

Once Walter Hendricks was back to work and Simon Tucker was no longer needed, Abigail hired him to build her the large nativity scene she needed for the front window. Once he had the pieces cut to her satisfaction, she recruited Jamie and Seth to help her paint them.

"You're the expert painter," she told Seth when he seemed poised to decline. "And don't deny it. I've seen your work on that sign you painted for my library."

Once he agreed, they had a fun afternoon, though unfortunately they got as much paint on themselves and the ground as they did on the pieces.

With that done, Abigail ordered a special heavy paper to make the stars from. She cut them in various sizes and didn't worry about making them perfect. "If you look up at the night sky," she told Jamie, "you won't see one star displaying five symmetrically shaped beams. If you ask me, these stars are much truer to what they should look like."

Freed from the constraints of perfectionism, Jamie enthusiastically lent a hand.

"What are you going to do with those?" he asked as she opened packages that contained sequins, glitter and ribbon.

"These are for when the stars come back to us. We're going to make sure they sparkle and shine before we hang them up."

* * *

Seth was both astonished and pleased by the change in Jamie. The boy was rarely without a smile these days, and he seemed full of energy and spirit.

Seth could hardly imagine his life without Jamie in it now. It was so heartwarming to see the youngster experience new things, learn new lessons. He still read to him every night—it had become one of his favorite parts of the day. They'd finished *The Swiss Family Robinson* and had moved on to *Twenty Thousand Leagues Under the Sea*. Jamie was now considering pursuing a seafaring life, though Seth suspected that would change with the next thing that caught his interest.

Seth never lost sight of the fact that he had Abigail to thank for this—Abigail, who had pushed and prodded him to learn more about his nephew, to spend more time in the boy's company. Abigail, who was such a generous soul, who always saw the best in people.

Abigail, whose heart he was destined to break.

Chapter Twenty-Four

The Monday before Thanksgiving, Seth was talking to Darby about a few preparations they'd need to make before the elevator engineer arrived the next week, when Everett Fulton walked into the lobby.

Abigail's brother shook his hand in greeting, then glanced around. "Is Abigail here? I thought I'd let her show off her new library to me like she's been wanting to do."

Darby spoke up before Seth could. "She went down to the dress shop a little while ago. Said she needed to check something on the new drapes she ordered."

"She probably won't be long," Seth added. "Can I interest you in a cup of coffee while you wait?"

"Of course."

Seth led the way into the dining room, stopping long enough to stick his head in the kitchen doorway and ask Della to bring them some coffee.

Once they were seated, Everett leaned back and gave Seth a polite smile. "Abigail seems to really enjoy the work she's doing here. I want to thank you for giving her this opportunity."

Seth shrugged. "It's Judge Madison you should thank. He's the one who gave her this opportunity, not me."

Everett nodded. "That's just one more thing our family owes that man. For someone who barely knows us, he's been an amazing benefactor."

Della bustled up, deposited their coffee in front of them, then returned to the kitchen.

Determined to say his piece, Seth met Everett's gaze head-on. "There's something I need to tell you."

"Oh? What's that?"

"I know who you are. Or rather, I know *what* you did back in Philadelphia that made you want to leave."

Everett leaned back heavily. "I see."

"I remember that story you wrote, the tragedy that followed it and the accusations that the story was unfounded."

"It's all true." There was deep regret in his tone and demeanor.

Then Abigail's brother took a deep breath. "I turned in that story without digging as deeply into the facts as I should have. No excuses—because of me, a good man and his family suffered. And even though his death, and that of his daughter, were ruled accidents, I know my story contributed to it in a real way. They were on that boat that capsized because they were trying to escape the scandal I created with my story. It's a burden of guilt I've carried with me ever since."

"Your sister doesn't know, does she?"

Everett shook his head, then his lips formed a twisted smile. "I told Daisy the whole story before I married her—I wanted her to know what she was getting herself into before she committed." He grimaced. "But Abigail has no choice, she's family. And I just couldn't bring myself to tell my little sister."

Seth could sympathize with that. But he remembered Abigail's story of how she'd been ambushed by gossip once before. "Do you ever plan to?"

Everett stared into his coffee. "I know I should, but the right moment just never seems to come up."

"Don't you think it would be better if she hears it from you than from someone else?" He held up a hand. "And no, I don't plan to tell her, it's not my place. But someday it could happen. How do you think that would make her feel?"

"You're right, of course." He tilted his head to one side. "You really care about my sister, don't you?"

Seth shifted slightly in his seat, uncomfortable with being on the other side of the interrogation. "She's my friend," he said.

Before Everett could respond, Abigail bustled into the dining room. "Everett, Darby told me you were here. I hope you haven't been waiting on me very long."

Both men stood and Everett stepped forward to take her hands. "Not at all. Seth and I have just been getting better acquainted over a cup of coffee."

He turned back to Seth. "Thank you for keeping me company. Now if you'll excuse us, I need to see my little sister's new library."

Abigail gave his hand a tap and rolled her eyes. "Listen to him. To hear my brother talk, you'd think I was still an adolescent instead of a grown woman."

Seth smiled at the teasing, disguised as chiding, she aimed at her brother. But as soon as they turned to walk away, he sobered.

Had he done the right thing, interfering that way? What Abigail's brother chose to tell or not tell her was none of his business.

Where was the businesslike dispassion he prided himself on? In a matter of weeks he'd be leaving this place, leaving Texas, and he would likely never see any of these people again.

But somehow that thought didn't make him feel one iota better.

As Abigail escorted Everett to her library she wondered just what it was she'd interrupted. There'd been a tension between the two men when she walked in, something almost tangible that stretched between them.

Not antagonism, exactly—which was good because she wasn't sure what she'd do if her brother and the man she was coming to think of as more than a business associate didn't get along.

But what was it?

"Nice sign," Everett said, interrupting her thoughts. "Did you have that made?"

She glanced up at the sign hanging over the library door. "Actually, Mr. Reynolds made it. Wasn't that nice of him?"

Everett's expression shifted, became thoughtful. "Yes, that was very nice of him."

Abigail led the way into the library, walked to the middle of the room, then spun around. "Here it is. What do you think?"

Her brother looked around appreciatively. "I think that you've definitely come up in the world. This gives you lots of room for your current collection, and lots of room to grow."

"And the best part about it is that I no longer have to take up room in the restaurant. Daisy can finally make full use of her space."

Everett waved a hand dismissively. "You know Daisy

never minded having the library there. In fact, she thought it added a little something extra to her establishment."

Before she could respond to that admission, Everett grew serious. He rubbed the back of his neck and then looked up to meet her gaze. "Abigail, there's something I need to tell you, something I probably should have told you a long time ago."

What was wrong? Few people knew Everett had spent his first eleven years in England. His accent was almost nonexistent most of the time, but it always became more pronounced when he was worried or angry, like now. "What is it?"

"I never told you why I left Philadelphia and came here."

She frowned at the unexpected choice of topic. "I thought it was because you wanted a fresh start, a chance to start up your own newspaper."

"That wasn't the whole story. The thing is, I did something when I worked for the newspaper in Philadelphia, something I'm not very proud of."

The deep regret she saw in his expression scared her. "Whatever happened, Ev, you know it won't change what I think of you."

He gave her a crooked smile. "You might want to wait until you hear what I have to say before you make a promise like that." He waved toward her desk. "Have a seat."

Twenty minutes later, Abigail was sending her brother away with assurances that she loved him more than ever.

Then she glanced toward the closed office door. According to Everett, Seth knew about this. She wasn't sure how she felt about that.

But she needed to address it, and there was no time like the present.

* * *

Seth looked up when Abigail walked into the office. "What did your brother think of the library?"

"He was impressed. He also liked the sign you made to put over the door."

So she'd told him about that. After Everett's probing into his feelings for Abigail, Seth wasn't sure that had been the best time for that revelation.

She nodded. "And after he looked around my library, we had a nice long talk about why he really moved to Turnabout all those years ago."

His estimation of the man rose several notches. "Oh?"

Abigail fisted a hand on her hip. "Don't pretend, he told me you know all about it."

He swallowed a wince. "Perhaps not *all* about it," he hedged. Then he studied her face. "How are you?"

She waved a hand dismissively. "I'm fine. Everett made a mistake—goodness knows I've made more than a few of those myself. Granted his had tragic consequences, but it's only by God's grace that some of mine haven't as well."

Was she remembering the time she'd run away from boarding school?

She sighed. "I'm more grateful than ever for how Judge Madison helped him get his fresh start here. Which I will now have the opportunity to say in person very soon."

Amazing how she could always find the bright spot in any cloud. Did nothing ever dampen her rose-colored view of life?

He sincerely hoped not.

Thanksgiving morning finally arrived and it was all Seth could do to contain Jamie's excitement.

The sun had barely come up before the boy was raring

to go. "When can we go? Noah says his family always gets there by nine o'clock."

"Just be patient. It's not even eight o'clock yet. Miss Abigail is supposed to come by and help collect the food we're bringing."

"Did someone mention my name?"

Jamie immediately popped up to greet her. "Miss Abigail! Are you excited about today?"

"I certainly am. And I'm most excited about hearing you sing in the children's choir program."

Jamie turned to Seth. "Miss Abigail's here—can we go now?"

Before Seth could answer, Abigail laughed. "First I need to help Mrs. Long get our hampers of food ready. But I promise to hurry." Then she raised a brow. "You want to help us? It might make the time go faster."

With a nod, Jamie turned and headed for the kitchen.

Abigail met his gaze with a saucy smile. "You coming?" Then, without waiting for an answer, she sashayed off to follow Jamie.

Seth grinned in appreciation. The woman knew how to get her way.

With a good-humored shake of his head, he followed them into the kitchen.

Once everything had been packed up in two hampers, Seth took one and Abigail took the other. Jamie was a bundle of nervous energy, chattering nonstop and unable to stay still for more than a few moments at a time.

As they stepped out onto the sidewalk, Abigail paused, lifted her face and inhaled deeply.

Seth couldn't tear his gaze away from her.

"Isn't this a glorious autumn day? Clear, crisp, invigorating…" Then she dropped her gaze, giving him and

Jamie a wistful smile. "It's one of those days that make me grateful I don't have to stay cooped up inside."

"Me, too," Jamie agreed.

Seth merely nodded, swallowing hard. She started forward again. Both hands clasped on the hamper's handle. "We couldn't have asked for a better day for the festival."

When they arrived at the schoolyard, which was being used as the festival grounds, Abigail pointed to a platform that had been erected to the left of the schoolhouse. "That's new this year."

"What's it for?" Jamie asked.

"Several of the fathers got together and built it for the choir to stand on. It's so folks who don't get a chance to stand in front can still get a good view of the children singing."

Why hadn't he known about that? Did folks think he wouldn't—or couldn't—help?

"You mean we're going to sing from up there?" Jamie's eyes were wide—Seth couldn't tell if it was excitement or apprehension.

Abigail ruffled the boy's hair. "Yes. And I aim to get as close to the front as I can so I can hear every note you sing."

Jamie grimaced. Then the sound of children's happy shrieks and excited chatter caught his attention. He pointed across the schoolyard. "There's Noah and Jack and some of my other friends playing ball over by the big oak. Can I go, too?"

Seth cut a quick glance Abigail's way, then turned back to Jamie. "Yes, of course."

The words were barely out of Seth's mouth before Jamie was racing off.

"It's nice to see him having such a good time." Abigail

touched Seth's arm. "The food goes inside the school-house."

He followed her inside Mr. Parker's classroom and paused on the threshold. The student desks had been cleared out and what seemed like dozens of women were milling about. Tables lined the walls, and they were fast being loaded with every kind of food imaginable.

Mitch Parker's wife, Ivy, bustled up to them with a smile. "Welcome. I'm helping organize the tables this year." She began pointing to the various tables. "Meats go over there, vegetables there, desserts there and if you brought anything to drink it goes over there."

Mitch set out the contents of his hamper as instructed, then looked around. "Do they use the other classroom for anything?"

Abigail took his hamper. "That's where all the desks from this classroom went." She stored both hampers beneath a table. "It's also a place where the babies and younger children can nap. Some of the older women take turns watching the little ones so the mothers can have the freedom to enjoy themselves."

As they went back to the schoolyard, Abigail gave him a mischievous smile. "I should warn you, I signed us up to judge the sack race and the three-legged race."

"Did you now?"

She nodded solemnly, but he didn't miss the twinkle in her eyes. "Of course. It's our civic duty as representatives of a major business in town to participate. I knew you would agree."

He shook his head. "It appears I have no choice."

"I'm so glad you understand." She waved him toward the left. "Now come along, the times of all the competitions are posted on the side of the building and we need to see when we're up." And with a sassy little flounce, she led the way.

Seth smiled as he kept pace with her. It seemed Miss Fulton was feeling feisty—more so than usual. It ought to make for an interesting day.

Abigail was having a wonderful time. Being able to show Seth and Jamie one of the highlights of Turnabout's year, and the best side of its community atmosphere, was a real joy. And to have Seth at her side in this rare moment of relaxation and fun without the pressure of the work at the hotel was lovely.

When the school bell rang at ten o'clock sharp, she grabbed Seth's arm and gave him a little tug. "Come on, we want to get a spot near the front."

He looked startled by her action and she started to pull her hand away. But then he closed his own hand over it and tucked it in the crook of his elbow.

Feeling her joy bubble up even higher, she walked beside him as they joined the crowd gathered in front of the platform. Reverend Harper stepped up first, delivering a message of gratitude and hope.

Once he stepped down, the children's choir went up to take his place. Verity Cooper, the choir director, stood on the ground in front of them.

Abigail stood beside Seth, her hand still on his arm, as they listened to the children sing "My Country, 'Tis of Thee" and "Now Thank We All Our God."

Seeing Jamie's shining face and hearing the gusto with which he sang out touched her deeply. Did Seth feel it, too? She stole a sideways glance his way and the pride and affection she saw in his eyes took her breath away.

And in that moment of perfect happiness, it struck her. She loved him—him and Jamie both. And with the kind of love she'd witnessed among the couples in her circle but never experienced herself. Until now.

And close on the heels of that thought was the realization that, if things went according to plan, the hotel would be ready to open in four weeks' time. After that, Seth and Jamie would return to Philadelphia and she would likely never see them again.

How in the world was she going to bear saying goodbye to these two who had become such a vital part of her life?

And how could she push those feelings aside, at least long enough not to ruin today's celebration?

Something was wrong. Seth could sense the change in Abigail, could feel the tension radiating from her, could see some of the sparkle fade from her countenance.

It had happened from one moment to the next while she was watching the children's performance. What had caused this? What had he missed?

But before he could dig deeper, the program ended and folks began milling about, collecting their children and moving on to other attractions.

Abigail turned to him, her expression a fairly good facsimile of her normal cheery demeanor. "Come on. Let's go tell Jamie how fabulous he was." And she was off, wending her way through the crowds to get to Jamie.

He followed, but once they reached Jamie, they barely had time to praise him before Noah ran up. "They're getting ready to start up the horseshoe tournament. Do you and your uncle want to play against me and my dad?"

Jamie turned to Seth, his expression a mix of eagerness and uncertainty. "Can we?"

Seth glanced Abigail's way, still trying to figure out what was wrong, not wanting to leave her alone.

But she waved them away. "You menfolk go on. I'm going to look for Constance—I need to ask her a question." And she was gone without a backward glance.

Seth turned back to Jamie. At least horseshoes was one game where a bad leg wasn't a disadvantage. He clapped his nephew on the shoulder. "Let's give it a go."

Abigail moved steadily away, trying not to meet anyone's gaze or draw attention to herself. She was happy that Seth and Jamie had found something they could do together.

And that she could have a little time to herself.

She chided herself for her mood—she knew she had no business being downhearted. Today was Thanksgiving, after all, a day to appreciate one's blessings, not get mopey about things outside her control. She just had to remember, everything was under *God's* control, and trying to wrest it back from Him with all her worrying and moaning about what she wanted but couldn't have was nothing short of a shameful lack of faith.

So, time to start focusing on her blessings. Starting with the fact that she still had four whole weeks of Seth and Jamie's company to look forward to, so she better not waste a moment of it. What was that verse Reverend Harper had quoted this morning—*This is the day which the Lord hath made; we will rejoice and be glad in it.*

Determined to do just that, Abigail went to watch the horseshoe tournament. When she arrived, Seth seemed gratifyingly happy to see her. And while he and Jamie didn't win, they obviously had fun.

By the time they walked away from the game, she had pulled herself back together.

Jamie, apparently unbothered by their defeat, declared himself hungry.

"How does that work?" Seth asked. "Does everyone sit down to eat at the same time?"

Abigail shook her head. "We used to, but the gathering has gotten too big for that. So now folks just pick their own time and groupings, and help themselves to the food." She waved a hand. "As you can see, some folks are already eating, others are just now wandering over to the schoolhouse to get their meal and others haven't gotten around to it yet."

Seth put a hand on Jamie's shoulder. "That sounds to me like we have permission to dig in."

The three moved toward the schoolhouse and joined the growing number who were ready to fill their plates. Abigail quickly retrieved one of their hampers and collected the dinnerware she'd brought for the three of them. Abigail helped Jamie serve his plate while she served her own as well.

Seth finished first and waited for them near the door. As they stepped outside, carefully balancing their overflowing plates, Jamie looked around. "Where are we supposed to sit?"

"Well, some folks spread blankets on the ground picnic-style, some take advantage of the tables spread out over the grounds and some stroll about with a plate in their hands, eating as they wander." Then she nodded toward the platform. "But I think we might do best joining those using the stage for a perch."

"Agreed." Seth led the way and Abigail was impressed that he managed to balance his plate one-handed.

Seth kept a close eye on Abigail as they ate, but apparently whatever had been troubling her earlier was resolved now. She seemed perfectly happy as she regaled them both with stories of festivals past and things they had yet to look forward to.

As soon as they'd finished their meal, Jamie raced off to join his friends and Mayor Sanders came over to tell Abigail and Seth it was time for them to assume their judging duties.

Judging the sack race and three-legged race proved more fun than Seth had expected. Not only did it give him a way to participate, but he also caught Jamie watching him with a touch of pride in his eyes.

Jamie participated in both games and took second place in the sack race for the under-twelve age group.

He also participated in the three-legged race, partnering with Noah, and while the pair didn't place, they were laughing so hard by the time they made it across the finish line that Seth didn't think they minded coming in next to last.

When their judging duties were at an end, Seth turned to Abigail. "Don't you participate in any of the contests?"

She shook her head. "I'm quite content to be a spectator this year."

"This year? Does that mean you've competed in the past?"

Her grin turned saucy. "I have been known to try my hand at the apple-peeling contest and the egg race."

"Now you tell me, once the egg race is over. But tell me about this apple-peeling contest."

"All the contestants are given an apple and a knife. The object is to see who can peel it so that they end up with the longest unbroken strip of peel."

He gave her an assessing look. "And are you any good?"

"Came in second two years in a row. And last year I lost by a mere quarter inch."

"Then I think you are honor-bound to give it one more try. Haven't you ever heard the saying that the third time is a charm?"

"I've also heard that three strikes and you're out."

He shook his head in disbelief. "Who would have guessed, Abigail Fulton is a quitter."

She halted in her tracks and fisted her hands on her hips. "You take that back."

My, but she looked magnificent when she got riled. "Prove me wrong."

She glared at him a moment longer, then grinned. "All right, but you have to enter as well. If I come in second again at least I'll have the satisfaction of knowing I beat you."

"Why, Miss Fulton, are you issuing me a challenge?"

"Absolutely."

"Accepted." He crooked his arm for her to take. "Shall we?"

Abigail liked this side of Seth, the side that could relax and have fun. It was a shame he didn't show this side of himself more often. They reached the tables where the apple-peeling contest was being held, just as the last call for contestants went out. They quickly took seats across from each other and waited for the bell to sound as they listened to the rules. Each contestant had three apples in front of them, which meant two extra chances if they weren't happy with their first attempt. At the end of twelve minutes it was knives down and whoever had the longest peel won.

Just as Abigail saw the mayor reaching for the bell, she caught Seth's gaze and gave him a sassy wink. It startled him so much he lost several seconds time when the bell rang.

With a grin, she settled down to business, tuning everything else out but the knife and the apple. A quarter of the way through her first attempt the peel broke. She tossed it aside and reached for another apple. This one went much better. She focused on taking her time and keeping the strip uniformly narrow and thin. This time she got through the entire piece of fruit without a break.

Glancing up triumphantly, she was surprised to see Seth watching her, a cocky grin on his face, a perfect strip of peel in front of him.

She should have known someone as meticulous as he was would be good at this.

A moment later time was called. The contestants who were obviously out of the running left the table, leaving five contenders—she and Seth among them.

Hazel Gleason, the judge for this event, came around with her measuring tape. Finally, she stood at the head of the table. "The results are in, and it's a close one. With a length of twenty-nine and six tenths of an inch, Asa Samuels wins third place."

Asa went up to receive his yellow ribbon amid applause from those gathered around.

Hazel stepped up again. "With a length of thirty and three quarter inches, second place goes to a newcomer in our midst, Seth Reynolds."

Seth looked genuinely surprised when his name was announced and the smile he gave her was almost apologetic.

Abigail stood and clapped for him as he joined Asa at the front and accepted his red ribbon. She was pleased to see Jamie had been watching and had run up to congratulate his uncle.

Hazel raised a hand as she prepared to speak again.

Abigail stood alongside the other two remaining contestants, one of whom was last year's winner, Lionel Jenkins.

"And the winner, with a peel that measures an impressive thirty-one inches on the nose, is Abigail Fulton."

Abigail was stunned. She walked up to the front to receive her ribbon and saw Jamie jumping up and down and Seth giving her the biggest smile she'd ever seen on his face.

Abigail accepted her ribbon and then turned to Seth. "I suppose the third time *is* a charm after all."

"Far be it from me to say I told you so, but…"

"Look at us," Jamie said proudly. "We all have ribbons to take home."

"So we do." Abigail stared at Seth over the boy's head. Did this, the three of them standing together and celebrating, feel like a family to him, too? Because it certainly felt that way to her.

It was getting on toward late afternoon now, and the sound of a fiddle tuning up drifted across the grounds. Like the pied piper, it drew folks from all corners to gather round.

Abigail smiled as she saw Constance and Calvin holding hands as they approached the area set aside for the dancers. It was about time the two of them acknowledged their feelings for each other.

Jamie excused himself to rejoin his friends and for a moment she and Seth stood in companionable silence. After a moment Abigail found herself swaying to the music. She'd always loved to dance.

"Feel free to join your friends if you like. I don't mind."

Abigail felt her face warm. It hadn't been her intention to hint that she wanted to leave him so she could dance. "Don't you like to dance?" she asked.

He gave her a crooked smile, and lifted his cane a few inches off the ground. "This third leg makes dancing a bit difficult."

"Nonsense. You might not have the most graceful stride, but I've seen you maintain extraordinary control when you need to." She raised a brow. "Besides, I didn't ask if you were good at it, I asked if you *liked* it."

He shrugged. "I've never tried."

She nodded. "Then it's time, don't you think?"

He glanced at the dance floor that was fast becoming crowded and she saw the trepidation in his expression. Taking his hand, she gave it a gentle tug. "Let's go for a walk." She wasn't sure if it was relief or disappointment she saw in his expression. Maybe a little of both.

But he didn't move. "You should stay. I'm sure there are any number of young men who would be happy to escort you out on the dance floor. I'll go check on Jamie."

"Jamie is fine. And I don't want to dance with any of the other young men right now." She tugged at his hand again and this time he gave in. She led him away from the crowds until she found what she was looking for—a nice level bit of ground, sheltered from the view of most folks milling about. "This looks like a good spot for your first lesson."

"Lesson?"

His reaction was almost amusing. "Dance lesson. We have relative privacy here but we're still close enough to hear the music."

He pulled his hand from hers. "I don't think this is such a good idea."

"You're not backing down from a challenge, are you?"

"Don't be ridiculous. I'm just being practical. You can't teach a frog to fly. You can't teach a pig to walk upright." He clenched his jaw. "And you can't teach me to dance."

She waved a hand dismissively. "Your logic is faulty. You are neither a frog nor a pig. And you have the advantage of having me as a teacher."

His lips quirked up in a crooked kind of grin. "And I'm sure you're a mighty fine teacher. But my leg is what it is and you can't change that."

"I don't intend to change it." She eyed him steadily. "Do you trust me?"

Seth hesitated a moment. *Did* he trust her? Finally, he nodded.

She rewarded him with a dazzling smile. "Good. Now, set your cane aside—you can lean it against the tree. Hold on to me to keep your balance."

Holding on to her would definitely not be a hardship. Whether it was a good idea or not was another matter entirely.

She took one of his hands and placed her other lightly on his shoulder. Then she directed him where to place his free hand. "Now, we're going to move very slowly and deliberately to start off. Listen to the music and let it guide you. I'll follow wherever you lead."

He liked the sound of that. And the warmth of her hand in his. Being this close to her was a kind of sweet torture.

"Keep your eyes focused on mine, not on your feet," she chided as they began. "Dancing is about anticipating your partner's moves, communicating without words."

He stumbled slightly but she paused, allowing him to lean his weight on her a moment and then they picked up the rhythm once more. He managed to get through the rest of the piece without stumbling again, though he was sure she'd never had a more graceless partner.

Somehow, that didn't bother him as much as it once might have. Holding her in his arms this way, feeling her warmth and supple movements, it was near intoxicating. He had a fierce urge to protect her and cherish her, to claim her as his own. He'd never felt quite this way about anyone before.

The music started up again almost immediately and he was ready to go again. This time, though, it was she who stumbled midstep and he barely managed to steady her without going down himself. But the movement brought them closer still, as if they were embracing. Abigail's eyes widened, filled with a liquid light. Her breath caught and the sound of it cut through the last of his control.

Seth actually leaned in to bestow the kiss he so desperately wanted to give her when the sound of nearby voices broke the trance.

He pulled back slightly and loosened his hold.

She straightened, her gaze searching his in confusion and, dare he hope, disappointment?

What had he been thinking? Anyone could have walked up on them—if they had been caught in a kiss, or even embracing, it could have had serious repercussions for her.

Not to mention the implied promise it would give, a promise he could never fulfill.

But oh, it would have been so memorable.

He released her and offered his elbow. "Thank you for the dance lesson. What do you say we go see what's left on the dessert table?"

With a nod, she placed her hand on his arm.

Was the tremble of her fingers due to the chill in the air? Or something more?

* * *

Abigail's thoughts swirled in bright kaleidoscopic fragments. The look he'd given her when they'd fallen into that embrace, a look full of a fierce tenderness and yearning... No one had ever looked at her that way before. It was something that would stay with her the rest of her life, no matter what else happened between them. He'd wanted to kiss her. That it hadn't happened was disappointing, to say the least. But what was important was that she could tell he'd wanted it as much as she had, as she did still.

The fact that he was back to being guarded and all gentlemanly didn't change things one bit. Because she had hope now, hope that if he felt the same for her as she felt for him, perhaps there was a way they could work things out, after all.

And hope was a powerful thing.

Chapter Twenty-Five

Seth exited the church Sunday morning still unsettled and on edge. He had yet to come to terms with his feelings for Abigail since their Thanksgiving day dance lesson a week and a half ago.

Abigail herself had seemed to suffer no such aftereffects, which should have been a relief but he found it left him even more out of sorts for some reason.

As had become their habit on Sunday mornings since Jamie had come to town, he let the boy play with some of his friends while he waited for Abigail to make her exit with the rest of the choir.

Several members of the congregation paused to exchange pleasantries with him. Strange how much he'd come to feel a part of this community. That had never happened on any of his other jobs, and some of those had lasted significantly longer.

Abigail stepped out of church just then, arms linked with Constance and her face alight with laughter. His heart skipped a beat at the sight of her. Goodness but he had it bad.

She approached him, her face still beaming with amusement. "Folks are getting excited about the elevator," she said. "I've had no fewer than five people come up and ask me when it will be complete."

The engineer had arrived Monday as promised and the project was well underway. But rather than taking the estimated seven days, Mr. Doyle had reported that it would take ten. Which meant a significant impact to Seth's overall schedule, but he was still hoping to finish up, if not by Christmas, then before the New Year.

As they moved to collect Jamie, Abigail cut him a sideways look. "I was thinking perhaps we could take advantage of the interest it's commanding and plan a reception of some sort once the elevator is in working order."

An interesting idea, but he decided to pay devil's advocate. It was always fun to watch her marshal her arguments. "What's the benefit for us, besides building some goodwill with the townsfolk?"

She gave him a haughty look. "Goodwill is always good to have." Then she grinned with an I'm-ready-to-convince-you look. "But yes, I had something more in mind. We can serve food from our kitchen, letting folks know about the new menu offerings to entice them to drop in more often. And we can hold the reception in our new guest parlor to let folks know it's available to rent for parties and such. The holiday season is upon us, after all."

"Now you're thinking like a businesswoman. I agree that it makes sense. Is it something you think you could take the lead on planning?"

"Absolutely."

When they arrived for lunch at Everett and Daisy's, Abigail went around to everyone, collecting their "memory stars." She'd passed them out the prior Sunday, giving strict instructions that she expected everyone to participate and wouldn't take no for an answer. That had elicited some good-natured grumbling from the menfolk, but Seth wasn't surprised to see that every one of them handed her a star with notes written on it. Few people could deny the intrepid Abigail when she made her won't-you-please-help-me requests.

Later, as they sat around the lunch table, Abigail explained her idea about the reception to the others present and received enthusiastic offers to help with the planning and spreading the word. She even convinced her brother to print an announcement in his newspaper for free.

Was there any project she wasn't afraid to tackle?

Abigail spent the next several days planning the reception. It was to be held on Saturday and she wanted everything to be perfect.

The guest parlor only lacked a few finishing touches to be complete, and Walter Hendricks promised to have it done before Saturday. Even the divider screen was ready. Chance had done an amazing job with the carving and the Hendricks men had constructed it exactly to her specifications.

She spent many an hour going over the menu with Della, always careful to give the woman opportunities to suggest changes and additions. Cora also contributed a few ideas based on family recipes and, in the end, they came up with something Abigail knew they could all be proud of.

By Wednesday afternoon the work on the elevator was officially complete and Mr. Doyle spent some time teaching the entire staff how to operate it. Except for Ruby. She declared it was a noisy mechanical closet and that she wasn't about to trust it not to crash down with her in it. And no amount of assurances as to its safety could change her mind.

Abigail was worried about how Seth would react. But,

with a resigned sigh, he merely told her she could continue to use the stairs so long as it didn't interfere with the performance of her job.

When he'd first arrived, Seth would likely have dismissed the maid and replaced her with someone he considered more suitable. She felt a small glow of satisfaction at this further evidence of how much Seth had changed since his arrival here.

Friday morning the two of them were working in companionable silence in the office. Seth was grateful, not for the first time, that they'd set up this place to work together. It was good having her nearby. Having the ability to bounce ideas and questions off of each other. Having the opportunity to just look up and be able to watch her at work.

Then he grinned as he noticed a faint shimmer on the floor around her. She must have spent time in the library this morning. She and Jamie had spent all afternoon in there yesterday getting her memory stars ready to hang. Unfortunately, not all the glitter had landed where it was supposed to.

But her display was up now and he had to admit it looked great. Already it was garnering a lot of attention and several people had inquired if they could add their own memory to the display. Abigail had left a stack of blank stars at the front desk for just that purpose, so her display was already growing.

Still smiling, Seth reached for the stack of correspondence that awaited his attention, then frowned when he noticed one of the letters was from Bridgerton.

He must have made some involuntary sound when he read it because Abigail looked up. "What is it? Not bad news, I hope."

"No, in fact just the opposite. It's from the headmaster at Bridgerton, assuring me they'll be ready to reopen Jamie's dormitory after the first of the year."

As he'd known would happen, Abigail didn't receive the news well. "I know it's none of my business, but do you really need to send Jamie back to boarding school? Can't you see how he's thriving being under the same roof with you?"

He himself wasn't nearly as pleased with the news as he should have been. But that couldn't be helped. "I told you, it's just temporary. In fact, I expect to be able to put down roots for the two of us very soon."

"So, you plan to stop all this traveling you've been doing?"

"If things work out the way I'm planning, then yes, eventually."

She looked skeptical, so he explained. "I'm in the middle of purchasing some property, a warehouse in a growing part of Philadelphia that I plan to convert and open as a hotel. I've already put down a considerable deposit and the balance comes due at the end of the year. Once I pay up, the Michelson property is mine."

He saw a flash of understanding light her eyes. "Is that why you need to finish this job by Christmas?"

He nodded. She was certainly quick. "The bonus I get for this job, along with some other considerations I'm offering, will allow me to pay the purchase price in full."

"And if you miss the deadline?"

He shrugged, though he felt far from nonchalant about the possibility. "The deal falls through and I not only lose the property, but my deposit as well."

She gave a decisive nod. "Then we need to make certain you don't miss it."

Then she pressed further. "You said eventually. So, there's more to this than just purchasing the property."

"I'll still need to come up with the funds to do the renovation. And I'll need to put in the work necessary to actually carry out that conversion, which means I also need to keep working for the judge to earn the money involved." He held up a hand to forestall the protest he could see forming on her lips. "But I figure by next summer at the latest, Jamie will be able to move in with me." And that thought was no longer quite as scary as it had been before.

Abigail, however, still wore a censorious expression. "That's a long time to make him wait. Especially now that he's had a taste of the kind of life the two of you could have together."

In Seth's opinion, Jamie was responding to Abigail's presence as much as his, if not more so. A home with both a surrogate father *and* a surrogate mother was what he really needed.

Not that he would say such a thing to Abigail—she might read too much into a statement like that.

Then another aspect of their conversation tugged at him. He studied her a moment, wondering again at her passionate dislike of boarding school.

Perhaps it was time to do a bit of prying of his own. "You know, I get the feeling there was more to your stay at boarding school than you let on."

She immediately stiffened. "What do you mean?"

Her reaction confirmed his suspicion that there was something there. "I'm only saying that your dislike of boarding schools seems based on more than just memories of homesickness and wanting more time with your brother. What happened to you there?"

She waved a hand. "Just foolish childhood melodrama,

and that's all in the past. Nothing worth bringing back up now."

He wasn't going to let her off that easy. "Humor me."

Her lips pinched together and he thought for a moment she would refuse him. Then she sighed and the starch seemed to go out of her. "Like I said, I was five years old when I first went to boarding school. At first I was terribly lonely and confused. But in time I settled in, made friends, got accustomed to the rhythm and routine of life there. I actually began to think of it as home."

She paused and after a moment he prompted her. "Then?"

"Then, shortly before my tenth birthday everything changed."

He resisted the urge to prompt her again. He sensed she needed to unfold the rest of her story in her own time.

Finally, she sat up straighter but she didn't quite meet his gaze. "One of the girls found out something about me." He saw the way her knuckles whitened as she clasped her hands together. "My parents were never married."

She shifted in her seat. "I suppose I knew, at least on some level, but it wasn't something Everett and I ever talked about, and since I was five years old when our mother died I didn't really understand all the implications. My father was out of the picture before I was even born so I never knew him. Everett and I considered ourselves orphaned after Mother died, and that was that.

"Once word got out, I was called names, words I'd never heard before but sensed were ugly and shameful. The girls who I'd thought were close friends of mine suddenly shunned me. I no longer received invitations to visit schoolmates' homes during holidays. Even some of the teachers began treating me differently." Her hands unclasped and now she was hugging herself. Was she even aware of her actions?

Seth's hands fisted with the urge to make someone pay for the hurt she'd suffered. He knew something of how that must have felt but her situation had been very different from his.

However, she didn't need his anger or his comparisons right now. Instead, he came around, kneeled by her chair and took her in his arms. "I'm sorry that happened to you," he said softly. "It's a testament to what a strong woman you are that you came through it with your beautiful spirit intact."

She relaxed into him for a moment, then she pulled back and met his gaze. "Did you hear me say that my parents were never married, that I'm a product of a sinful union?"

He brushed the hair from her lovely face. "That reflects on your parents, not on you. And doesn't the Good Book teach that we are to judge not?"

She gave him a watery smile. "You are a good man, Seth Reynolds."

Would that that were true. He stood and leaned back against the desk. "I'm surprised your brother didn't withdraw you from the school after that happened."

"I never told him."

"What? Why?"

"I think, in my mind, I was afraid if Everett heard that he'd turn his back on me, too. I know it seems foolish now—Everett would have been appalled had he known and would have yanked me right out of there—but to my nine-year-old mind it was a valid concern."

He took her hands. "I suppose I understand now why you're so opposed to boarding-school life, but you have to know Jamie isn't experiencing anything like that."

She stared up at him with a concerned, earnest expression. "Do you know that for sure? Have you talked to him about it? I mean *really* talked, not just a superficial how-are-you-doing? kind of question. Because as far as Everett was concerned I was just feeling homesick for him."

Was she right? Had he really taken the time to find out how Jamie was doing? Would he know if things had gotten difficult for the boy?

He squeezed her hands. "I give you my word, Jamie and I will have that talk very soon."

She stared into his eyes for a long moment as if trying to see past them to his very soul, and then she nodded, apparently satisfied.

That evening, before Seth opened the book he was reading to Jamie, he remembered his promise. "Jamie, tell me what it is you like best about Bridgerton."

The boy tensed. "Are you planning to send me back soon? You promised I could stay for Christmas."

"Of course you can stay through Christmas. I gave you my word." Then he grinned. "And Miss Abigail would be very cross with me if you weren't here to help her decorate." He smoothed the covers. "I just wondered what it was you considered the best part of being at Bridgerton."

"Oh." Little furrows appeared on Jamie's forehead, as if he was concentrating very hard. "I suppose it would be Billy Peters. He's my roommate and is a right sort of fellow."

"So you've made friends there?"

His nephew nodded, and Seth could detect no hesitation. It was reassuring.

Then Jamie added, "But I like my new friends, like Noah and Jack, better."

Not as reassuring, but not an indication that anything

was seriously wrong. Besides, whether or not Jamie went back to Bridgerton, they would be leaving Turnabout by the end of the year.

So he shook off that feeling and went back to his need to learn more. "Now tell me what it is you like the least about Bridgerton?"

This time there was no hesitation. "It's the feeling of the place."

That took Seth completely by surprise. "What do you mean?"

"It feels, I don't know, like someplace you visit, I guess, not at all like a home."

That was a surprisingly mature assessment, even if it was voiced with a child's vocabulary. "And *this* place?"

"Oh, yes, this feels like a home. Don't you think so, too?"

"You do know this isn't our home, don't you? That when this job is over we'll be leaving?"

"Do we have to?"

"I'm afraid so."

"But I like it here. The people are nice and there are lots of mommies and daddies around."

Seth knew just what the boy meant—it was the sense of community, the feeling that people cared about you.

"And what about Miss Abigail?" Jamie asked. "Won't we ever see her again?"

"I'm sure Miss Abigail will want to write to you."

"It won't be the same."

"No, it won't." That reality seemed to affect Jamie as deeply as it did him. Then he gave his nephew a bracing smile. "But we have Christmas in Turnabout to look forward to, so let's not spoil it with worries about what comes after."

He'd set out to discover how Jamie felt about Bridgerton and he'd accomplished that much, at least. The boy longed for a real home and loving parents in a community of people who cared about him. Seth wasn't in a position to provide him with either. But perhaps he could give him the next best thing...

The reception on Saturday was an overwhelming success. Nearly everyone in town showed up, thankfully not all at once.

Darby had the role of elevator operator and he kept busy the entire day. But the guest parlor and food garnered nearly as much interest.

"With food like this you'll be putting me out of business," Daisy said, tart in hand. "I'm going to have to see if Della will share her recipe."

Abigail laughed. "I think your restaurant is safe. And that tart recipe is one Cora shared with us, not Della."

Daisy winked. "Good to know. I'm heading over to your kitchen now." And with that she was gone.

"It appears your event is a success."

Abigail turned to see Constance approaching. She gave her friend a hug. "Oh, I'm so glad you made it."

"I wouldn't have missed this for the world—it's a chance to ride in an elevator, after all."

"But you've ridden in them before."

Constance gave her a sly smile. "But Calvin hasn't."

With a grin, Abigail nudged her friend with a hip. "I assume the two of you are officially walking out together now."

Constance nodded, her expression blissfully happy.

Abigail gave her another hug. "I'm so happy for you. Calvin is a good man."

Before she could say more, Hannah Greer came up and asked about making a star for the window display.

Excusing herself from Constance, Abigail led Hannah to the table where the blank stars and several pencils waited for just that purpose. As she crossed the room, her gaze sought Seth, as it had so many times today. He stood across the room, cornered by a group of men who were no doubt discussing the workings of the elevator. It had been that way all day, but he had handled it with patience and polish.

As if he felt her watching him, his gaze slid in her direction and he gave a small smile of acknowledgment and approval before turning back to his conversation. It had been done so quickly and smoothly that she doubted the men he was speaking to had even noticed.

But she had. And that one glance lent a wonderful buoyancy to her spirit that no doubt translated to her steps.

Surely, *surely*, he wouldn't look at her that way if he was planning to leave in a few weeks.

Chapter Twenty-Six

As they headed down the sidewalk toward Daisy's after service on Sunday, it occurred to Seth that he was going to miss this when his time here ended. Walking together this way, one could almost imagine the three of them were a family.

"Oh, I almost forgot," Abigail said suddenly. "After lunch today a group of us are going out to select our Christmas trees. I thought it might also be a good idea to get one for the hotel, too, if you and Jamie would like to come along."

Jamie's eyes widened in excitement. "Can we, Uncle Seth?"

Concerned about his ability to swing an axe given his issues with balance, Seth turned to Abigail. "You're going to go chopping trees on the Sabbath?"

She rolled her eyes. "I didn't say we were *cutting* them, I said we were *selecting* them." She waved a hand. "A tradition around here is that sometime in December families go to the woods and scout out the best trees for their homes. When you've found the one you want, you tie a bright colored ribbon on it and tag it with your name. Then, when you're ready to decorate, you or someone you hire goes out and cuts it down and brings it to your home or business."

Seth turned to Jamie. "In that case, I think we can definitely go find us a tree."

After the meal, when the cleanup was just about done, Mitch Parker claimed everyone's attention. "I've made arrangements with Ned Littleton to borrow his hay wagon for the afternoon," he announced. "There should be room enough for all of us if most of you don't mind climbing up in back."

Abigail caught Seth's eye with a won't-this-be-fun look.

"I think I'll have to pass this year," Daisy said, rubbing her swollen stomach. "But the good news is you can leave all the little ones with me."

"Ira and I certainly don't plan to go traipsing about the woods looking at trees," Mrs. Peavy added. "So we'll help Daisy with the children. The rest of you go on and enjoy yourselves."

Fifteen minutes later, the cleanup was complete and Mitch was back with the transportation. He set a crate behind the wagon to use as a stepstool before moving around to help Ivy climb up front so she could ride next to him. As everyone else scrambled in the back and settled themselves in for the ride, Abigail signaled Seth with a touch on his arm to hold back. "I like to sit on the end with my legs dangling out," she said with a sheepish grin. "I always ride there for the Christmas-tree-selection trip—it's a tradition for me."

"Then by all means, we will sit on the end."

Once everyone was settled in, Mitch set the wagon in motion.

Eve Dawson started singing "Deck the Halls" almost

as soon as they got underway, and it didn't take long for everyone to join in. When they finished that carol, someone suggested "I Saw Three Ships" and they were off again.

Abigail swung her legs in time to the singing. She loved the sound of Seth's voice, so strong and sure. It was the first time she'd heard it up close, since her position in the choir kept her separated from him during the church services.

A sudden bump in the road brought her up against him and he put an arm around her shoulder to steady her. If the jostling hadn't already stolen her voice, the feel of his arm around her would have done the trick.

His gaze met hers with a concerned smile that brought butterflies to her stomach. He didn't release her right away, which was fine by her. Instead he resumed singing, as if it was the most natural thing in the world.

Just past Mercer's Pond Meadow, Mitch turned the wagon onto a narrow track that wound its way through the woods. After about twenty minutes he pulled the wagon to a stop and then turned around to face them. "This seems like a good place to start from."

While Mitch secured the wagon, everyone else disembarked in a more or less organized manner. She noticed Seth winced as he landed, but other than that gave no sign that anything was amiss. Was the pain so much a part of him that he could ignore it so easily?

"Does everyone have their tree markers?" Eve asked.

Abigail pulled a roll of wide yellow ribbon from her pocket. On the end she'd embroidered the word *Hotel*. Others pulled out various ribbons and cords.

"Then it looks like we're ready."

Mitch, who'd apparently decided he was in charge of the outing, took Ivy's hand. "Meet back here when you've made your selection, but make sure you don't take more than two hours. We want to make it back to town before dark."

Jamie waved to the others as the individual families set out amidst friendly boasts and challenges concerning who would find the best tree. "Which way should we go?"

Abigail smiled down at him. "You pick a direction."

With chest puffed out at the importance of his task, Jamie looked around, and then pointed to his left. "How about that way?"

"Excellent choice."

Though obviously excited, Jamie was also incredibly picky. He found some flaw in every tree they stopped to study—some were too skinny, others too sparse, still others too uneven.

"It's got to be perfect," he kept saying.

Finally, he paused in front of a smallish cedar that caught his eye. It was nicely formed and filled out, with large clusters of the berry-like cones common to that species. The whole tree, from ground to tip, was barely four feet tall.

He glanced up at Seth, his eyes bright. "I like this one."

"It is a fine-looking tree," Seth said cautiously. "But it's a bit small for the hotel lobby. Perhaps in another few years…"

"But we won't be here to see it then."

Abigail spoke up quickly, not wanting to dwell on that aspect. "Yes, it's a bit small for the lobby. But it's not too small for your suite."

Jamie's eyes widened and he turned to Seth. "Can we?"

Seth had picked up on Abigail's reaction to Jamie's statement. It was one he shared as well. Was it possible he could really change the inevitable?

But Jamie was still waiting for an answer, so he smiled down at the boy. "I suppose two trees *are* better than one."

As Jamie gave out a triumphant whoop, Abigail pulled out her roll of ribbon. Offering his pocketknife, Seth helped her cut off a nice length. And when his hands not quite accidentally brushed against hers, he smiled to see the pink coloring her cheeks.

Quickly turning, Abigail tied the ribbon to the top of the tree with a flourish. "That's how whoever we send to cut it will know it's ours."

"What about the lobby tree?" Jamie asked anxiously. "There won't be any embroidery on it."

Abigail put her finger to her chin. "We'll just need to find some other way to mark it." She looked from one to the other of them. "Do either of you have anything in your pockets we might be able to attach to it?"

He and Jamie both shook their heads and she gave a long-suffering tsk.

Then she smiled. "That's okay, I have a plan."

Of course she did.

"What is it?" Jamie asked.

She ruffled the boy's hair. "I'll show you when the time comes." Then she waved a hand forward. "Now let's see if we can find the perfect tree for the lobby."

Jamie gave her a challenging look. "I picked this one, it's you and Uncle Seth's turn."

With a grin, Abigail nodded. "All right. Let's see if we can do as good a job as you did."

Seth raised his hands in a gesture of surrender. "You're in charge of hotel decor. I defer to your expertise."

"Very well—challenge accepted."

After studying and discarding several possibilities, Abigail paused in front of another fir. "This is it!"

Jamie, however, didn't share her enthusiasm. "But it's kind of flat on one side and the limbs are crooked on the other."

Seth had to agree that her choice was an odd one. He couldn't wait to hear her explanation.

She gave Jamie an incredulous look. "But don't you see, that's what makes it the right choice." She waved a hand dismissively. "Perfection can be so boring. By picking one that has obvious imperfections but lots of character, we will have the absolutely marvelous challenge of showing everyone how beautiful it can be when we lavish it with loving attention."

Her unexpected words took his breath away.

Perfection is boring—did her philosophy extend to people as well as trees? Could she see through his own physical imperfections to find something to love?

Or was he reading too much in her words?

He caught her cutting a quick look his way, a look filled with a meaning he was almost afraid to believe.

Then she looked away, studying the tree with just a little too much concentration. There was a vulnerability in her demeanor that made him ache to go to her.

But Jamie spoke up, and the moment was lost. "So how are you going to mark it special without the embroidery?" his nephew asked. "You promised you'd show us."

"So I did." Abigail reached up and took off her bonnet. With a quick tug, she removed the perky blue ribbon that circled the brim and formed the tie under her chin.

"I'll just twist this with the ribbon I brought and that should make it unique enough to identify the tree as ours."

"But you've ruined your bonnet," Seth protested.

"Just temporarily. I can replace the ribbon with another one once I get home."

Abigail fussed with the ribbons until she had marked the tree to her satisfaction. Then the two of them each took one of Jamie's hands, and they headed back toward the wagon, singing carols. When they arrived, they found the Parkers and Everett already there. The Barrs came up right behind them and Jamie and Jack immediately began boasting to each other about their finds. Jack seemed decidedly deflated when Jamie reported that they had claimed not one but two trees for the hotel.

When the Dawsons arrived a few minutes later everyone piled in the wagon and they headed back to town.

Seth was frustrated by the fact that he and Abigail hadn't had any time to talk privately.

Although he wasn't sure what he would have said to her if they had.

Yes, he did. It was time to tell her the truth. The truth about the hotel-manager job.

And, if she would still listen, the truth about his feelings for her.

Chapter Twenty-Seven

On Monday Seth was prepared to have that discussion with Abigail, or at least as prepared as he'd ever be.

Surely, if he explained how important hiring Michelson was to his and Jamie's future, she would understand. Perhaps, if he also explained that he wanted to share that future with her as well, she would even embrace the opportunity. Because he now dared to hope that she actually returned his feelings. It was something he'd never allowed himself to hope for before, that someone could love him just as he was.

But problems with one of the materials shipments claimed his attention first thing, and when he was done with that he found Abigail had stepped out to run some errands. It was nearly lunchtime before they finally had a moment alone.

Deciding to wait until dessert was served, Seth let Abigail chatter on about her day. Why had he ever thought the sound of her voice distracting and foolish? Now he looked forward to her colorful reports with pleasure.

Darby stepped into the dining room when they were halfway through their meal and approached their table. "Sorry to bother you, Mr. Reynolds, but I thought you'd want to know. There's a Mr. Bartholomew Michelson here to see you. He's waiting in the lobby."

Seth felt his whole world tilt off balance. What was Michelson doing here? He wasn't supposed to leave Philadelphia until the day after Christmas.

Abigail gave him a puzzled smile. "Michelson? Isn't that the name of the property you're planning to buy?"

Seth nodded, trying to figure out how to stop the rock slide that was hurtling his way.

Before he could pull his thoughts together, he saw Michelson himself step into the dining room. "There you are, I thought I heard your voice."

Seth set his napkin on the table and stood. "Bartholomew, this is quite a surprise."

The man grasped Seth's hand and gave it a firm shake. "I know I'm a few weeks early, but I just couldn't wait any longer to see the place. And it occurred to me that if I'm going to be hotel manager, I probably ought to be in on some of the staffing decisions as well."

While Michelson was speaking, Seth watched Abigail from the corner of his eye. Her confusion was rapidly replaced by disbelief and betrayal.

As if in a dream, he continued to make polite conversation, as if his world wasn't unraveling. "You should have wired me so I could have a room ready."

The man waved a hand. "It was a spur-of-the-moment thing. And there's no need for special arrangements, any room will do."

He seemed to notice Abigail for the first time and gave her a short bow. "Pardon me, I should have introduced myself. I'm Bart Michelson. My apologies for interrupting your meal."

"Pleased to meet you, Mr. Michelson. I'm Abigail Fulton."

"Ah, Miss Fulton. You're the decorator, are you not?"

"I am." She stood and set aside her napkin, her movements deliberate. "And there's no need to apologize. I was finished anyway."

Michelson shook his head. "Please, don't let me run you off."

The smile she gave Michelson was overbright. And she still hadn't met his gaze. "I'm sure you and Mr. Reynolds have a lot to discuss. And since I have matters to attend to myself, I'll leave you get started."

Seth couldn't let her go like this. "Miss Fulton—"

"I'll have a room prepared for you right away." Her words were addressed to Michelson, as she was ignoring him altogether.

And before he could say more, she walked away.

Michelson was saying something, but Seth didn't try to listen. "Excuse me, I need to tell Miss Fulton something." He waved toward the table. "Feel free to order something to eat while you wait."

He had to explain things to her, had to try to wipe away the hurt he'd put in her eyes. He wasn't sure he could make it right, but he had to try.

Seth caught up with Abigail just as she finished giving Ruby instructions.

"Abigail—"

She cut him off again. "I'm sure you and Mr. Michelson will have quite a bit of planning to do in the coming weeks. Since my work is nearly complete, I can easily work from my library, giving Mr. Michelson my desk in the office. I'll have my things cleared out by the end of today."

Seth raked a hand through his hair. "That's not necessary. I—"

"I insist. Now, if you'll excuse me, I should make a few arrangements in the library to prepare for the move."

Without giving him a chance to respond, she turned on her heel and headed to the library.

Determined to have her hear him out, Seth followed. He found her standing with her back to the door, shoulders bent and her hands gripping the edge of her desk.

"Abigail, please, let me explain."

She spun around to face him. "Explain what? That this was your plan from the beginning and that you had no intention of giving me a chance?"

"Bartholomew Michelson has experience with the job of hotel manager that you simply don't, no matter what your aptitude."

"Yet, you let me believe I had a chance."

"You were the one who kept insisting you would change my mind. I never promised you anything."

He knew it was the wrong thing to say as soon as he saw her flinch.

"You're right. I did this to myself."

"That's not what I meant. Look, I know I should have tried harder to explain, but this is important to me. Hiring him for this job is part of the deal I struck for the Michelson property. It was decided long before I knew you."

"And now that you know me, has anything changed?"

He raked a hand through his hair. "Let me explain."

"There's no need. I thought this time it would be different but I should have known better."

"What do you mean, *this time*?"

She waved a hand, her expression settling into bitter lines all the more alarming because he'd never seen her like this before.

"No one ever chooses me. Not my brother when my mother died. Not my friends when the truth came out at boarding school. Not Everett when I first showed up at his door. Not anyone, not ever." She waved a hand, her expression desolate. "You'd think I would have learned my lesson by now."

"Abigail, that's not—"

"Please go."

Seth wanted to protest, wanted to shout out "*I* choose you." But her expression hardened further and she spun around, turning her back on him.

He'd waited too long. She wouldn't listen to him. Not now.

Perhaps not ever.

With defeat turning his hope to ashes, he left the room.

As soon as the door closed behind Seth, Abigail crumpled, letting the sobs come. She'd dared to hope he returned her feelings. How could she have been so wrong?

It wasn't even that he'd given the job she wanted so desperately to someone else, though that did sting.

If he'd truly loved her, he would have trusted her with the truth, would have told her so she could have dealt with it and moved on. But he hadn't thought enough of her to allow her that dignity.

Why wasn't she ever enough?

Abigail took the only step left to her. By later that afternoon, she was ready to talk to Everett. There was no way she was going to give him a chance to turn her away as well.

She cornered him in the newspaper office with a request to hear her out. "I wanted to let you know that I've spoken to Mrs. Ortolon about taking Hilda's place at the boardinghouse come the end of the month, so I won't be as available to help with the children or the businesses in the future."

Everett studied her with a probing look for a long moment and it was all Abigail could do not to squirm.

"For some reason, I thought you would end up working at the hotel," he finally said.

She shook her head, keeping a bright smile on her face. "That didn't work out."

"But Mrs. Ortolon? Are you sure that's the right job for you?"

"It's a place to start. After all, I can't live here forever. And since the job comes with a room at the boarding-house, you and Daisy can take my room and use it when the new baby comes."

He raised a brow as if figuring out a puzzle. "Is *that* what this is all about? Abigail, you will *always* have a place here, for as long as you want it. Daisy and I both love having you around, and not just because you're such a big help." He took her hands. "You're family, Abby, as much as Daisy and the kids are, and family sticks together."

"But the space is—"

He grinned. "You're not the only one who's noticed how tight things are getting. I was saving this to surprise you with for Christmas, but I can see now that it won't wait. Come with me."

Curious, Abigail followed her brother past his printing press to the storeroom located in the rear. He threw open the storeroom door with a flourish and waved her in ahead of him. Abigail stepped inside and studied the much-changed space. Where once there were stacks of boxes containing paper and ink, along with cleaning supplies, assorted odds and ends, and who-knew-what that had accumulated over the years, there was now a mostly open space.

Along one wall was a bookcase and upholstered chair. The single window on the far wall now sported a pretty curtain rather than the utilitarian shade it had previously borne.

She turned to her brother. "What am I looking at?"

"Your new room. It's not finished yet—there's a new bed on order and we plan to bring down some of the furniture from your current room. Daisy and I figured you needed a place of your own, a place where you would still be close at hand so you could take meals with us and be part of our family time, but where you could also be a bit apart and have more privacy when you want it." He studied her face. "What do you think?"

Abigail threw herself at her brother, hugging him around the neck. "Oh, Ev, I love it! I love even more that you and Daisy would do this for me."

"We love you, Abby." He grinned sheepishly as she released him. "Daisy is going to pout for days when she finds out I showed this to you without her."

Then he turned serious. "So you see, you don't need to take the job at the boardinghouse. If you still want to find work, find something you enjoy. Don't take something you don't like just because it will provide you with a place to live, because you have that here with us."

Abigail felt tears prickling her eyes. Someone had finally chosen her.

Chapter Twenty-Eight

Over the following days, Seth felt as if he were walking around in a nightmare.

True to her word, Abigail had moved her things into the library and he rarely saw her at all. She never took meals with him anymore. And when they did happen to be in the same vicinity, she smiled politely, took care of her business as quickly as possible and left. She didn't appear angry or hurt, as she had immediately after Michelson had shown up, but was merely indifferent to him.

And that cut deeper than her anger would have.

Michelson was now sharing the office with him and the man looked ridiculous sitting at the small desk Seth still thought of as Abigail's.

But Michelson just laughed it off. "I can work with this for a few weeks. Once you're gone I'll have that one to work from."

Once he was gone. Christmas was less than a week away. And instead of looking forward to the culmination of his goals, he was absolutely miserable.

Thankfully, Abigail didn't treat Jamie any differently than she had before. He still caught them laughing together and discussing books and Christmas. But Jamie was a sharp kid and he noticed.

The day their trees arrived, Jamie begged Abigail to help them decorate them. At first she tried to beg off, insisting it was something families did together and that she would be helping Daisy and Everett with theirs.

"But you're like my family, too," Jamie pleaded. "Besides, you promised to shower it with love and make it beautiful."

Seth saw her heart melt at the little boy's plea, saw her glance his way, hesitate and then nod. "All right, Jamie. But just the big one. You and your uncle should do the one in your suite together."

Jamie, who obviously knew that he'd gotten all he was likely to get, nodded. "Where do we start?"

"Give me a couple of hours to gather up some supplies. In the meantime, you tell Mrs. Long to pop up lots and lots of popcorn for us."

Then she turned to him and Seth's heartbeat kicked up a notch when he realized she was willing to include him in the activity. "Why don't you take Jamie and see if there are any scraps of wallpaper or shiny metal left over from the construction that we might be able to transform into ornaments. Use your imagination."

He nodded and turned to Jamie. "It'll be like a treasure hunt."

Abigail did her best to make the afternoon a fun one for Jamie. For just a few hours she tried to pretend that she and Seth had only ever been friends and that he hadn't taken her heart and then discarded it.

Deep down, she knew she was as much to blame as he was. She'd wanted the job of hotel manager so much she'd ignored his talk of having another candidate in mind. It wasn't his fault he didn't love her as she did him. Not everyone could find that kind of reciprocal love.

So she smiled and laughed and even teased a bit as they strung popcorn, tied ribbons, fashioned paper angels and turned scraps of wood, metal and wallpaper into unique ornaments.

When they were finally done, the three stepped back to admire their work.

"We did it," Jamie said. "We turned that crooked old tree into something beautiful."

"I told you," Abigail said. "It just takes a little love and a keen eye to bring out the beauty in anything or anyone."

"And a person who cares enough to look for it," Seth said softly.

Abigail nodded but refused to turn and meet his gaze. It was best he not see what might be reflected there.

Instead she studied the tree. "It's a shame, though, that we don't have a tree topper. Something special to crown it with. I'll have to see if I can come up with something."

"I know!" Jamie's voice vibrated with excitement. "I'll be right back." And before she or Seth could say anything he'd dashed off toward his room.

There was an awkward silence once the two of them were alone and for once Abigail didn't know how to fill it.

Seth decided he had to say something. "Thank you for doing this for Jamie. I know it wasn't easy for you, feeling about me as you do, but it means the world to him."

"Making memories is my theme this year, remember?" She was proud that her voice held steady. "And I don't dislike you, Seth. I just need to keep my distance."

"Abigail, I—"

Thankfully, Jamie's return interrupted whatever he'd been about to say. She wasn't sure she could take hearing another apology from him.

The boy held up a shiny silver rattle, round on one end and with a long keylike handle on the other. "Will this work?"

Abigail took it from him and examined it. "There's an inscription here. 'James S. Shaw, March 3, 1891.'" She looked back up at him. "Is that you?"

Jamie nodded. "Momma said it was a christening gift and that I should save it for when I have my own kids. Poppa's name was James, too, so everyone calls me Jamie."

"And what does the *S* stand for."

Jamie cut a quick glance his uncle's way. "Seth."

Seth felt as if he'd been punched in the gut. The last thing he'd expected of Sally was that she'd give her son his name.

Had she done it out of remorse?

Seth realized he didn't know much about Sally and her husband at all. When Jamie had been dropped in his lap, he'd been too surprised to learn he had a nephew to ask many questions.

Truth be told, he didn't want to know. He realized now that it had been wrong not to give Jamie a chance to speak of his parents. And perhaps it had been short-changing himself as well.

Asking about the name was a good place to start. "So your mother named you after me?"

"Uh-huh. Momma said she carried a piece of you with her always and she wanted me to have a small piece of you, too."

"She and I hadn't seen each other for a very long time," he said carefully.

Jamie nodded. "Not since you both were little kids and they pulled her away from you."

Is that how Sally had described it? He supposed it was true as far as it went.

Jamie sighed. "I wish she had known you weren't really dead."

He heard Abigail inhale sharply at that, but he kept his focus on Jamie.

"She told you I was dead?"

Jamie nodded. "It always made her sad to talk about it, but she said she wanted me to know all about you, so she told me stories about the things the two of you used to do, the trouble you would get into, like the time you tied a bell on the tail of the neighbor's cat."

Seth smiled at the memory. He and Sally had had bread and water for supper for three days over that one.

Something didn't seem to be adding up here.

"Tell me a little about your father. I never had the opportunity to meet him."

"Poppa was a blacksmith and he was strong, stronger than the fathers of all my other friends." Jamie's voice was filled with pride. "Momma took in sewing, but she could do that from home."

Seth's image of his sister took another blow. "Are you saying your mother had a job?"

Jamie nodded, obviously puzzled by Seth's tone.

"What about your grandparents?"

Jamie looked uncomfortable. "Poppa didn't have any family. Momma didn't talk about her family much, except for you. She said her stepparents didn't really understand about true love but we shouldn't be angry with them, we should feel sorry for them."

Had Sally's adopted family cut her off? Is that why Jamie had ended up with him instead of them?

"Did she ever mention the letters I wrote to her?"

Jamie's nose wrinkled in confusion. "You mean the letters she wrote to you?"

"What do you mean?"

"She told me she wrote you lots of letters when she first got adopted. She was worried about you 'cause you were hurt so bad."

Seth glanced at Abigail and saw a soft sympathy in her eyes. It was almost too much on top of everything else.

What in the world was going here? Seth was beginning to doubt that Sally would have gone to the trouble of weaving so elaborate a fantasy just to have stories to tell her son. After all, why mention him at all?

Had someone been intercepting both his and Sally's letters? But why?

Perhaps it was time he found out.

But for now, Jamie needed some reassurances.

He smiled down at the boy. "Anytime you want to talk about your parents you let me know. And I've got some stories I can share with you about your mother that I'll wager she never told you."

Jamie's eyes lit up at that.

Seth reached for the rattle Abigail still held. "But for now, why don't we figure out how to mount this fine-looking rattle on the top of our tree?"

Seeing the glow of approval in Abigail's gaze made him forget, for just a heartbeat, that things had changed between them.

Then her expression shifted and the pain came crashing back.

The next morning, when Michelson caught sight of the tree, he described it as quaint. "Don't worry," he told Seth, "next year I'll make certain we have elegant glass ornaments and silver garland."

He pointed to the front window. "And I'm sure I'll be able to come up with something better than glittered paper stars for the front window."

Glad that neither Abigail nor Jamie had been around to hear that, Seth turned a stern eye on the man. "Actually, this tree is decorated with ornaments made mostly by me, my nephew and Miss Fulton. And that front window display has been generating quite a bit of goodwill for the hotel."

Michelson smiled indulgently. "That's good. But we can do so much better, don't you think?"

Before Seth could respond, the man changed the subject. "What do you think about having the staff wear uniforms? It would add an air of formality around here, something it's sorely lacking."

Seth stiffened, then tried to remember that this was exactly the way he himself had been thinking when he first arrived.

"I tell you what. Arthur Madison, the hotel owner, is supposed to arrive on today's train. Why don't you run the idea by him?"

Michelson clapped him on the back. "Splendid. And I have some other ideas I may just run by him as well."

Seth nodded and then quickly excused himself to take care of business elsewhere. Because the more he was around Bartholomew Michelson, the more he doubted that he was the right man for the job after all.

Abigail had been on pins and needles all morning. She'd wanted to be there to meet the train when Judge Madison arrived, but had known that honor rightfully belonged to his granddaughter and her family. But Reggie had promised to send him round to the hotel as soon as he'd had a chance to rest up from his travels.

So Abigail had stayed in and around the lobby for the past hour, determined not to miss his arrival. And at last her vigil was rewarded when he walked in the door with Reggie on his arm.

As soon as the introductions were complete, Reggie kissed his cheek and took her leave.

"Judge Madison, it's so wonderful to finally meet you." Abigail didn't even try to keep the gushing tone from her voice.

The judge patted her hand and gave her a warm smile. "Abigail, my dear, I assure you the pleasure is all mine."

"Allow me to show you my library," she said, pointing the way. "The one I have you to thank for."

"I like your sign," he remarked as they passed under it.

She hoped he didn't notice that her smile wobbled a bit at that reminder. "Mr. Reynolds made it. It's quite nice."

As they stepped back out in the lobby, he looked around appreciatively. "If you've done as good a job on the rest of the rooms as you have on the lobby, I most heartily approve."

"I'm so glad you like it. It was a very satisfying assignment. Thank you so much for trusting me with it."

"And how was it working with Seth? Did the two of you get along?"

"Mr. Reynolds is quite the astute businessman. I learned quite a bit watching and listening to him. And speaking of Mr. Reynolds, I'm sure he's waiting to give you a proper tour of the place. Come along, I'll show you where his office is."

The judge eyed her curiously, as if trying to read something in her expression. "Is something wrong, my dear?"

"Of course not. In fact, finally getting to meet you has made me so very happy."

He patted her arm. "It pleases me as well. Now, let's go find Seth and have a look at the place."

Abigail led the way to the office and then stepped aside to let her companion enter first.

Seth stood as soon as they entered and came around the desk to meet the judge halfway. "It's very good to see you, sir. I trust you had an easy trip of it."

Abigail felt her world shift slightly off center. It was her first time back in the office since she'd moved her things out, and she found the room looked both the same and different. Mr. Michelson had definitely put his mark on it.

And speaking of Mr. Michelson, the man had stood and was offering his hand to the judge.

"Allow me to introduce myself, sir, I'm Bartholomew Michelson, the new hotel manager."

The judge shook his hand and exchanged pleasantries, all the while studying the man dispassionately.

Feeling out of place, she stepped back toward the door. "I'll leave you gentlemen to your business. I have a few matters in the kitchen to attend to."

But Judge Madison held up a hand. "Just a moment, if you don't mind."

Abigail halted and Judge Madison turned to Mr. Michelson. "If you will excuse us, I have a few business matters to discuss with these two."

Michelson nodded affably. "Of course. But there are a few ideas I'd like to discuss with you when you have a few moments. I'm entirely at your disposal."

Once the man had made his exit the judge turned back to them. "Now, I'd like both of you to give me a tour of the place and show me what you've been doing the past couple of months."

Resigned to the fact that she would need to keep up her

act that everything was okay between her and Seth, Abigail joined the two men as they headed out of the office.

"Seth, has something happened to upset Abigail?"

Seth sat back in his desk chair, resigned to explain his failure to the man he admired most in the world. He'd hoped the judge wouldn't pick up on the tension between him and Abigail during the hour-and-a-half tour they'd made of the premises, but he should have known better.

He fiddled with a pencil on his desk. "Abigail had her heart set on getting the hotel-manager job from the very first. But I had already made a commitment to Bartholomew Michelson."

"That's what you meant before, about hiring the right person for the job being part of what would get you the Michelson property."

Seth nodded. "He wanted to get out from under his father's shadow, and his father agreed it was time for him to strike out on his own. So they were willing to make a trade, this job for Bartholomew in exchange for a reduction in the money owed. But I would never have made that deal if he hadn't been highly qualified for the role."

The judge waved a hand dismissively. "That doesn't concern me. I know you're an honorable man."

Seth winced. "Perhaps not so honorable as you might think."

The judge didn't press, just raised a brow in inquiry.

"I let Abigail hold out hope she had a chance to earn the job. I didn't realize how serious she was about it. In the beginning, I didn't feel the need to put a lot of effort into explaining the situation."

"And later?"

"Later, I didn't want to hurt her."

"And when did she find out?"

"Several days ago, when Michelson turned up unexpectedly."

"I see."

Seth shifted, afraid the judge saw a little too much.

"Seth, my boy, it sounds to me as if you've made a regular mess of this situation."

Seth nodded miserably. "She won't listen to a word of explanation from me. And, even though she remains polite, she still wants nothing to do with me."

"Not a good frame of mind to be heading into Christmas with." He stood. "Oh, well, cheer up, my boy. You're finally getting what you've always wanted. You can leave all of this behind you and build your own business empire."

He moved to the door. "I'm going to talk to Abigail about reserving that fancy new guest parlor for Christmas day. I want to have a grand party for all of my friends here in Turnabout. Who knows when I'll be back this way?"

Then he paused and gave Seth a look that seemed to carry significance. "I seem to remember you telling me that you were prepared to sacrifice even your queen if it ensured you achieved your goal. I wonder, do you still feel that way?"

And without waiting for an answer, the judge made his exit.

Seth slowly sat back in his chair.

The judge was right. He could collect his end-of-job bonus, turn the keys to the place over to Bartholomew Michelson and get on the train back to Philadelphia with Jamie. The Michelson property would be his free and clear in a matter of days.

He was within a hairbreadth of becoming the success he'd vowed to become all those years ago as he stood outside the gates of Sally's adopted home.

But who was he going to impress?

Sally—she was gone.

The caretakers at the orphanage he'd grown up in—why would he want to impress them?

All those people who had turned their backs when he was looking for work—he couldn't even remember their names.

The people who mattered, whose approval he really cherished, didn't look for him to prove anything. Judge Madison had always afforded him the respect of a friend. Jamie didn't care about what he did so long as they were together.

As for Abigail—ah, Abigail was a different story altogether. What she required of him was something he'd deliberately, stupidly, withheld.

And now it was too late. He'd sacrificed his queen before counting the cost.

How could he have been so blind for so long?

He was still pondering the supreme mess he'd made of things when he tucked Jamie into bed that night.

"Uncle Seth, I wish we didn't have to leave Turnabout. I really like it here."

And there it was, another reminder of what he'd lost. "I know. And I really like it here, too. But my work is finished and it's time for me to move on."

"Why don't you just get another job here?"

"I'm afraid it doesn't work that way. For now, I work for Judge Madison and I go wherever that work takes me. But one day soon, I'll own my own hotel and be able to work just for myself. Then you and I can build a real home for ourselves."

"Why don't you just buy a property here instead of one back in Philadelphia?"

It was clear there would be no appeasing the boy.

"I'm sorry, Jamie, I really wish things could be different, but that just isn't possible."

Jamie turned over on his side. "Miss Abigail says anything is possible, it just might mean changing the way you look at what it is you want."

That sounded like Abigail. Unfortunately, he didn't have her gift for looking at things in unconventional ways.

Still, if he looked hard enough, was it possible to win back his queen?

Abigail smiled as brightly as she could, keeping the lie pasted on like a mask. Saturday should have been a grand day.

The hotel had taken first place in the decoration contest and Judge Madison had been there to accept the prize. Mr. Michelson had unaccountably been called back home for an emergency of some sort, so he wasn't there to witness it.

The parade through town had been fun to watch. And the weather, though sunny, had finally turned appropriately cold for this time of year, which in Turnabout meant it was in the mid-forties.

There were hayrides to look forward to this afternoon and a bonfire tonight with fiddle playing and caroling. Under other circumstances it might have been fun, but Abigail wasn't in the mood for celebrations.

Had Seth bought his and Jamie's train tickets yet? Was he eager to get on with his life, with his pursuit of a business empire of his own?

She prayed he would keep Jamie with him, or would at least find more time to spend with the boy if he did send him back to boarding school. Those two needed each other.

Just like she needed both of them.

Abigail had managed to slip away from her friends and family and now stood back from the milling crowds, watching people enjoying themselves.

Perhaps she could leave unnoticed, retreat to the library or the new room Everett and Daisy had prepared for her, and lose herself in a book.

She'd just started in that direction, when someone hailed her. Turning, she saw Constance waving at her.

Feeling as if she'd been found out in a minor crime, Abigail joined her friend. "What is it?"

Constance linked her elbow with Abigail's and started leading her toward the other end of town. "I need you to come with me. And hurry."

Suddenly alarmed, Abigail picked up speed. "What's wrong?"

"Nothing's wrong, I just need your help with something."

"With what?"

Constance gave her a sideways look that Abigail couldn't quite interpret. "It's hard to explain. I need to show you."

Her normally pragmatic friend was acting very strange. "Where are we going?"

"To the church."

"Oh." Abigail's suspicion was somewhat mollified. Nothing untoward could be happening in a church.

Deciding she wasn't going to get any straight answers, she quit asking and tried to keep pace with her friend. By the time they reached the church steps, Abigail was feeling a bit breathless. What in the world had required this rushing about?

"We're here now. What was so important?"

"Inside" was all Constance would say and she pushed past Abigail to open the door.

Abigail followed her inside, for a moment unable to see clearly as her eyes adjusted from bright sunlight to the muted interior.

As soon as she recognized the man standing by the last pew, though, she stiffened and turned on her friend.

But Constance was ready for her. She gave her a quick hug and a smile of apology, then quickly slipped back out the door without a backward glance.

Abigail decided it was time to rethink Constance's best-friend status.

Then she turned to Seth. "That was quite a production to get me here. You could have just asked."

He moved closer, giving her one of those crooked smiles that always tugged at her heart. "I wanted to see you alone. And I wasn't sure you'd come if I did the asking."

"Well, I'm here now. But I warn you, I'm in no mood for apologies."

He nodded "Fair enough. Though goodness knows you deserve one."

"Well?"

"I wanted to let you know the job of hotel manager is yours, if you still want it."

What was going on? "But Mr. Michelson—"

"He wasn't the right person for the job. I realized that almost as soon as he arrived. He might have a lot of experience with big-city hotels, but he knows absolutely nothing about fitting into a community."

She stepped forward, concern overriding caution. "But Seth, what about your deal? What about the property you want to buy?"

"I'm afraid that's dead. They already have another buyer."

"Oh, this is all my fault." She closed the distance between them completely, placing her hands against his chest. "I don't need that job. This deal means too much to you. Get him to come back, tell him it was all a mistake. I'm sure you can work something out."

He closed his hand over hers, pressing them more firmly against his chest. "The deal means nothing to me, not anymore."

"But the money you've invested—"

"Is my worry, not yours."

"Oh, Seth, I'm so sorry."

"Don't be, I'm certainly not. I have a new project, something with better potential, something I'm really excited about."

Of course. He'd merely exchanged one project for another. "I'm so happy for you."

"I hope so, because I traded Judge Madison my interest in the Michelson property and the bonus he owes me for a fifty-one-percent interest in the Madison Rose."

"What? You mean you're staying?"

He nodded. "Jamie has found a home he loves here. And I have as well."

Seeing the look in his eyes, feeling the strong beat of his heart under her hands, a wild sort of hope took hold of her. Could it be—?

He gave her hand a squeeze. "I know you don't want apologies, but I've been every kind of fool and pigheadedly blind on top of it. I hurt you and I can never forgive myself for that. But I want you to know… I. Choose. You."

He stared into her eyes as if he could see all the way to her soul. "I love you, Abigail Fulton. I love your sunny smile and your schoolmarm scolds. I love how deeply you care about others and how unaware you are of your own considerable worth. I love you and I will always choose you, no matter what. Whether you will have me or not."

She felt as if her heart would burst. "Oh, Seth, I love you, too. I—"

He put a finger to her lips. "Those are the sweetest words anyone has ever said to me." His eyes caressed her face in an almost tangible way and she thought for a moment he would kiss her.

To her disappointment, he didn't. "Before we proceed, there's more I need to say to you."

When she nodded, he removed his finger. "I don't want there to be any more secrets between us." He held her gaze. "You know about my limp, of course, in fact you know more about the whys and wherefores of it than most. But the reality is that the sight of the scar itself is very ugly and unsettling. I'm not in any sense of the word a whole man. It's important to me that you understand that before we go any further."

The sweet, honorable, totally clueless man. She touched his cheek. "Oh, Seth, you're wrong. You are a whole man in *every* sense of the word. I have, in fact, seen your scars and they neither frighten nor disgust me. They only prove to me how much you've suffered and how strong you must be to live with them without excuse or complaint."

Seth was flabbergasted. "You've seen them? When?"

Her cheeks pinkened adorably and her gaze dropped. "That morning I found you on the floor of your room. Your nightshirt was…well, it revealed your scars. But don't worry, I covered them so no one else could see." Then she peeked back up at him. "By the way, if that was just some kind of convoluted marriage proposal you just offered, I accept."

Seth let out a roar of laughter and grabbed her in a fierce embrace. If he had his way, he'd hold her this way forever. "Oh, my darling, darling Abigail—what a treasure you are. You are well and truly stuck with me now. There is no way I will ever let you go."

Abigail's eyes twinkled and she gave him that sassy smile he loved so much. "Prove it."

So he leaned in and captured her lips with his.

Epilogue

Seth sat on the sofa in the hotel office with Abigail close by his side. She'd arrived bright and early this Christmas morning so she could see the look on Jamie's face when he received his Christmas present.

When the boy had learned that he and Abigail were to be married and that they were planning to settle down here in Turnabout as a family, Jamie had been over-the-moon excited and had declared that he had everything he needed, there was no need to get him any gifts for Christmas. Already he was calling Abigail Aunt Abby.

However, Abigail had other ideas. And of course she'd been right. When the two of them presented Jamie with a wriggly, clumsy puppy this morning, the boy had nearly started crying with happiness. He was currently down on the floor getting better acquainted with his new pet.

Seth cut a glance at the woman who would soon become his wife. "I've just realized that it was a total lack of foresight on my part not to have boughs of mistletoe hung throughout the hotel."

She gave him one of those innocent, wide-eyed looks that held more than a touch of mischief. "Why, Mr. Reynolds, I have never known that circumstance to deter you before."

With a grin, he leaned down and gave her a quick kiss, in deference to Jamie's presence. As soon as they straightened, Abigail gave his hand a squeeze and stood. "I believe I hear people arriving."

Jamie scrambled to his feet, cuddling the puppy in his arms. "Come on, Nemo, time for you to meet everyone."

They entered the lobby to see the judge and the Barr family arrive, all of them loaded down with brightly wrapped packages.

Christmas greetings were exchanged as everyone made their way to the dining room. Jamie's friend Jack and his sister, Patricia, exclaimed over the new puppy and each wanted a turn to hold the exuberant ball of fur.

Before long the rest of the close-knit Sunday lunch group had arrived and the room was filled with conversation and mirth.

Seth considered these people his friends now. He was one of them and proud to be so.

Judge Madison approached him with a warm smile. "Well, my boy, I see you've finally discovered the *real* secret to success."

Seth nodded. "Yes, sir, I have. It's finding someone to love and be loved by."

"Make sure you don't ever lose sight of that."

Abigail sidled up next to Seth, linking her arm with his. "Don't worry," she said to the judge, though her gaze never left his, "I plan to remind him on a regular basis."

Seth was both humbled and elated by the love he saw reflected in her eyes. It was all he could do not to sweep her up into a crushing embrace.

She caressed his cheek, then turned to Judge Madison. "We've decided on a New Year's Day wedding. It would make us both so happy if you say you'll stay to celebrate with us."

The older man's smile softened. "I wouldn't dream of missing it."

Abigail gave Seth's arm a squeeze, then let go, moving to link her arm with that of Judge Madison.

She waved a hand, encompassing the whole group in her gesture. "Look around, this is all your doing. It's thanks to you that these families came together." She turned and met Seth's gaze, reaching for him with her free hand. "That Seth and I came together."

"I merely set the wheels in motion. I can't take credit for more than that."

Abigail raised up on tiptoe and kissed his cheek. "That, my dear friend, was the catalyst for all the love and joy present in this room. Without you, none of us would have found our true loves." Then she squeezed his arm and stepped away, returning to Seth's side.

Abigail's words filled Arthur Madison's soul with a sweet, quiet joy the likes of which he hadn't felt in a very long time. His darling wife, Rosemary, gone these fifteen years, would have dearly loved being a part of this.

Perhaps he could find a place here in Turnabout himself. After all, it would be nice to see his great-grandchildren grow up. And there was a lot he could still do for this town that had such a special place in his heart.

In another week it would not only be a new year, but also a new century. Perhaps it was also time for a new chapter in his own life.

* * * * *

*If you loved this story,
pick up the other books in the*
TEXAS GROOMS *series:*

HANDPICKED HUSBAND
THE BRIDE NEXT DOOR
A FAMILY FOR CHRISTMAS
LONE STAR HEIRESS
HER HOLIDAY FAMILY
SECOND CHANCE HERO
THE HOLIDAY COURTSHIP
TEXAS CINDERELLA
A TAILOR-MADE HUSBAND

*Available now from Love Inspired Historical!
Find more great reads at www.LoveInspired.com.*

Dear Reader,

I hope you enjoyed Abigail and Seth's story. I've known since Abigail first showed up in book two of this series as an adventurous fifteen-year-old that her story would likely be the one to wrap up this series—I just had to wait for her to grow up. Seth is her opposite in many ways and he's also her perfect match. I fell a little bit in love with him as I wrote his story.

It was a bittersweet moment for me when I wrote "The End" on this story. This is the last book in the Texas Grooms series (for now—never say never), and saying goodbye to Turnabout and the community was unexpectedly difficult. But I am looking forward to turning the page on a new chapter in my writing life and I hope you'll come along with me and see where it leads.

For more information on this and other books set in Turnabout, please visit my website at www.winniegriggs. com or follow me on Facebook at www.facebook.com/ WinnieGriggs.Author.

And as always, I love to hear from readers. Feel free to contact me at winnie@winniegriggs.com with your thoughts on this or any of my other books.

Wishing you a life abounding with love and grace,
Winnie Griggs

Get 2 Free Books,
Plus 2 Free Gifts—
just for trying the
Reader Service!

Love Inspired. HISTORICAL

*Hoping to make his dream of owning a farm come true,
Jeremiah Stoltzfus clashes with single mother
Mercy Bamberger, who believes the land belongs to her.
Mercy yearns to make the farm a haven for unwanted
children. Can she and Jeremiah possibly find a future
together?*

Read on for a sneak preview of
AN AMISH ARRANGEMENT
by Jo Ann Brown,
available January 2018 from Love Inspired!

Jeremiah looked up to see a ladder wobbling. A dark-haired woman stood at the very top, her arms windmilling.

He leaped into the small room as she fell. After years of being tossed shocks of corn and hay bales, he caught her easily. He jumped out of the way, holding her to him as the ladder crashed to the linoleum floor.

"Are you okay?" he asked. His heart had slammed against his chest when he saw her teetering.

"I'm fine."

"Who are you?" he asked at the same time she did.

"I'm Jeremiah Stoltzfus," he answered. "You are…?"

"Mercy Bamberger."

"Bamberger? Like Rudy Bamberger?"

"Yes. Do you know my grandfather?"

Well, that explained who she was and why she was in the house.

"He invited me to come and look around."

She shook her head. "I don't understand why."

"Didn't he tell you he's selling me his farm?"

"No!"

"I'm sorry to take you by surprise," he said gently, "but I'll be closing the day after tomorrow."

"Impossible! The farm's not for sale."

"Why don't you get your *grossdawdi*, and we'll settle this?"

"I can't."

"Why not?"

She blinked back sudden tears. "Because he's dead."

"Rudy is dead?"

"Yes. It was a massive heart attack. He was buried the day before yesterday."

"I'm sorry," Jeremiah said with sincerity.

"Grandpa Rudy told me the farm would be mine after he passed away."

"Then why would he sign a purchase agreement with me?"

"But my grandfather died," she whispered. "Doesn't that change things?"

"I don't know. I'm not sure what we should do," he said.

"Me, either. However, you need to know I'm not going to relinquish my family's farm to you or anyone else."

"But—"

"We moved in a couple of days ago. We're not giving it up." She crossed her arms over her chest. "It's our home."

Don't miss
AN AMISH ARRANGEMENT
by Jo Ann Brown, available January 2018 wherever
Love Inspired® books and ebooks are sold.

www.LoveInspired.com

LIEXP1217